Tactical Scars

by Arrow Wren

DORRANCE
PUBLISHING CO
EST. 1920
PITTSBURGH, PENNSYLVANIA 15238

Dorrance Publishing Co
585 Alpha Drive
Pittsburgh, PA 15238
Visit our website at *www.dorrancebookstore.com*

ISBN: 978-1-6480-4525-7
eISBN: 978-1-6480-4503-6

Tactical Scars

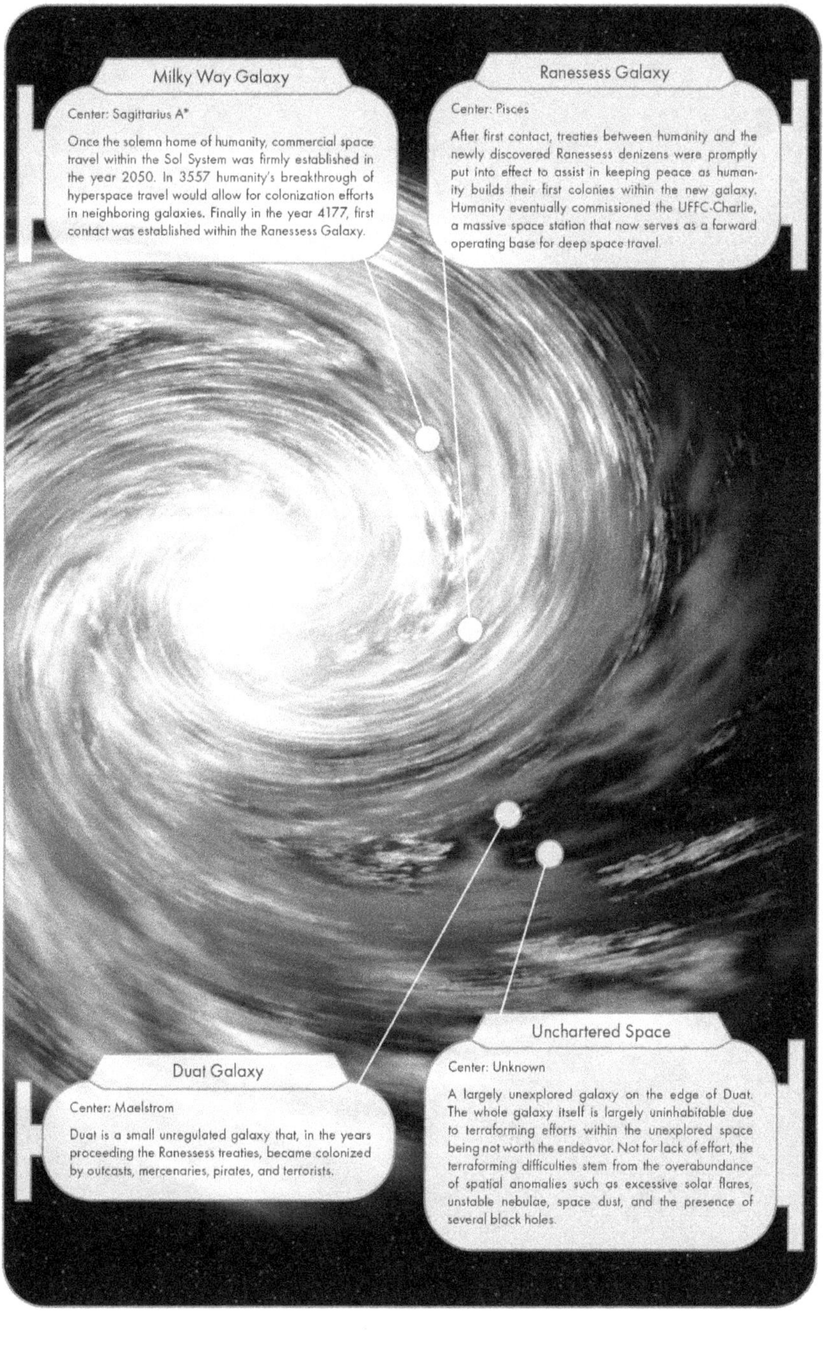
Milky Way Galaxy
Center: Sagittarius A*
Once the solemn home of humanity, commercial space travel within the Sol System was firmly established in the year 2050. In 3557 humanity's breakthrough of hyperspace travel would allow for colonization efforts in neighboring galaxies. Finally in the year 4177, first contact was established within the Ranessess Galaxy.
Ranessess Galaxy
Center: Pisces
After first contact, treaties between humanity and the newly discovered Ranessess denizens were promptly put into effect to assist in keeping peace as humanity builds their first colonies within the new galaxy. Humanity eventually commissioned the UFFC-Charlie, a massive space station that now serves as a forward operating base for deep space travel.
Duat Galaxy
Center: Maelstrom
Duat is a small unregulated galaxy that, in the years proceeding the Ranessess treaties, became colonized by outcasts, mercenaries, pirates, and terrorists.
Unchartered Space
Center: Unknown
A largely unexplored galaxy on the edge of Duat. The whole galaxy itself is largely uninhabitable due to terraforming efforts within the unexplored space being not worth the endeavor. Not for lack of effort, the terraforming difficulties stem from the overabundance of spatial anomalies such as excessive solar flares, unstable nebulae, space dust, and the presence of several black holes.

Chapter One

YEAR 5019, JUNE 5

DR. HORACE MILLS – OSIRIS

"Everyone ready?" Command Sergeant Major Lucas Wilts took lead of our team. He managed to squeeze his heavily muscled body into a skin-tight leotard space suit. His suit left… little room for imagination. Major Robyn Cage, on the other hand, fit nicely into hers, while Staff Sergeant Samuel Ravin and I looked as packed in ours as Wilts did. We all wore these suits, a requirement set by U.F.F.C. regulations.

Atop all of our suits were tactical vests. Each packed with weapons, ammo, and radios. Ravin carried the overfed bag of explosives, med-kits, and any spare gear that we would need in case of an unforeseen event. He was the last one to join our team and got stuck doing all the grunt work. He was a good sport about it; everyone else, in his opinion, "did it wrong anyways."

We were aboard our ship, Osiris, getting ready to pass over a trading vessel that had been discovered trading goods to the Formers' home planet Sobek, a planet where thieves and criminals ran to claim sanctuary; a law adopted by the Formers that created a "legal" procedure that allowed any criminal to remain unprosecuted by secular law as long as they remained on Sobek.

Generally, all ships found guilty of this illegal trade were detained, and everyone aboard is tried and sent to jail. This trading vessel, however, would survive one more trip down to Sobek before officers would take any action. In the meantime, we would use it to gain access to the planet without being detected. The plan? Jump out of our perfectly safe ship, "dive" twenty miles down, and hitch a ride on the outside of the ship.

Wilts bent over and secured his hands on the emergency latch that would lead us into space.

"Ravin, Mills, Cage," he said. "Maintain the formation discussed in the brief. Check in every mile. Move."

Our suits were equipped with a switch activated magnet that kept us from being sucked out as the latch clanked to the other side. Air hissed all around us from the oxygen breach, drowning out all other noise. Fully open, the small hatch was large enough for us to slip through. Ravin clicked off his magnet and jumped, screaming and waving his arms dramatically: "Wrong lever!"

I followed after him, switching off my magnet. The vortex of air gave me an extra boost as I positioned myself toward the trajectory of the ship. Cage and Wilts followed suit.

"Playtime's over. Let's get to work." Wilts' voice filled my helmet along with static. During his first jump outside of basic, he'd miscalculated and missed his mark. Luckily, an admiral aboard the mission ship noticed, sending an emergency shuttle for rescue. Since then, he never joked around with jumps; he wasn't fond of space after that either. In fact, he was a bit paranoid. But that didn't stop him from being an exceptional soldier, space fright and all. We were the same age, seventy-three, the oldest of our team. We'd spent so much time in cryosleep that we didn't look our age, perhaps no more than forty.

Unlike Wilts, I enjoyed diving out of ships. The concept of it was practiced every day in basic, day in and day out, over and over. It had become a rush, an extreme sport that got my adrenaline pumping. I wasn't the only one who felt this way. A record of almost three hundred civilians have been reported missing due to lack of training and supervision.

If you missed your landing and no one saw, that was it; you were toast. It is this very idea that makes Wilts' blood run cold on every jump. Sure, you could float around and hold out hope that someone will find you before the oxygen runs out. If you didn't, and decided to take off the helmet and end it all, the liquid inside your body could begin to boil, your skin would swell, and within fifteen seconds, you'd be dead. On the bright side, your body would mummify, leaving a clear identification of who you were in case someone happened to stumble upon you.

Wilts and I held the same solution in hand, to eat a bullet before the oxygen would run out. We had a lot of things in common, no wives, no kids; our families though were quite different. Unlike mine, where I was the first to join the military, Wilts wasn't. His father was a retired general of the U.F.F.C. and was beyond happy to discover he was having a son. At the age of ten, Wilts could fire nearly any weapon, and by age eleven he could clean and reassemble it. Holding true to his father's wishes, in high school, he joined the ROTC program and shipped out for basic at eighteen.

Our dive to the ship below took ten minutes, a cruel ten minutes for Wilts I'm sure. Like most ships, this one was a dark brown, and from above, it gave the illusion of a hole ripped into space. An unsettling thought to have to say the least.

I positioned my body toward the center of the ship. My left hand made contact first, and with a secure grip, I came down softly, avoiding a solid drop. The rest of the team followed suit. We wouldn't activate our magnets again until orbit.

I looked out and could see Sobek in the distance. It was at one point a beautiful planet. In many ways, it reminded me of Earth, my birth planet. Full of oceans and seas, plentiful forests, diversity of species, all forms of life working together, thriving. That was until the Formers had made this their home. Millions of years of evolution undone in less than two centuries.

Sobek was turning into a desert, getting dangerously close to rejecting all life. Oceans were drying up, deforestation was constant to make room for the ever-growing population, and species were becoming extinct one at a time, one after another. If nothing changed in the next hundred years, the planet would die taking as many with her as she could.

The Formers had demanded for years to have a planet for themselves where they could practice their traditions without secular law. Unsatisfied with the planet the U.F.F.C. had chosen for them, they made the decision to fly in during the early stages of terraforming on Sobek, murder the workers, and claim it for themselves.

The Formers were already a hot topic among the races of Man since they followed the Old Traditions of Earth, traditions that had or should have died out over thousands of years ago. Their actions that day stirred up conflict, not only within the races of Man, but in all other alien races. The idea that a group of Men had murdered innocents over thousand year-old customs and were given no more than a slap on the wrists along with the planet itself didn't go over well.

The Old Traditions were discontinued, and for good cause: the impact they had was devastating. The consequences they had on the world and society were taught in educational systems all over the galaxies, in hopes of preventing history from repeating itself.

The consequences affected the planet on a global level. It was a custom to breed without question; the more the better. Unable to support the overpopulation, Earth began to give out. Oceans acidified; fresh water became scarce; food was hard to come by, and the air pollution was changing the atmospheric composition along with many other side effects.

Societies were divided as people fought over the little indiscretions that each culture had within their traditions, causing war between lands.

Those who ruled, ruled for power and instilled fear. Fear that would, on many occasions, cause people to enter states of psychosis. The fear would stop society from seeking out knowledge. For those who did, they were sought out by the masses, and in some cases, they were murdered.

As the Formers' cult grew, they became increasingly violent to those who refused to join, as they did thousands of years ago. The public had become exhausted with the threats they'd receive on a daily basis both verbally and physically. Soon, they'd refused to accept anyone who was involved with the Formers, pushing them out from society. With nowhere to go and the constant struggles they received from the law, they decided it was time they had a world for themselves.

Sobek had become that world, a safe haven for all who practiced the Old Traditions. As the years passed, it became nearly impossible for anyone, even the U.F.F.C. to land there. Any ship that landed and wasn't authorized or claimed sanctuary were attacked, and everyone aboard was killed. As more and more criminals claimed sanctuary, agreeing to practice their laws, their desire to convert became stronger.

Over the years, several Men fought for power to rule over Sobek, but it was Audwin Holland who became the first official ruler. He instilled fear in everyone on Sobek and in several thousand off-world. His goals were simple: reform as many Men as possible and rule over all alien races. If he couldn't rule over them, then he would abolish them from the universe along with anyone who resisted. The justification he had for his actions came from the Old Traditions, as it was Man's duty to rule over all land, animals, and beasts.

It was in the last century and a half they truly came into power. Their cult was growing rapidly, and new leaders came, bringing more to the table. It was known that the Formers were targeting alien races, some more than others, but by the time the U.F.F.C. realized what they were doing, it was too late.

One of the oldest alien races had been eradicated, the Pharaohs. Pharaohs, in their eyes, held the greatest threat. They were a spitting image of Man besides a few little characteristics. Their skin, hair, and nails were solid gold, their eyes a deep emerald green and their blood was mercury-based. If anyone spent too much time with them, they would start to get mercury poisoning.

Besides the physical characteristics that separated them from Man, the Pharaohs were highly intelligent and quickly worked on medicines to prevent any future poisonings to other races.

I was lucky to work first hand on many medical treatments with them. They were coworkers, and they were friends. This war had become personal for me when the Formers attacked. The Pharaohs didn't believe in war or violence. Out of all the species that co-existed, theirs was the only one without war. They were the true definition of pacifists, but that peaceful nature had destroyed them.

The current leader of the Formers, General Douglas Warts, used it against them thirty years ago, killing every last one of them. He encouraged all his fellow members to track any and all Pharaohs down, murder, and skin them, but not always in that order. The families of the deceased didn't get angry, even as the skins of their loved ones were being sold on the black market.

Since the genocide of the Pharaohs, Warts had been hiding on Sobek, popping up every now and then to gather more followers by traveling planet to planet, preaching the reign of mankind, before running home.

The thought that angered many was how the U.F.F.C. would not infiltrate Sobek to stop any further actions that they intended to do. Unfortunately, by law, the U.F.F.C. couldn't; laws were set up years before that, preventing any domination or meddling into another's world without rightful cause. Somehow, their actions thus far were not "rightful cause," at least until now.

A message was sent out, hitting every military receiver in the galaxy. Three statements spiked an alarm, "General Warts. Bio Weapon – Charlotte's Kiss. Planet to be attacked – Babi."

It was unclear what this message was meant to be. A warning perhaps? A threat? It was well known that Warts in his younger years had dedicated his time to science and genetics, graduating top of his class. He had all the qualifications to build a bioweapon. What he lacked though, his henchmen would get for him or die trying.

The U.F.F.C. decided to take it as a threat and refused to have another alien race massacred. I wish I could say it was for the safety of Babi, but in reality, the U.F.F.C. couldn't handle the repercussions if the public were to revolt against them. Everything done would be kept under wraps, and Babi wouldn't be notified of the threat.

Very few knew about the illegal missions my team was given. This one was no different, we are to infiltrate Sobek and capture Douglas Warts, record all data of Charlotte's Kiss, obtain any samples of the bioweapon, and escape in one piece, all-the-while not getting caught.

"Everyone hold on, we are entering orbit." Wilts' voice pulled me from my thoughts.

The speed of the ship increased as it entered orbit, and the force from the gravitational pull hurled the ship to the planet, rocking it from side to side. It was at this time we could activate our magnets. The metal of the ship creaked and popped with the sudden increase of heat. The sound of our suits latching down wouldn't be noticeable.

The ship landed with ease at the docks, I unsealed my mask, letting the thick, heavily-polluted air fill my lungs, making it difficult to breathe. Keeping our bodies flat, we crawled toward the end of the ship to the emergency exit while the workers scurried around. Cage snuck through first, eradicating the few crew members who were inside. One by one, we followed her in, stripped the crew members of their clothes, hid the bodies and played dress up to blend in.

There. My eyes focused on crates that were labeled for delivery to Warts' operating base. "Mama." I motioned for Cage to get the other end of a large crate for us to carry out, while Ravin and Wilts took another.

Outside the ship, for as far as I could see, was brown cracked clay from the heat of the sun and ship engines. It reminded me of an old lake bed, with no vegetation or water. There were, however, spare and broken parts from ships that docked and trash that strong gusts of wind blew around.

My boot crunched over an old cup as a group of men who stood guard outside the ship eyed us, each covered up from the sun, weapons in hand. *Mercenaries*. Hired guns. The larger man of the group wobbled over towards us, his shotgun moving from one trembling hand to the other.

"Lemme see." We stopped. Wilts turned and ducked his head as if to block out the rays of the sun. "Take it over to the far truck." I watched him closer, taking note of his trembling body along with the large welts and red rash that was on his face and neck.

"You got it." I gave a friendly smile but kept my eyes on the men as we veered over to the truck. The closer we got to the truck, I could see the layers of duct tape that held the thing together.

"How fast will we die when the fossil fuel death trap explodes?" Cage whispered under her breath.

I chuckled, "Not fast enough."

We loaded up the crates, while Ravin moved to the driver side and swayed the man to exit before he snapped his neck and pushed him back inside. He looked like nothing more than a sleeping passenger.

Ravin then climbed in the driver's seat while the rest of us hopped in the back settling in for a long ride to catch ourselves a criminal. Most docks were not far from civilization; the ever-growing technology kept the force of ship take offs contained, while the ones here were at least a century old.

Ravin enjoyed the cool air from the A.C. while the rest of us baked in the back. Even as the wind whipped its way around us, there wasn't an escape from the heat. Sweat was dripping down our heads and into our eyes, causing the dirt on our faces to stick. I didn't bother to wipe it away, Wilts on the other hand cursed under his breath at each attempt.

"Fuck this planet. Let's bomb this forsaken shit hole and end this bullshit."

"I like it." I tossed him another handkerchief.

"We can live right there by the dead tree," Cage motioned over to the corpse of a small tree.

I nodded.

"We'd have room for guests, too." I played along with her scenario.

"You two can stay here. Ravin and I will visit on holidays." Wilts adjusted his feet.

"And birthdays." Ravin shouted through the back window of the truck that was no more than a piece of plastic.

I gave a dry laugh. How people lived here really was a mystery for me.

Despite the heat, we approached the rundown town, with families traveling and buzzing about. We kept our heads down as Ravin weaved through the traffic. The building was easy to spot. It was well taken care of while the other buildings corroded with faded and chipped paint, as well as shattered windows and splintering wood.

Ravin drove around to the back to the loading zone for shipments. Five men walked to the truck, weapons at low ready. I set up and lined my scope up with my target, as did Wilts. Together we fired, the glass from the windshield shattered. Ravin didn't flinch. Direct hit. The suppressors on our weapons kept us quiet.

Cage fired taking out the third, while Wilts and I took aim at the last two. They were on the ground before any of them knew what happened to the other.

Ravin parked the car, and we jumped out, dragging the bodies out of sight of any civilians who could potentially pass by. Stripping out of the crew's clothes, we entered the building. Wilts took point at the front of the line, and Ravin held up the rear.

It was unclear what room Warts was in, but it didn't matter. We shouldered our weapons and went in. The inside of the building contained new furniture. *Shit*, it even had the smell of fresh paint. Up ahead towards the front of the building was our first target. The concierge, who had access to the main computer system to turn off all alarms and hopefully a blueprint to Warts' office.

We came in unnoticed until Cage broke from formation taking the woman by surprise, she placed the barrel of her gun next to the woman's head, loading a new round into the chamber for extra effect.

"Keep your fucking hands where I can see them." She spoke each word clearly.

I broke from formation next to secure the door. I looked back to see the concierge face down on the floor sobbing quietly. Cage was already logged onto the computer shutting down the alarm system.

"Where is Warts?" Wilts asked, hovering behind her.

"I'm not sure yet, I don't know this system. It's older than…" she hesitated a moment and looked at him. "Well, you."

"Please, don't kill me. I-I can tell you what room General Warts is in." The woman peeked her head up, the makeup she had caked on was running down her face. "Please."

"Shut the fuck up."

Ravin struck the stock of his weapon to the side of her face, forcing her to cower closer to the ground.

"Come on, Mama." He motioned for her to hurry up.

She tsked at him. He was the only one who could get away with rushing her. "Alright," Cage stepped away from the computer to let Wilts in. "He's here."

"Excellent. Let's go. Ravin dispose of the witness."

Without a thought, Ravin pulled the trigger. The force of the bullet sent her blood, skin, and brains spraying out. Keeping his weapon in one hand, he lifted her up by the collar and stuffed her under the desk. The blood wasn't visible from any of the windows. She wouldn't be found for quite some time. Without a second to spare, we fell back into formation.

The building was mostly hallways with closed off rooms. Every few doors, the sound of voices leaked out. We moved slowly in order to sneak past, making our way to the southeast corner of the building. Wilts took point, leading us into the next hallway. Raising his hand, he signaled for us to halt, followed by a motion for Ravin to open the door. Lining himself up, Ravin gave a final nod to make sure we were ready.

Three men inside the room struggled to unholster their weapons. It wasn't a surprise, Formers had little-to-no military training or fighting experience. It didn't stop the two men who rushed us. I fired, two in the chest, one in the head. Cage's fire mimicked mine, while Wilts shot a single bullet at the third man.

"Target acquired," Wilts spoke, closing the distance to General Warts who lay crumpled on the ground, his white lab uniform staining with blood. The bullet from Wilts' gun shattered his shin.

"You fucker!" His words spit out. His dark brown hair fell over into his eyes that watered from the pain. What was interesting was the similar red rash he had on his skin that the man from the docks had.

"No skin to skin contact with him until we find out what that rash is." I stepped over him as I spoke.

Wilts walked up; his weapon shouldered while he took his large boot down on the bullet wound. "Where is Charlotte's Kiss?"

Warts cried out, unable to answer.

In the center of the room was a large wooden desk where Cage was already attempting to get into the computer. As our communications specialist, the girl could hack into anything. Before she joined the U.F.F.C., she worked with telecommunications giving her more than a basic understanding of nearly every system. Working on anything with a hard drive had become second nature to her.

"I'm in already," she said. "They have no firewalls. On anything." She continued to click opening different files, chuckling in disbelief. "Here." She stepped back giving me reign over the computer.

Anything medical or science was my expertise. It was one of the main reasons why my team was chosen for this operation. No other U.F.F.C. soldier had the experience I did, not only was I a doctor, but I had several degrees in science and psychology.

She'd already pulled up the files that had anything remotely to do with biological weapons. I clicked in a thumb drive and immediately started downloading. From the looks of it he'd been working on this weapon for years. Talk about dedication. *Wait …no.*

"Sergeant," I called out to Wilts. "We need to leave."

"What's the problem?"

"I'm not sure, somethings not right. The message we received warning us about Charlotte's Kiss came from this computer."

"Fuck! Get everything you can, we are out of this room in five. Ravin, any movement?" He almost shouted.

"Not a peep." Ravin secured the door and darted over to the window. "Clear."

"Charlotte's Kiss?" Wilts asked.

"It's still in the process of being created from the looks of everything. I'll wipe the computer; they'll lose all their data on it."

"No, don't you fucking dare!" Warts attempted to get up. Wilts slammed the butt of his gun into his head, knocking him out cold.

"Mills, injured civilian." Cage's voice came from the far corner of the room gathering our attention. She'd been searching the room, and was standing over a crate she'd pried open.

"Ravin, med-kit." Whoever was stuffed inside the crate, was too big for it. Their limbs were broken, and several joints were dislocated in order to cram them inside. Doing my best, I kept their neck straight hoping to avoid any more injuries. No movement. "Female. Human." I laid her mangled body down. No pulse, but her body was still warm. "Administering CPR. I need a shot of adrenaline."

The woman was naked and every inch of her body was bruised. Fresh round circles showed the pattern of burn marks given by cigarettes and an open fracture on her right leg. From the look of it, it was an old injury. Blood began to pool out between her legs with each compression.

The adrenaline jump started her heart, I didn't waste any time. My job now was to keep her alive until the ship. She was losing blood fast. *Intraosseous infusion is her best bet.*

"Wilts, she needs blood." He was a universal donor and had clean blood, he rolled up his sleeve as Ravin set up an IV.

I pulled out a ball of gauze. Her breath was shallow and she appeared to be unconscious. I opened her legs, the movement woke her. She tried to roll over to her stomach.

"Ma'am, can you hear me?" She pushed my hands away. "Ma'am, my name is Horace Mills. I'm a doctor, I'm with the U.F.F.C. I need to stop the bleeding." I couldn't tell if she heard anything I said, she didn't stop her attempt to flee. "Hold still."

I looked over to Ravin who'd finished up with Wilts. "Hold her." I ordered. He reached for her wrist but thought better of it and pinned her arms. I pulled her legs apart again, pushing the cotton in, ignoring her cries from the pain.

"Ravin, send a call to Osiris, get the infirmary ready. There is a civilian car outside. Get us to it. Move. Cage, get everything on the computer even remotely related to Charlotte's Kiss. Wipe it clean." Wilts handed me his bag of blood.

"You're going to be okay," I whispered to her. "He won't hurt you anymore."

Chapter Two

Year 5032, September 10

Sergeant Samuel Duke – U.F.F.C Space Station

My team, put together for rapid response missions, was summoned and gathered in the tight conference room. I was advised of our mission one hour ago by General Elba, the General of the United Federations Fleet Command (U.F.F.C.).

I was skeptical when I saw the unknown signal appear on my screen. "This is Master Sergeant Samuel Duke."

"This is General Elba. I've had a file sent your way. Review it and assemble your team, and Sergeant Duke, this transmission never happened." His voice came in patchy.

"Yes, sir." *Why was the General calling me?* I was nowhere near the paygrade to even speak his name. "May I –"

"Everything is in the file." He signed off. *What the hell?* I'd heard he wasn't the most patient of people. Needless to say, I understood why.

Sure enough, after he clicked off, a file appeared in my system. Classified in large, bold, red letters covered the front page of the documents. I flipped to the next page, heart racing. What was I getting looped into? Five words filled the page, Scars Tactical Team. Bioweapon C.K.

Scars. The top U.F.F.C. special ops tactical team, they were considered to be the best. Their missions didn't exist half the time. It didn't matter; they got the job done, no matter the cost. It was what made them incredibly dangerous and also what gave them the darkest past. They looked at rules like guidelines and went off script. They were well known for years and became a sensation a little over a decade ago. News feeds and papers covered their story, broadcasting it across multiple star systems. This must have been what their last mission was before they were stripped of their ranks and incarcerated within days.

Their team leader, Command Sergeant Major Lucas Wilts, had a reputation. He was a brute and had the opportunity to lead two tactical teams before this incarceration. To keep a closer eye on him with his second team, the previous General of the U.F.F.C. assigned a Colonel to babysit. That Colonel was Raymond Elba, the current General of the U.F.F.C.

A direct recipient of their actions thirteen years ago when Wilts and his team were given a mission. What that mission was, was unclear. It was one of the few that was kept off record. What was known was how Scars subdued everyone aboard their ship, including Elba. Each one, drugged, tied up, and helpless to the mayhem that was about to come.

Wilts flew their ship to Sobek, destroying nearly half of the planet through bombing, they murdered thousands. Nearly half the population was wiped out. Satisfied with what they'd done, they flew back home, willingly confessing to their crime and refusing to give an explanation. It was rumored throughout U.F.F.C. that this was a bout of space sickness that caused them to do what they did.

A sickness thought to occur when someone spent too much time in cryosleep. It's been known to send the strongest soldiers spiraling out of control. The history of the sickness starting at the beginning of space travel.

The more I thought about it over the years, I didn't buy that excuse. Every member losing their marbles at the same time...not a coincidence. What had brought me to that conclusion was a little-known fact that every hostage aboard their ship didn't have any signs of physical assault, not even a bruise.

I finished flipping through the file he'd given me. It contained the original mission the team should have completed. Well, it contained parts of it. Most was blacked out, leaving the bare minimum of what was expected of the team at that time and what my team was supposed to do now.

It was late, and most of my team had gone home for the night. One by one, they filed in taking their seats. I stood up and passed out copies of the file.

"We received a response mission. It's classified, so do yourselves a favor and keep your god-damn mouths shut." I looked specifically at Captain William Atkins. He was my signal support specialist; it was the one thing he was good at. He'd bounced from team to team, each team leader refusing to work with him. Until he got tossed to me. He was in his early eighties, but looked fifty from all his time in cryosleep. He kept his blonde hair long, and from the looks of it, he hardly washed it. He divorced his wife a few years ago and didn't bother to keep in touch with her or his kids. He gave me a hard stare but nodded. "The mission was given to us by Top... General Raymond Elba." As I suspected, his name got their attention.

"How is he? I haven't seen him in almost a year."

I cocked my head to the side and looked at my Staff Sergeant, Angel Mills. She'd been with my team the longest, roughly eight years. She was in her fifties but looked to be in her mid twenties due to her own time in cryosleep. She was small, a bit over five feet, lean, toned, and packed with muscle. On the left side of her head, she had a quarter section of her long curly brown hair shaved, due to the thick scars obtained from a head injury on a previous mission. Angel was my grunt. An expert in weaponry, explosives, and I'd bet my left nut she could lay Samuel Ravin from the Scars team flat on his ass. The bitch could kick ass.

"You...you know General Elba?" I asked with surprise.

"We have brunch once a year." She smiled at me, while I waited for her to continue. "I can't really talk about it." She waved her hands in the air. "What's the mission he has for us?"

I looked at her a bit longer before I continued.

"General Elba has assigned us a mission that was written up thirteen years ago. The mission was originally assigned to Command Sergeant Major Lucas Wilts and his team. You may better know them as the Scars Tactical team."

No one spoke, turning their heads to look at one another, as if to confirm what they'd heard.

"Sir," Angel raised her hand. "Scars?"

"Yes," I confirmed. I paused a moment before I continued on, "Thirteen years ago they were given a mission to find and obtain a bioweapon that was designed by General Douglas Warts, the leader of the Formers. I'm sure you are all familiar with him as well."

"Warts? He's been quiet for the last decade," Cameron spoke up.

Private First-Class Cameron Jones was sitting next to Angel. He was my doctor and the newest to join my team. He was fresh out of training, not even twenty-one. Six feet tall, still skinny. Still new. The poor kid jumped at anything and was more gullible than a five-year-old. Angel enjoyed messing with him. My favorite joke to this day happened when she bought a small fish tank to put on our ship and told the poor guy it was full of ghost shrimp. He is still looking for them. He kept his dark curly hair a bit longer than required. I didn't mind; it was out of his face and didn't interfere with his job.

I nodded.

"A wave was sent from Sobek to the U.F.F.C. warning us of the weapon Warts was creating. Wilts' team found passage to Sobek, and according to the file," Waving the one held in my hand. "They were to find the weapon, and find Warts to bring him in for questioning. The problem was, they destroyed the weapon and anything related to it and threw Warts out the airlock. You don't have much to say when you're dead."

"If they destroyed everything related to the weapon, why is the mission being reassigned? In a way, they did their job." Angel brought up the question.

"Three weeks ago, high grade lab equipment went missing. General Elba believes the equipment that was stolen is tied to the mission."

"Someone stole hardware, and he thinks it's related? That's a bit of a stretch, sir." Angel had a point.

"I agree, but I can't refuse the mission, and we have to remember Elba was there when everything went down, I bet he knows something vital, and that's why he's concerned."

I moved to the front of the room and clicked on the screen that brought up a grainy video. Robyn Cage appeared handcuffed to a chair. Her face held no emotion, eyes following her interrogator around the room.

"We waited until it was night before we took over the ship. It was at that moment Wilts turned the ship to Sobek. We dropped all of the bombs that were aboard the ship. We didn't even wait for the smoke to clear before we hit the ground."

"What did you do when you got on the ground?" She didn't respond. "Speak!"

The man slammed his hand on the metal table. She didn't flinch.

"We opened fire."

"Why?"

"We waited until it was night before we took over the ship. It was at that moment Wilts turned the ship to Sobek. We dropped all of the bombs that were aboard the ship. We didn't even wait for the smoke to clear before we hit the ground."

I paused the video. "Robyn Cage. Wilts' signal support systems specialist. Thirteen years ago, she was a Major. Unlike the rest of the Scars team, she started her career in the military later in life. She has a husband on her home planet, Set. She's the only female Wilts' has had on any of his teams. If that doesn't tell you how tough she is, I don't know what will. Don't underestimate her."

"I heard she used to go 'bed-to-bed' with higher ups, gathering pillow talk to keep the team one step ahead of everyone else." Cameron shifted uneasily in his chair as he spoke. It was the logical thought process. After she'd joined, Scars began knowing things that only leaders knew.

"That was only a rumor," Angel jumped in to defend.

"Rumor or not, she slit the throat of the man who accused her of it." I looked at Angel.

"That, or he didn't sleep with her," Atkins whispered the comment under his breath.

I silently agreed with Atkins. It really wasn't known why. She didn't say, and the man was dead and couldn't give his side of the story. "Well, if you think she's scary, you'll love Staff Sergeant Samuel Ravin."

"He sought out the position, if I remember correctly," Cameron spoke.

I nodded.

"He was the one who carried out a lot of the dirty work. He's well trained in hand-to-hand combat and martial arts. Both his civilian and military files are layered with criminal activity from fights starting at the age of ten. Several incarcerations, how he wasn't discharged before this incident is unknown, but unfortunately, it's not uncommon."

I continued on, "The last person on Wilts' team was his doctor, Chief Warrant Officer Three, Horace Mills. He joined the U.F.F.C. as an infantry soldier and worked alongside with the Pharaohs on several medical treatments we use today."

Angel adjusted in place, crossing her legs in the seat.

"They used to call him the Battlefield Guardian. It was said he could save a man with a six-inch hole in his chest out in the field with a basic medical kit."

"A highly skilled doctor," I commented. "And like Cage, he repeated word for word that she said here during his interrogation. They all did. Even when physical interrogation was given."

"They were tortured?" Angel asked in disbelief.

"Yes." I walked over and gave her shoulder a quick squeeze. "In a little over twenty-four hours, we will arrive on Ammit to question Wilts and his team. We need to know what the bioweapon is, what it does, and what happened."

"Are you out of your fucking mind?" Atkins stood up to speak. "They aren't in their right minds. Wilts murdered his first team, he chopped them up like kibble. When they found him, he had their ears strung around his neck."

Angel laughed at his shrieking voice.

"That's a rumor too, but he *was* drenched in their blood, surrounded by what was left of them."

"I still don't understand why he wasn't charged for that." Cameron shook his head.

"Space sickness," Angel offered up sweetly. "Very common."

Atkins tossed his hands in the air.

"See! And you want us to go to Ammit and poke the bear?"

"Yes."

"Sir? If they didn't say anything before, why would they say anything now?" Cameron asked. The top of his head was beginning to sweat.

"Elba believes that if they are offered the possibility of parole, there is a *chance* they will cooperate. They've been in prison for a long time."

"This team killed thousands, and we are going to let them walk?"

"No, kid, it's a power move. If they refuse, then we adjust, adapt, and overcome. Figure it out for ourselves. It never hurts to ask. Besides,

I guarantee Elba knows more than he's sharing and will spill it when he can't keep it secret anymore."

"And the equipment that was stolen, what was it?"

"The equipment that was taken can be used to build a particle accelerator."

"It's not uncommon for those to be used in medical research… It could be something they need to put the weapon together. And Elba hasn't given you any clue as to what the weapon is designed to do?" Cameron was flipping through the file.

"Nope. We go to them and see what we can get." I pointed to Cage on the screen.

"I think this will be fun, imagine all the dirt we might get." Angel was smiling.

"Ships up in thirty." I gave her a wink.

Ammit wasn't too far from the U.F.F.C. base where we were stationed. It would take a little over a day before we would arrive. Ammit was one of the few ice planets. By night, its temperatures dropped down nearly half as cold as space itself, while during the day, it warmed up enough to melt the top of ice caps. The building was built with metal sheets and was kept heated enough to keep the inmates thawed out at night. It was here the prison for the galaxy's worst criminals was built. If any tried to escape, they wouldn't get far.

I sent word to the warden of the prison to have each one of Wilts' team members set up in their own holding cell for questioning prior to our arrival.

"Warden, has Wilts or any of his old team members attempted to escape?"

"No attempts have been made." The warden's voice came in patchy over the call.

"None?" Part of me couldn't believe it.

"None sir. However… Several prisoners have gone missing since their arrival. No bodies, no blood. They've disappeared."

"No one disappears, sir. Send me the files on the prisoners who've gone missing."

"Yes, sir."

"What about their behavior? Are they violent?"

"They only get violent if you antagonize them. Most prisoners learned to steer clear of them straight off. They'll fight each other however."

"They fight each other?"

"Yes, sir. All the time. At first, the guards tried to stop them. I've now ordered the guards to leave them alone. This prison has lost a lot of guards from them."

"Do you know what happens before or after each fight? What's triggering it? Anything?"

He was silent. If the static wasn't audible, I would have guessed he clicked off the call. "I don't know what happens before, but after, they patch each other up and carry on."

I dropped my head into my hands, this warden was unbelievable.

"Sounds like they are sparing, sir, not fighting." He tried to speak but I cut him off. "Send me their individual files as well. I'd like to have a look at them. We will be in orbit at 0500." I ended the transmission.

He was clearly intimidated by them. *Some warden…* I thought. He was supposed to be in charge of the toughest prison. This was getting a bit too perplexing. I leaned back in my chair, going over the files that he sent me, comparing them side by side with their military and civilian files. Something wasn't adding up.

"Duke?" Angel's voice caught my attention, drawing me away from my thoughts. She was standing in the doorway. "You missed dinner." She set a tray down in front of me. "Penny for your thoughts?" she asked sitting across from me.

I smiled at her. She was gorgeous. Her hair was pulled back, exposing her porcelain skin. Her green eyes always made her stand out in the crowd.

"Thanks, Babe. Take a look at this."

I pulled up an interrogation video of Doctor Mills. He was chained to a metal chair, his face swollen from punches. "This was day five of his interrogation."

He looked over to the soldier who struck him across the face and spat.

"You hit like a bitch. Why don't you bring Cage in here, she could at least teach you how to hit like a girl." Mills laughed.

"What happened on your mission?" The soldier towered over him, doing his best to be intimidating.

"Ah, well you see…go fuck yourself."

He laughed for a second before the soldier's fist struck him again, snapping his head to the side.

"You murdered thousands."

"You make it seem like I should give a shit. If I didn't run out of ammo, I'd have kept going."

"Sick bastard." The soldier slammed Mills' head onto the table.

I paused the clip and looked over to Angel, her eyes had gone wide and her jaw hung open. "It goes in a loop. He never says more than what you hear here. I've watched the other interrogations of the other members. They all said the same thing. 'If I didn't run out of ammo, I'd have kept going.' Their confessions are the same."

I opened the files of the missing prisoners.

"There is more. All of these men," I pointed to each one. "Are prisoners who have disappeared once the Scars team arrived at the prison. I checked the history, every inmate before them that has escaped was found. They were dead, but there was always a body."

"And you think Scars has something to do with it." It wasn't a question.

"Yes, I just –" I sighed scratching the back of my head. "I need to find the connection."

She smiled and started to thumb through the files.

"All the inmates committed different crimes. Embezzlement, theft, fraud, murder."

"All on different cell blocks."

"Did you check their financials?"

"Yes."

"What's the smile about?"

"I checked Wilts and his team's accounts, nothing out of the normal."

"But."

"Every last credit from the inmate's accounts are gone."

"You think the inmates paid them to help aid in escaping?"

I nodded.

"But, no money trail. Their money, much like them, has disappeared."

"Alright, Scars has been sneaking prisoners out, and helping them disappear all for the right price, but not taking a penny for their work? Why wouldn't they escape themselves then?"

"I was hoping you'd have an idea. What am I missing?" I leaned forward to her.

"Just where the money has gone, and why."

"Thanks, Babe." I kept my voice monotone and raised my eyebrow. "I never would have guessed."

She laughed. "Would they even have the means to pull this off?"

"Appearances would say no."

"But?"

"But, there is more to all of this than meets the eye."

She looked down at the files, fiddling with the corner of the pages. "What if we take a step to the side. What about their last mission? Anyone with a brain knows something is missing."

"Of course. Problem is, they covered their asses so well, no one's been able to find out what it is."

"But, whatever it was…"

"Whatever it was, it isn't over. Here," I pulled out Wilts' file and flipped through to the pictures. "Look at this. Take the day he was admitted, compare it to the yearly lineup after."

"He got a tattoo. Lots of inmates do."

"They all did." I showed her the other photos of his team. "The same tattoo. All on the left rib cage. Wings made of bone and webs. What else did they all have when they got admitted?"

She looked back down at the photos. "A rash, it's gone in their yearly photos." She looked back up.

I nodded.

"When they returned, Elba had the same rash. It means something. They've even kept their training up from the sounds of it. Almost like what they did isn't over. They've had no unnecessary fights with other prisoners and no attempts to harm guards – *except* in defense. No attempts to escape. Why?

"The doctor – Mills has saved over fifty inmates who were attacked. His friends keep him safe while he's providing life-saving measures. He's been thrown in solitary several times for shaming the prison doctors. I believe they are helping prisoners escape, while they are willingly rotting away in prison. It doesn't add up. Why would you willingly rot away?"

"Let's switch it up again."

"Quit avoiding the questions, you've always had an answer when I ask for your help."

"You're from Sobek." Her voice was tentative, knowing this was a subject I didn't care to discuss much, much the same way she didn't like to discuss her childhood.

"You know I am, what are you getting at?" The tone in my voice gave her a warning to proceed cautiously.

"Is this mission going to be personal for you?"

"No. It's not." I kept my words short and crisp.

"Liar." She leaned forward. "I know you lost your brother Derrick from the attack."

"He was my twin."

"I'm really sorry." She paused, reaching over to take my hand. I smiled and brought her hand to my lips to give it a kiss. "Sometimes things aren't always as they seem, and that's why things don't add up. It's not my place, but maybe you should keep that in mind. It might get you farther. I think it's safe to say this is personal for *them* as well as for you. Something happened that made *everyone* involved act out of character. Yes?" I nodded in agreement. "*Or* maybe…they acted in character."

"Explain."

She tsked out of frustration.

"I think they are protecting something. Their job is no different than ours. Protect all lives and keep the peace by any means necessary. Lucas may have psychotic actions, but he's never broken that. None of them have."

"He murdered his team," I couldn't help but add.

"To be fair, we don't know why he did that."

I sighed while leaning back in my chair. She wasn't wrong.

"Find out what they are protecting, and we have a leg up."

"Exactly."

The descent onto Ammit went according to plan. Tut, my ship, was given to me when I was assigned to be a rapid response team leader. The captain of my ship was an older man by the name of Morcant. He reminded me of the old ship captains thousands of years ago on Earth who sailed the seas. He definitely fit the description, dressing out of uniform and doing as he pleased.

He wore a white hat and a white V-neck shirt that dipped low enough to expose his graying chest hair. His shirt was tucked into blue pants and his black boots came up to his knees. To complete the look, he had a tattered knee-length blue jacket. Part of me wished he had a wooden leg and a parrot.

"Captain." I greeted him as I stepped onto the bridge. He was standing looking out the front window of his ship. Always a quiet man, he nodded his head to acknowledge me.

Ammit was a beautiful sight to see covered in ice. Still too early for the planet's suns to melt any ice, the lights of our ship sparkled against the blue crystals. Large glaciers cultivated the terrain that made up most of the planet. The prison itself was built on one; scientists charted its path to keep trade and prison shipments up to date.

Descending down, the only building on the planet grew in size. The Captain's years of flying led to a smooth landing within the large warehouse that was built for the exchange of any goods and protected traders and new prisoners from the freezing temperatures. The large doors opened from the ceiling allowing the ships to descend in.

"Get the ship fueled, and be ready to go when we get back." I saluted the Captain before meeting my team in the cargo bay.

My team was prepped. A deep black with gray accent replaced the dark hunter camo design used for previous military uniforms on Earth. I smiled as I saw Cameron and Atkins looking nervous as hell. Angel, on the other hand, seemed excited. Then again, she thought being in a building about to explode in ninety seconds was exciting. The idea of being in the same room with men who were considered the most dangerous in the galaxy? This was Christmas to her.

The bay doors opened exposing the inside of the prison with the warden and six guards waiting for us.

"Warden." I nodded at him. "I appreciate you working with us. Do you have the prisoners ready?" I asked.

He was a fat man with a receding hairline. His blue suit was wrinkled, and his tie was pulled too tight around his neck.

"Yes, sir. Follow me." He tripped over his feet and nearly fell. "Excuse me. I uh, have all four of them in separate cells. These men are dangerous. I can't stress that enough."

"I'd like to talk to Lucas Wilts first."

"Of course." He guided us through hallways and upstairs to the top section of the maximum-security wing. "He is through this door. Um… Before you go in." His face was covered in sweat; I didn't know if it was from the workout of going up three stories of stairs or the fact a stone-cold killer was on the other side of the door. "They are here because they want to be. I have no doubt in my mind that if they wanted out of this prison…they would be. On more than one occasion, Robyn Cage has hacked our security system with a watch she pickpocketed off a guard. She turns off the systems and opens the doors causing riots. They sit and watch the inmates fight for entertainment."

I chuckled under my breath. I guess you'd have to find some way to keep busy in a place like this.

"Take positions outside the door." I turned to my team. "If it's not me, shoot. Angel, you're in charge."

A buzzing noise shot out over the speaker, and the door clicked open.

My eyes were instantly drawn to a giant in an orange jumpsuit sitting in the middle of the room behind a table, both sleeves torn off. I doubt they would have fit his arms if they were still there. His head was shaved and deep scars were carved into his face and arms. I understood now where his team got its nickname.

"Call if you need us." The warden said as the door locked shut.

"Lucas Wilts, I'm Master Sergeant Samuel Duke. I'm here to talk to you about your last mission."

He leaned back in his chair and yawned. It was for show. His eyes were alert, sizing me up. I pulled out the chair across from him.

"You and your team were given a mission, and looking at your track record, you've never failed to complete one. Hell, you've even taken an IED to complete a mission. You were in a coma for three months. Remember?"

He smirked.

"No. I was in a coma."

Ignoring his comment, I continued. "I need to know what happened on your last mission. To make it easier for you, I'll tell you what I already know. I know a message was sent out, warning the U.F.F.C. of a new biological weapon. You were to obtain the weapon along with Douglas Warts, who *you* threw out the airlock. Now, it's believed the weapon – C.K. is in the process of being designed again, and you and your team are the only ones who know anything about it."

He didn't budge; he continued to stare at me, enjoying the idea of the power he had over me.

"With your cooperation, I can get you and your team out of here and back to civilian life in exchange for information."

His laughter shook the walls.

"You are one dumb motherfucker. Do you expect me to believe that *you* or anyone else is going to let any of us go? You don't have that authority, and anyone who does wouldn't dare."

"I don't, but General Raymond Elba of the U.F.F.C. does, and *he* is that desperate. You remember him, don't you?"

"Bullshit."

I leaned forward, putting my weight against the table.

"Not for me to say, but what I will say is this," I gestured to him. "All this seems a bit staged. Scripted. I watched the interviews. What dumb motherfucker would attempt a mass genocide of an entire planet, murder an informant of the U.F.F.C., and willingly walk into custody?" The smile that was on his face faded. "Now, I can't prove it, but I think there is more to this. Warts knew, so you killed him. It can't be related to the bioweapon. No." I studied him, "You don't seem stressed about it." I could see his jaw clench shut making me smile. "It was a distraction. Get the focus of the U.F.F.C. to believe that whatever you did, you did it because of the bioweapon. What are you hiding? What are you *protecting*?"

He didn't move. His brown eyes focused on me, and if looks could kill, I'd be six feet under right now.

"Duke, is it?" He asked leaning forward, I nodded. "You should fuck off before you end up like Warts."

I leaned back and slouched down in my chair, getting comfortable. I didn't bother to hide the smile on my face. "Try it, Toots."

He jumped up, sending his chair crashing into the back of the room. In an impressive move, he ripped the handcuffs apart. I kicked the metal table towards him as hard as I could, knocking him back a few inches. I was up with my chair in my hand, I stepped up on the table and sprung myself over, swinging the chair down, smashing it into his upper body. I was really expecting that I'd need to hit him a few more times, but surprisingly he went down. I dropped the chair and put a bit of distance between us.

"Tell me what you know."

He was up with his fists ready. I widened my stance, preparing myself for a fight. Before he could take a step closer, the buzzer from the door opening filled the room. Twenty guards charged in with loaded weapons and electric nightsticks.

"Get on the ground. Now." Every guard in the room was shouting. He didn't look intimidated. "On the ground. Now!"

"Saved by the bell, Toots." I taunted.

He lunged towards me, but I didn't flinch. The guard closest to him fired his gun. *Rubber bullets.* He didn't even seem phased. Turning his head, he looked over to the man who fired the bullet.

"Motherfucker, are you out of your pea pickin' mind?" He knocked the man out with a single punch, causing the rest of the guards to spring into action.

Wilts knocked them out like flies. More guards rushed in, in an attempt to secure the prisoner. I had to duck out of the way as he picked up a guard and tossed him clear across the room at me. I mimicked his fake yawn, doing my best to look bored.

"Sergeant Duke?" I glanced over to see the warden flinching nervously outside the door. *What did he want?*

"What is it, Warden?" I walked over, but kept my eyes on Wilts and tapped on my watch edging up his anger.

"What are you doing?" The warden snatched my arm and dragged me through the door locking it behind us.

I yanked my arm away.

"My job."

A loud scream and thud escaped from behind the door.

"How's it going in there, Sarg?" Cameron asked nervously, looking at the door.

"Well, I asked him for help. He said no. One thing led to another, and I hit him with a chair."

Angel hunched over laughing.

"Sir, you catch more flies with honey."

"Think you can do better?" I asked her.

She wiped away the tears in her eyes and gained back her composure.

"Are you giving me permission, sir?"

"Knock yourself out, but don't hurt him."

She smiled before pulling out her tablet.

"Care to see how it's done?"

"Cocky much?"

"Confident. Open the door, Warden." She was standing next to the door waiting patiently.

"He needs to be apprehended –" His voice was shaking as much as his body.

"I'm going to hit you with a chair if you don't open this door." She turned towards him and popped her hip out. "Open it."

His eyes got wide as he looked to me for permission.

"Go on."

He hesitated for a split second before he opened the door. The irritating buzzing noise filled the air again. Five men rushed out of the room nearly knocking Angel over. She still had a smile on her face as she walked through the door. I was a step behind her.

Wilts was standing in the middle of the room surrounded by unconscious guards. He wasn't even sweating, he looked over to me, and then to Angel.

"Command Sergeant Major Lucas Wilts. I am Staff Sergeant Angel Mills – no blood relation to your soldier Horace Mills, I believe you've met my commanding officer?" She casually stepped over the bodies.

"Now, before you completely disregard us," She was standing in front of him handing over her tablet. "Here is our mission. It was given to us by General Raymond Elba."

Wilts took the tablet from her but didn't turn his eyes from her. A gorgeous woman was standing inches away from a man who has been stuck in prison for the last thirteen years, and I doubt Cage put out. I held my hand over my gun; I didn't have rubber bullets.

"You will mind your eyes with my team, Wilts." I gave my first and only warning.

He looked up from Angel to me.

"He's your C.O.?" I could hear the disbelief in his voice.

"Yes."

"I like him." Wilts turned his attention to the tablet and quickly browsed over the secure file. I closed the distance between us.

"Will you help us?" Angel asked again.

"Absolutely." He folded his arms across his chest and smiled. "You look awfully young to be a Staff Sergeant."

What. The. Fuck.

"Now you'll help us? A piece of ass walks in and it's a one-eighty?"

"She asked nicely. You catch more flies with honey. Didn't your mama ever teach you that?"

"I'm going to hit you again." I took two steps to the left and picked up a chair.

"Duke. You're pouring vinegar on my honey." Angel knocked the chair from my hands and turned her attention back to Wilts. "I happen to be very good at my job, and I sleep with the occasional commanding officer. Except for this guy, he likes a different kind of ass."

My jaw dropped.

"You know, Horace feels the same way. One time, he had to seduce this total hot mama, poor guy couldn't get out of their fast enough. Jumped from a twelve-story window to get away." They both erupted in laughter. "He said she was into some really kinky shit. We had to hogtie Sammy down. He kept trying to turn the ship around when he found that out, the poor bastard-"

"Excuse me."

"Don't worry, I'll introduce you." Wilts didn't even look up and continued his conversation with Angel.

"We have a job to do." I gritted out my words.

"Relax, Toots, I said I would help. Warden, bring my brothers in." Wilts shouted the last bit to get the warden's attention.

I stood dumbfounded, unable to comprehend what I was seeing. I don't know why I was surprised; Angel made friends with literally everyone she met. Why should a psychotic murderer be any different?

The door buzzed open, Atkins and Cameron walked in leading Wilts' team in, one by one, each accompanied by two guards. Samuel Ravin, thick with muscle, came in first, the top of his head almost hit the doorframe. He was dressed in the same orange jumpsuit with chains around his wrists and ankles, his hair was a light brown that clashed with his bright blue eyes.

Horace Mills was after him. His body was bulkier, and he was as tall as Ravin. His hair was black, matching his beard, and his pale skin was evenly toned making his dark blue eyes that were surrounded by laugh lines stand out.

Robyn Cage entered last. She was a bit taller than Angel. Her hair was short, and her jumpsuit fit nicely. I couldn't see the muscle on her, but I was smart enough to know it was there.

"Up against the wall," the first guard shouted. They complied easily.

"Lower your weapons," I called out to Atkins and Cameron. "They'll help."

"Help with what?" Mills didn't sound happy and stepped out from the wall. His guard slammed a nightstick into the back of his knee, forcing him to the ground. In the blink of an eye, Ravin knocked out his own two guards with a headbutt and an elbow to the head. The guard who assaulted Mills had his neck snapped by Ravin in the next second.

Cage knocked her two guards out and smashed their heads in with their own nightsticks. Mills took care of his other guard. During this commotion, the warden ran out and locked the door. *Pussy*.

"Stand down." I ordered my team. I didn't need them to fuck up the cooperation Angel had gotten. Cameron's eyes looked about ready to pop out of his head.

Wilts walked over to Mills, "You good?"

They bumped their forearms.

"Yes."

"Mills, this is Duke. He is –"

"For the love of all that is holy, can we *please* focus," I cut off his words. "The bioweapon from your previous mission is believed to be recreated. If it gets out, thousands will die."

"Impossible," Cage cut in, stepping towards me fists balled.

"There were a lot of things that shouldn't have been possible on that mission, Robyn." Mills placed a comforting hand on her shoulder.

"Impossible or not, we can't let it go unturned."

Mills turned his attention to me.

"Who gave you this mission?"

"Top."

"Raymond Elba," Angel queued in immediately.

Mills' attention turned to her.

"Who are you?" He spoke with a smile.

"Staff Sergeant Angel Mills. No blood relation."

Wilts came to stand beside her, wrapping his thick arm over her shoulders.

"Adorable as fuck, right?"

"How do you make friends so easily?" Cameron shook his head. Angel laughed and leaned into Wilts.

"Adorable indeed." Mills brushed his hand across her cheek before he let out a sigh.

"So the bastard made it to General, huh? Took him long enough." Mills chuckled before turning to Cage. "I owe you a grand."

In an almost too perfect scenario, the Warden came back in, dripping in sweat.

"Sir, Duke…um…I just got a call…from General Elba. He said they…were…um…free to go. He filled out the release papers. I…have them in my office. He will be here in thirty minutes with Osiris."

"What?" I almost shouted. *They were free?*

"I-I-uh, his authority overrides mine." He looked like he was about to piss his pants making Wilts laugh. Elba… *he was is in on this.*

"Shit," Cage kicked the wall. "Just give the grand to Ravin." Ravin was grinning like an idiot but clearly proud of the bet he'd won.

"General Elba, asked us for help. We will help him," Wilts addressed his team.

"Can we trust this team?" Cage eyed us before planting her eyes on Angel, who was still under Wilts' arm.

"One way to find out." Ravin turned his head to the warden. "Can I get the keys bud? You know what? Never mind."

He held the gaze of the warden before he dislocated his thumbs and slipped the cuffs off.

A rush of white flushed over the warden's face, making Angel laugh. She walked over to the warden and took the keys from inside his jacket. Angel proceeded to release the cuffs from the rest of Wilts' team.

Each of Wilts' team members was given their old clothes, and paperwork to fill out as we waited in the warden's office. The eight of us made it a tight fit in his small office. A small window looked out to the icy planet; at the right time of day, it would be the perfect spot to watch the sunrise.

The walls in his office were decorated with pictures of important people he'd met and certificates on a job well done on running the prison.

"Any of you got a cigarette?" Ravin asked pacing back and forth behind the warden, who was shifting uneasy at his desk. The grin on Ravin's face told me he was enjoying making the warden nervous.

"I do." Angel pulled out a pack and tossed it to him.

"When did you start smoking?" Cameron asked. Valid question. In the eight years I worked with her, not once did I see her even eye a cigarette.

"I don't." She went back to talking to Mills over by the window.

"Thanks, honey. Got a light, Warden?" He towered over him.

A shaking hand pulled out a lighter and struggled to get it lit. Ravin leaned down closer to help him light it.

"Thanks, buddy." He was going to give the poor guy a heart attack.

Ravin took a drag and blew the smoke out on the left side of the warden's head. A low whimper escaped through his lips.

Ravin chuckled, clearly proud of himself, before he walked outside the door to finish the cigarette. Thoughtful action of a man who murdered hundreds.

A loud ring sounded from the computer, indicated an incoming wave. Still shaking from Ravin's game, his voice cracked when he answered the call. "Warden of Ammit."

"Send out my teams." General Elba clicked off. I was beginning to have doubts that this mission was simply about a bioweapon.

"Thank you," I spoke to the warden who had a look of relief on his face that he no longer had to be in the same room with these men.

We headed to the warehouse. My ship was already released, and Osiris was docked in its place. It was a large ship and was originally given to Wilts before he was incarcerated. Three stories high with escape shuttles on the wings. The cargo bay was open, and General Elba was waiting to greet us.

"Gentleman." He gave a nod. "Lucas, it's been a long time." He extended out his arm to Wilts.

"Long time indeed, brother." He clasped his hand and pulled him into a hug that resembled old friends reuniting after years apart. He greeted all of them with the same hug. The only one who got a bit of extra affection was Ravin, who he threatened to shoot if he caught him smoking aboard his ship.

"Sir," I stepped up and saluted him. "I didn't realize you would be on this mission with us." I didn't try to hide the frustration I was feeling towards him.

"This mission has a personal touch for me. As I'm sure you can imagine, I want to make sure it's done right. Have your team settle in and meet in the common area."

"Yes, sir."

The inside of the ship appeared larger than the outside led on. It ran smoothly, a light humming noise of all the parts working together filled the air. The ship was a Tesla, designed to be efficient, not only in battle but in living. Bunks resembled rooms from back home. The common area was also first introduced in this model. Five minutes on board, and it really did feel like home back on the space station.

The common room on this model was connected with the kitchen, making it a bit larger. A large couch was facing a coffee table, while recliners and a loveseat formed a circle around it. On the far wall, shelves lined up and down the wall, each one filled with books and board games, and a foosball table was placed in the far-left corner to top off the room. I was the last one to report in.

Angel was sitting next to Ravin on the loveseat, while Mills sat on the arm of the seat next to her, all three engaged in a conversation. Wilts and Cage sat on the couch with Cameron and Atkins. General Elba was standing up waiting for me. I took a seat in one of the recliners and turned my attention to Elba.

"Let's begin, we don't have a lot of time. This mission is beyond classified. As far as all of you are concerned, this never happened. According to your files, you all are on leave right now." He took the time to eye everyone in the room. "Duke, I chose your team for a reason to take this mission. You have something the other teams don't, but don't think for a minute that if one of your team members gets out of line, I won't throw them out the airlock myself."

"Understood, sir." I said.

"As all of you know, I believe C.K. is in the works of being made to wipe out any and all life that doesn't follow what the Formers believe. It's unknown what it does, or how it works. All evidence was destroyed by yours truly." He gestured over to Wilts and his team. Ravin jumped up and bowed. "Douglas Warts, the man who designed it, died years ago. Yes?" We nodded. He continued, "I'm going to guess no one here is an idiot and actually believes that." *I knew it.* "Wilts."

Wilts stood up and walked over to the wall behind the foosball table. In a hidden compartment, he pulled out a thick file that was covered in dust.

"This is what we are protecting." He dropped the heavy file on the table in front of me. "Thirteen years ago, we were sent to Sobek to retrieve Douglas Warts and all information on his weapon. Easy mission. When we hit planet-side, Warts was in custody within an hour, all of the information for his bioweapon was recorded and wiped from his computers. He named the bioweapon Charlotte's Kiss or C.K. That was when…" His voice trailed off and he stared down at the file. "We found a prisoner."

Prisoner? I pulled the file closer to open it.

"Jesus Christ…" I felt sick and looked up to Wilts. "What the fuck?"

The look on his face said he understood. I looked back down to the picture of the prisoner. I couldn't tell if it was a man or woman, it was just a face. A face that was bashed in, the eye on the left side of the head was bludgeoned, the right eye was swollen shut, and the nose was flattened to the face. The jaw was clearly dislocated and hanging open. The skin of the poor soul was black and purple.

I flipped through the file, that was the only picture of the face. X-rays showed fractures. Pictures of hands with fingers smashed and bent. In several locations, the skin itself was rotting, cigarette burns lined the body.

"Mills spent almost three days helping her," Wilts' voice grew deeper and gritted out his words.

"She's still alive?" I was shocked. "How?" Technology has come a long way but even this looked impossible. I'd only seen this type of cruelty once before...

"Yes," Mills spoke up but remained seated. "She's still alive. She was chained up so long the skin on her wrists grew over the cuffs." The look of pure hate crossed over his face, followed by everyone else, even Elba's. "She was four years old when she got chained up. Six years old, he tore her hips out of their socket because she kept squirming to get-away. Fifteen, she became a woman, and mad that she 'made a mess,' he ripped her uterus out. When he couldn't get it up, he used a knife on her. Every bone in her body was broken more than once. One of the last things he did was take a whiskey bottle and bludgeoned her face in." His voice grew angrier with each word.

Cameron jumped up and ran to a trash can before throwing up.

"Why? Why was he doing that to her?" His voice broke on each word.

"There was no reason for what he did. He did it because he could. He liked to hear her scream," Cage spoke. "He used some bullshit from the Old Traditions to justify what he did to her, the same way they justified the genocide of the Pharaohs."

General Elba paced behind the couch as he spoke.

"It was then we wanted to throw the bastard out the airlock, but... it didn't seem to justify what he did. So, we tortured the bastard. Well, we still are torturing the bastard. Everything he did to her, we are doing to him. If I recall correctly, he still has about seven years left before we kill him."

"Warts is still alive? The record says you threw him out the airlock." Atkins looked a bit uneasy as he spoke.

"That is what I told everyone. If they think he is dead...no one will look for him." Elba had a sly smile on his face. "It was all part of the plan."

"Plan, sir?" Angel asked. Her voice was softer than normal, once again fidgeting with her fingers.

"Yes, Mills estimated the girl to be in her early twenties when we found her. That leaves seven more years before we actually kill him. We are headed to his location. I figured his time with me has added up to around the age she was when he mutilated her. Ravin did call 'dibs.'"

I looked at Ravin who looked more than pleased at the idea.

"Have you questioned him yet?" he asked.

"No, I figured you would love to do that.

"Where is she? Is she on the ship?" Atkins asked.

"No." Elba eyed him. "Let me make myself very clear. I read your file Atkins. I don't like you, one bit. There is no way I'd willingly put you and her in the same room. Her identity will remain a secret. We are the only ones who know where she is, and it will remain that way."

"And the rest of the plan, sir?" I asked. "I understand you were a brilliant doctor, Mills, but how is she still alive?" I shook my head. "*Why* is she still alive?"

General Elba didn't answer, instead, he turned to Mills, who took a moment to speak. "Once I got her stable, I ran blood tests. I wanted to know who she was, to get her back to her family. There was no file on her. Not uncommon, considering most Formers don't report their births. However, I got a partial match in the system based on her DNA. I found her father." He paused, filling the room with anticipation. "Warts."

Warts? Warts! *He* was her father? Impossible. A father didn't do that to his child. I jumped out of my seat, cursing. The thought that he was being tortured in the last thirteen years helped my anger, but it wasn't good enough. If he did that to her what did he do to...

"Where is her mother?" I asked. I didn't feel like sitting anymore.

"We don't know where or who her mother was but we know *what* she was." I turned around and looked at Mills who spoke. "Care to take a guess?"

Chapter Three

YEAR 5019, JUNE 8

SERGEANT MAJOR LUCAS WILTS – OSIRIS

"Tell me what I want to know." The Former pressed the tip of his knife deeper into the corner of my eye as he spoke. "And I'll make this quick." His yellow, decaying teeth smiled down at me.

"Fuck you." I said my words slowly, looking him directly in the eyes. I wasn't going to beg.

He let out a growl as rage sparked to life in his eyes. "When I am done with you, no one will recognize who you are." His coffee stained breath filled my nose. I was going to die; I knew I was going to. Soon, I'd welcome it. I held his gaze, as he moved to the other side of the table, blade dancing from hand to hand.

Snarling, he dug the knife into me, slicing it through my flesh. My jaw clenched, swallowing the scream that was

> *tearing at my throat.* Get away! Get away! *My mind screamed these words over and over as I fought against the restraints that held me. The blade continued to carve its way down my face, through my eye and to the edge of my jaw.*

I balled up my fist and slammed it into the punching bag, it flew back. I swung another blow as it hurled itself back at me. My mind painted the memory on the bag; somehow, if I could hit it hard enough, it would disappear entirely.

The air around me was growing thick, sticky. I hit harder, the vibrations traveled up my fists and to my arms. His laughter filled my head, echoing against my skull. *Get away!* Black spots danced across my vision; I couldn't get away. The blood was running down my face, dripping onto the floor. I would be dead soon.

I hunched over trying to catch my breath. The bag swung back and forth, the chain it hung by protesting. I straightened, shifting my weight into my left leg before spinning around and kicking with my right. The chain screamed louder. *Why wouldn't it stop?* I hit it again. And again. *It needed to stop.* I wailed on the bag. Blow after blow.

My breathing became shallow as my eyes burned from the sweat that dripped into them. The lights flashed in the hallway, distracting me from the pain and pulling me from the depths of my memory. All the lights on our ship were motion censored. *Someone was there.*

It was early morning, everyone was in bed, and those who were running the ship were too busy to be taking a midnight stroll. *Had someone managed to get aboard our ship?* I made my way to the door, palming a blade. Looking out in both directions, another light flickered on in the next hallway.

I tightened my grip on the handle, keeping my steps quiet. As I maneuvered, looking left and right, my boot slipped. *Blood.* It was everywhere, getting thicker as I began sprinting down the hallway, following it. *Whoever was bleeding was moving in the opposite direction of the infirmary, towards Mills' room.* Someone was injured and needed help.

I stopped when I saw who it was. *The girl.* She was awake. *But how*? Unaware that I was near, she continued dragging her body down the hallway.

"Hey," I spoke softly. Putting the knife away, she slowly turned her head towards me. "Let's get you back to the infirmary and find out why you are bleeding." *Why was she awake?* I couldn't help but think to myself. I moved slowly, the fear in her eyes growing with each step that brought me closer to her.

Three days ago, she was fighting for her life. Now it seemed, she had a sense of vitality to her that wasn't there before, that shouldn't be there now. After the surgeries, Mills had said it himself, she shouldn't be alive.

Kneeling beside her, I reached out, making her flinch.

"Come with me." I kept my voice low, pulling her into my arms.

I continued down the hallway, hardly noticing her attempts to get away. I shifted her into my right arm and pounded on Mills' door with my free hand. "Mills. Infirmary."

I didn't wait for him. Marching to the infirmary, I noticed the tipped over medical bed she'd been in. "You have to be a bit more careful." I set her down on the one next to it and waited for Mills to arrive. "I don't want you to hurt yourself."

She didn't look at me, and she didn't make a sound, but her mind was working. Her eyes darted over to the door. Her body was trying to decide whether to fight or flee, but she wasn't able to do either. A feeling I knew too well.

"Here." I pulled out my compact opal knife, an heirloom my father had passed down to me. I squeezed the handle forcing the blade to spring out, making her jump. "Take this." I place it in her hands, wrapping her bruised, shaking fingers around it. "The next time *anyone* tries to hurt you, use this." I lifted the blade to my neck, next to my carotid artery. "The deeper you cut, the faster they will bleed out." I helped her squeeze the handle to retract the blade. I lifted her chin up to catch a glimpse of her green eyes. "Got it?"

"What happened?" Mills sprinted through the door. His hair was everywhere while dark circles surrounded his eyes.

"I found her in the hallway… Bleeding."

He paused for a second, taken aback as he looked at her.

"Get me towels from that cabinet over there." He jogged over to the sink, shoving his arms under the hot water. He grabbed some medical tools and lined them up next to her. "I need to stop the bleeding. Lift her up."

She jumped once again as the tips of my fingers brushed against her skin. Horace placed a towel underneath before I set her back down.

"Alright sweetheart, I'm going to give you something to make you feel better." He gave her a friendly smile as he spoke, reaching for her hand to reinsert her IV that she'd torn out. The knife dropped from her hands when he moved toward her.

He pulled away giving her some distance, watching her for a moment. I was unsure what he was seeing. His degrees in behavioral psychology were most likely coming into play as he studied her. He leaned down to pick up the knife, the blade glistening in the light. Flight kicked in, as she proceeded to back away. She would have fallen off the bed if I hadn't grabbed her.

"First rule, sweetheart, don't lose your weapon. Now I have it, and if I wanted to, I could hurt Lucas and I could hurt you." He pointed the tip of the blade towards me. She stopped struggling, and listened. "He's been really kind to you, hasn't he?"

She nodded. My heart broke when she positioned herself in front of me. He flipped the blade around with ease, offering the handle to her. "Take the knife."

He waited, but she didn't move.

"Take the knife." It was the same voice I used on new trainees, a voice that made her tremble. Reaching out she took the knife in her hand. "Good girl." I softened my voice then whispered in her ear. "He's a doctor, honey. He's not going to hurt you. See my scars? He helped me get better, and he's going to do the same for you. Okay?" I placed a soft kiss on her head.

I turned my attention to Mills.

Cautiously, she held out her arm, letting him reinsert an IV.

"Do I scare you, sweetheart?" he asked her softly. She didn't move. "Are you scared of Lucas?" She shook her head this time, I couldn't help but smile. Mills couldn't either, "Not at all? Not with all the," He gestured to the scar that covered my face. She shook her head again, "Well in that case we will keep him around." He turned his attention to me. "Can you help her lean back?"

"Sure," I rubbed my hand up and down her arm.

"Come on," I pulled her back and adjusted the pillow for her head. "Are you really not scared of me?" With a sweet smile, she shook her head. "Thank you." I whispered to her.

Mills came back with another needle and inserted it into the other end of the IV.

"Has anyone told you that you have beautiful eyes?" He asked. She gave him a nervous smile but shook her head. "No? Well, they are absolutely gorgeous." He filled up the needle again. "There is an old saying that the eyes are the window to the soul, and if one is to look long enough, they will see who is *really* in there. Right now, I see a very beautiful woman who is terrified, confused, and in a lot of pain." He began to refill the needle. *What was he doing?* "These meds I am giving you will make the pain go away, and it's going to make you a bit sleepy. When you wake up, we will explain everything to you. In the meantime, you don't have to be afraid. No one here is going to hurt you." He set down the syringe. "Quite the opposite actually."

Her eyes shifted to the door and back to the IV.

"Get some sleep," I said. "And I'll see you when you wake up."

Slowly, she nodded her head. I watched the clock ticking, waiting for her head to bob and her eyes to droop shut. Mills had already hooked up a bag of blood.

"Why is she awake? You put her into a medically induced coma."

"I did." He looked me dead in the eyes. "There is no way she should be awake. There is no way she should even be *alive* right now."

"Why is she?" I demanded an answer from him.

"Her eyes, what do they remind you of?" He started to disrobe her. I watched him, "Are you telling me –"

"I'm hypothesizing," he cut me off. "Her eyes, the way her body burned through the medicine, and the way her body hasn't broken down from the trauma it was given. The rash on Warts."

"If she is –"

"I know, I'll start running tests. Now, go wrap your hands, get some rest, and let me work."

"This stays quiet."

"Roger."

I gave his shoulder a squeeze, and I continued back down the blood-filled hallway, passing by Mills' opened door heading for Ravin's. I slammed my fist against his door. "Get up, the halls need to be cleaned." The door vibrated from what I'd guess was a boot he tossed. I opened his door, and flipped on the lights. "Get up."

"No."

"Now, princess."

I shut his door behind me and continued on to Cage's room. Her lights were turned off, leaving only the faded blue light from a star-shaped night light. I left the lights off and removed my shirt. It was drenched in sweat and blood, I tossed it to the trash before slipping into the latrine to wash.

I let the steam from the hot water fog up the mirrors, refusing to take a look at myself as I stepped out. I switched off the light before opening the door. My eyes searched for Robyn's silhouette on the bed. I crawled up behind her, waking her up.

"Can I sleep with you tonight?" I kept my voice low, brushing my lips against her ear.

She nodded, her eyes half-open.

I held her gaze, taking her face in my hand. Robyn was by far the most beautiful woman I'd seen. Her skin was a shade of mocha, while her eyes resembled charcoal. I pressed my lips against hers, the blood rushed between my legs. My fingers slid through her hair, gliding along the neck to her large breast that spilled out of my hand. Her hands pulled me closer and traced over my scars, leaving a trail of goosebumps on my skin.

I kissed along her jaw to her neck. The aroma of her shampoo filled my nostrils, making me crave her all the more.

"You are beautiful." I rubbed my nose against hers, while my hands pulled her closer.

"I am not. I'm ugly and homely." She pressed her lips into mine, winding her legs around my waist.

I rubbed against her, "You are delusional."

She laughed giving a snort.

"I am not."

"You are." I pulled down her pajama bottoms. "All women are."

She gasped, smacking my shoulder before laughing more. "We are not."

I kissed her nose.

"How would you know?" I stole one more kiss. "You're delusional."

I adjusted my body, moving my way down hers' pausing from a loud crash echoing outside the hallway. The noise continued, one after another.

"What the fuck is that?"

"Uh, that would be Sammy."

"It's 2:00 in the morning, why is he having a tantrum?"

I cleared my throat, trying to get it to loosen up.

"The girl woke up. She tried to get away. Her wounds reopened. She bled in the hallways."

"Is she okay?" She pushed me away, sitting herself up. "I thought Mills put her to sleep."

I brushed her hair behind her ear.

"She'll be fine. Mills is with her now. He thinks he knows why she woke up."

"Why?"

"Her body burned through the medicine. Some races will do that."

"She's human, Luke."

"Mills is an excellent doctor. You know that, the dosages he'd given her before were correct for a human woman her size."

She shifted.

"I know he is. I'm not doubting him. It's just that – the closest race to us is gone. What race does he think she is?"

"He's thinks that with her eyes, the rash on Warts, and-"

"That's not possible. I need to see for myself." She tried to get up.

"Robyn, I promise you, she is going to be okay." I took her hands and pulled her back into bed. "Mills is working and doesn't need to be distracted with questions that can wait until he's done."

"Okay." She let out a breath. "I just-I know how it is to be treated the way she was. Not to the extent, but –"

I took her face into my hands and kissed her.

"I know. She doesn't have to worry about that now, and neither do you." I pulled her closer. "I promise."

Chapter Four

YEAR 5019, JUNE 20

DR. HORACE MILLS – OSIRIS

I couldn't believe it. She *wasn't* human. Well, not fully at least. There had been small traces of mercury in her blood, suggesting anyone with prolonged contact with her would need treatment for mercury poisoning. *It explained the rash and other symptoms that Warts had.*

Her appearance suggested she was human. Her skin wasn't gold, and at first glance, one couldn't see the strands of gold that blended in with her dark brown hair. *A hybrid? How was this possible?* I thought back to research I had done as a consultant decades ago. Research on creating hybrids. Hybrids for those of two different races who wished to start a family. There had been no positive outcomes. Stillborns with deformities had been and still are the closest thing we've managed to come to. No one was able to conceive simply because the DNA between the races was not compatible.

This brought up the question if she was genetically modified and grown as a donor baby to be used for experimentation. *How did Warts do it? What did he do differently?* The tests I'd ran on her DNA told us who the biological father was, but her mother, her mother was still unknown. This would explain why normal amounts of medicine weren't working for her, how she was able to heal at such an abnormal rate.

I'd regressed her medicine, so she could wake up. All of her bones had fully healed, and the bleeding had stopped. Rubbing my jaw, I stared down at her; her face was still swollen but was healing at a good pace considering the state it was in before.

I gently shook her.

"Sweetheart, wake up." Her eyelids slowly opened, showing her emerald eyes. "Hey," I kept a firm grip on her in case she tried to make a run for it. "Do you remember me? Horace Mills?" I gave her a minute to wake up and take to her surroundings. "You're aboard a U.F.F.C. ship and in the infirmary." I brushed a strand of her hair around her face. "You're safe here." I wasn't too sure how much she remembered from waking up the first time.

She shifted her eyes to the table next to me, I'd left the knife Wilts had given her lying there next to my stethoscope.

"Let's sit you up." I kept a grip on her arm and moved my other hand to the back of her head and helped her up. "Slowly, you might feel a little dizzy." Once up, I scooted her legs over the side of the bed to face me.

Her hands slowly came up, stopping as she caught sight of them. I'd removed the restraints that were put on her and set her dislocated and broken fingers back. She closed her hands making fists and wiggling her fingers.

"Can you tell me your name?" My voice must have startled her, but she slowly looked up at me. "Do you have a name?" She turned around and looked at the door, her hand taking a fistful of my sleeve to keep balanced.

"Lu-Lucas?" She looked back at me.

"Lucas?" I smiled. "He's eating lunch. He'll be happy to see you are up, and I bet you are starving. Why don't we go join him?" The mention of food caught her attention. "Come on." I urged her closer to the edge of the table. Her hand kept a grip on me, she moved slowly, her legs almost giving out from her weight.

I wrapped my free hand around her waist.

"Take your time." She balanced, swaying from side to side. "And don't forget your knife." Unsure, she reached out and took the handle. "Put it in your pocket."

She fumbled to get the knife into her pocket and looked at me, waiting once she did.

"Let's go."

After a moment she took a step, swaying again.

"I won't let you fall."

She took a few more steps, and she smiled. It was small and lasted only a moment.

"Ch-Charlotte." She paused to speak, looking at me.

"It's nice to meet you Charlotte."

She kept close to me, stopping at the door, peeking her head out to look down the hallways before stepping out. I led her through, then down the hall and towards the kitchen.

As we got closer, the sound of Ravin and Cage's banter filled the hallway.

"Who-who is that?" She pulled back.

"That is Sammy and Robyn." I guided her toward the entrance. "They won't hurt you."

"Ravin, you're eating, why the fuck do you need a cigarette?" Cage was the one who asked the question. I could imagine Ravin taking a double hit to spite her comment.

"Well, Mama, I can be a dragon when I smoke. See?" Finding his joke funny his laughter spilled out into the hallway. He always used this joke when someone asked him why he was smoking. He'd blew the smoke out his nose and puffed up his cheeks. *Cute little fucker.* The problem was, he knew that.

"In here." At the door, I could feel her pulling away again, she didn't want to go in. Wilts was at the sink, washing his dish and turned his head. "Look who's up? Lucas you remember Charlotte."

He gave her a big smile. It was then she slowly took a step in.

"Rise and shine." He walked closer towering over her. He leaned down giving her a quick kiss on the cheek, before making his way to a chair in the corner of the room to finish reading his book. A quick smile brightened up her face as her fingers brushed against where he'd kissed her.

"There's an empty seat next to Robyn, and across from her is Sammy." I pulled the chair out for her. "It's alright."

She looked over to Ravin, he gave her a Cheshire grin putting the cigarette out on the bottom of his shoe.

"Sit down, honey, Robyn won't bite." Charlotte hovered a second before sitting down on the edge of the seat. "I'll get you some food."

Her shoulders slumped forward, exposing the outline of her spine. In an effort to help pull back the hair that had fallen into her face Cage reached over, causing her to jerk.

"I'm sorry, I was going to move your hair out of the way, so it won't get in your food." Cage moved a bit slower and pulled her hair over to the side, folding it into a braid to tuck behind her ear.

"Here you go. Ice cream. It's the softest thing we have for you to eat at the moment. I'll be sure to cook soft food for dinner tonight." I set the bowl in front of her. "Eat up."

Ravin and Cage began eating again, but their eyes had a hard time looking anywhere else but at Charlotte. I couldn't blame them; they too were trying to wrap their brain around the idea of who and what she was.

"Are you going home on leave, Cage?" I asked the question, turning the attention of the room over to her.

"No. I don't think so. I mean, I should, but every time I go home the house is trashed and I have a fat husband on the couch in his underwear." She cleared her throat, a habit she'd picked up from Wilts.

"Instead, we were actually thinking of going to Earth." She gave a look to Wilts. "We haven't been there together and thought it would be a fun vacation."

"What part?"

"Somewhere in the States. Somewhere...colorful."

"Colorful?" I laughed at her word choice. "Well there is the north-west section of the States. It gets beautiful fall weather. The leaves change, but it's wet. *All* the time." I thought back to my first time there as a child. I could still see the leaves stomped and compressed on the wet ground. "I don't think it stopped raining the entire time I was there. Somehow when it wasn't raining, it was still raining..." I shook my head.

"That doesn't sound too bad. I love the rain."

I chuckled. Set, her home planet, was a desert, and rain never happened. Families who've lived there for generations haven't even seen rain. Water had to be imported from other worlds and was re-cycled constantly.

Set was originally a mining planet, never meant to be terraformed, as a result all resources were almost gone making it the perfect spot for desperate families who couldn't afford to live anywhere else. Her family was one of the first to settle there years ago.

"You don't need to go home to file for your divorce?" Ravin asked.

"No," Cage had married her husband out of school as a business merger for her family. For the first part of their marriage, she worked two full time jobs to support him. Exhausted to the bone, she got the courage to quit one of her jobs and ask him to pick up the extra slack. He didn't take it well. She spent the next three days in the hospital; it was that next day she joined the U.F.F.C. and shipped out to basic the following week.

"He's going to get upset and make a scene." She looked down and pushed her food around. "I'm going to hack into the court system and fill everything out, forge a couple signatures, and be done with it."

"Say the word, and I'll kill the bastard." Ravin offered this every time at the mention of her husband. Unfortunately, each time she said no.

"He's mine, Sammy, but you are more than welcome to help." Wilts didn't look up from his book as he spoke.

"No," Cage laughed. "And lets not talk about murder in front of our new friend. She's already nervous." She wrapped her arm around Charlotte. "They are kidding, their sense of humor isn't for everyone." Cage gave her a friendly smile. "Eat."

She kept her eyes down and didn't move.

"Do you not want to eat it because it's vanilla?" Ravin grunted his way out of his chair. "I don't blame you, the only people who like vanilla are…" He shuddered. "They're just not right." He made his way to the cabinet to pull out a bottle.

"Don't be hatin', Sammy." Wilts put his book down and looked up from the corner.

"I'm not saying there's anything wrong with being vanilla, which you clearly are." Ravin's comment made him laugh, "Why this strawberry mama is with you I'll never know."

"Does that make you chocolate?" Cage asked, finishing her plate.

"Mills is chocolate, I'm-I'm more of a…"

"Rocky road." I offered.

"Because people either love me or hate me?"

"No, because you're nuts," Wilts laughed, as he spoke.

"It's endearing." I blew him a kiss, "What do you have?"

"This, my fine friend, is," He paused, being as dramatic as possible. "Chocolate syrup." He set the bottle down in front of Charlotte. "This will make it taste better." He walked back over and sat down.

"Hold on, real chocolate?" I asked.

"Yup." He kicked back in his chair and raised his eyebrows. "You're welcome."

How did he get that? Real chocolate, the cook inside me was jumping. Chocolate was rare, and only came from Earth.

I pulled down a bowl, "Do you want any, Mama?"

"Yes, please." She pushed her plate away to make room. I filled two bowls up and doused them in chocolate and gave some to Charlotte.

"Eat up, sweetheart, before it melts."

"*See*," Ravin gave a dirty grin to Wilts. "Everyone loves chocolate." He sang the last bit.

Wilts tsked towards him.

"Sammy, you and Lucas are going to make us fat with all these sweets you keep bringing on the ship," Cage interjected.

"What about the homemade bacon grease meals Mills cooks? Three times a day, I might add," Wilts countered her claim.

"Let's not say anything hasty," Ravin was sitting up in his chair. "We love your cooking, Wilts' blood sugar is low, he's talking crazy."

I laughed, "I think his sugar fine –"

Colonel Elba walked in giving a mocking cough, "As you were." Shifting our attention over, he was dressed in his uniform. "Just getting a little grub." He gave us a nod and a smile at Charlotte. "Look who is up, you better eat that," he said. "It's gonna melt."

She shifted a bit in her chair and brushed her fingers against her jaw. She looked over to me, I set my bowl down and turned to talk to Elba.

"Colonel, I'm almost done reviewing C.K. I was also –" My voice got caught in my throat as I felt Charlotte's hands pull on my belt.

I jumped back and clenched her hands in mine. All I could do was stare at her, unsure how to handle what was happening. "What are you doing?"

Deep down I knew, but I didn't want to believe it.

"Di-did you want to sit down?" Her voice came out raspy.

"No, no. What. Are. You. Doing." I couldn't stop the anger from spilling over in my voice.

"Where-where do you want me?"

I released her hands and slammed my fist into the cabinet behind me. The hate I was feeling for the Formers had reached a new high. Doing my best to calm down I turned back to her.

"Eat *your* food."

She didn't move; even with her puffed face, I could see the confusion that was embedded on it. "Wh-what do you want?"

"I want you to eat your food."

She didn't move.

Ravin reached over, placing her spoon into the melting ice cream. "Eat." He said. She struggled to get up from her seat. "Sit your ass down, and eat." He didn't shout, instead he pulled his voice from his diaphragm. It was a clear warning, her hand shaking as she picked up her spoon. I was too stunned to sit down, and everyone else couldn't look away.

"Sergeant Ravin. This is the fifth cigarette butt of yours I've found today. Get off your ass and clean the ship from top to bottom." Elba walked over and flicked the butt at Ravin. "You might want to start in the holding cell. There is a piece of shit in there that needs to be taken care of."

That last part caught his attention and actually put a grin on his face. "The code, sir." Ravin was up and ready to go.

"Of course. Four, six, seven, three." Elba had to shout the last bit out to Ravin who was already down the hall.

"Sir," Wilts stood up. "Some of those might have been mine."

"Then why don't you get off your ass and help Ravin." He didn't have to be told twice, he was out the door as fast as Ravin was.

I looked over to see Cage comforting Charlotte.

"Horace, you scared her." It was my turn to be scolded by her.

I knelt down next to her, "I'm sorry, Charlotte, I didn't mean to scare you."

"I didn't mean-mean to make you mad." I had to strain my ears to hear her. "Please –"

"You didn't make me mad. I have a temper sometimes. Can you forgive me?"

She nodded before I was finished talking.

"Thank you, sweetheart. Eat."

Chapter Five

Year 5032, September 11

Sergeant Samuel Duke – Osiris

"Alien," Cameron said. "With these injuries, she should be dead; unless she had some sort of modified genetic work or wasn't completely human."

"You idiot." Spit shot out as Atkins spoke. "Formers despise aliens, why would he go and fuck one?"

Angel shot up and slammed Atkins' head onto the table.

"Call him an idiot again and I'll break your legs." She sat back down.

"I'm in love." Ravin whispered under his breath to Mills, before turning to Angel, "Are you seeing anyone?" He brushed the edge of her chin with his fingers as he spoke making her laugh. Unentertained by Ravin's thinking, Mills jammed his elbow into his side. "Ouch!"

"Could you use your other head for a moment?" Mills turned his attention back to the matter at hand. "Jones is right. Her mother was alien."

"Formers don't fuck aliens." Atkins pinched the bridge of his nose as he leaned forward.

"They don't. But they rape them. It wouldn't be the first time it's happened. Aliens are looked at as property to the Formers, and they will do whatever they want to them." I looked at Mills. "They usually sell the men and rape and kill the women. I've never heard of this though, are you sure she's a hybrid?"

"I'm positive."

"What race was the mother?"

"Pharaoh."

"That's impossible. If she was in her early twenties, that means they were wiped out eight years before her birth."

He agreed, "Which means that Warts had at least one Pharaoh as a prisoner. He used the DNA from the mother and the girl to create C.K." Mills stood up and began to pace. "He used them as his guinea pigs, loading them up with different chemical cocktails. But the girl held the key to his weapon. Her DNA was what he needed to make the weapon."

"That's why you destroyed all evidence of the weapon. Scientists would have figured out about her or at least of a hybrid." Cameron ran his hand through his hair.

"That doesn't make sense. So, what? He tested the weapon out on her? How does that have anything to do with exposing her?" Atkins joined in.

"Her DNA would have been found within the weapon," Cameron explained.

"Spot on." It was Wilts who complimented him. "If we handed over the weapon, it would be no different from handing her over. She would have gone from a prisoner to a science experiment. Besides that, there is the possibility that the Formers would hear a rumor of a hybrid and come running demanding that she be killed. The whole situation for her was fucked. So, we did what we could to hide her from everyone."

"Do we know what it was about her DNA that made the bioweapon work? Better yet what is the weapon supposed to do?" I looked over to Mills.

"C.K. is highly contagious, transmitted by air, and everyone that comes in contact with it becomes a carrier. Once infected the virus lays dormant, giving it an incubation period of one week before the signs of infection appear."

"What's it target?" Cameron asked.

"The nervous system, specifically the brain. It brings on hallucinations – visual and audial. Forty-eight hours after the incubation, the virus begins to eat the brain in a similar manner of untreated syphilis, but it specifically targets the amygdala, resulting in increased aggression."

"Jesus." I muttered his name under my breath.

"As the brain starts to eat itself," Mills continued on. "The body starts to rot."

"What do you mean rot?"

"The way the virus attacks is through the nervous system. While the brain is eating itself, each nerve in the body is becoming infected, depending on where the nerve leads will depend what part of the body starts to die."

"Are you telling me that he created a weapon to create god-damn zombies?"

"I wouldn't call them zombies," I shook my head in disbelief at Mills. "They are alive. Similar in the aspect that they are rotting and depending how far along they are, a bullet wouldn't stop them because they wouldn't be able to feel the pain."

"But you guys destroyed it. Right?" Atkins was on the edge of his seat. "The report says you destroyed it."

"We couldn't destroy it because we got to him in time before he could finish putting it together." Elba paced behind the couch as he spoke. "Warts needed an erroneous amount of pressure to combine the new compound he designed."

"The equipment that was stolen a few weeks ago is what was needed to build a particle accelerator." Angel spoke, "That's why you're worried."

"Yes." Wilts was the one who spoke. "Warts didn't talk; we honestly don't know if anyone else is aware of what he was doing. If this is related to C.K., we need to take care of it before someone builds it and tries to find out what happened to Charlotte."

"Is that her name?" I directed my question to him.

His jaw tightened, but he gave a sharp nod.

"The bastard thought it was poetic."

I shifted through the pictures again, "What did you do with her? I mean no disrespect, but there is no way she can be mentally stable. Her quality of life is gone."

Mills was the one who answered me.

"The mind can be very powerful, and it finds ways to adapt, comprehend, and deal with trauma. We helped her find a way to deal with her situation."

Elba jumped in.

"To be more precise, it was Mills who helped her, in all aspects of healing from physical to mental. He was the one who spent the most time with her. If he felt in any way she was unable to thrive, he would have taken care of it and given her peace." The tone of his voice told me not to press the matter.

"Yes, sir."

He continued, "Cage worked on creating her a file. Spruced it up, gave her a regular childhood. An only child, a loving mother and loving father. She joined the U.F.F.C. in her early twenties and was a part of the infantry team. On a mission, she was captured by a group of Formers, and taken as a prisoner of war."

"After a month, she was rescued, and the injuries she'd obtained allowed her to be medically discharged. After that, the U.F.F.C. would take care of her. Weekly disability checks, counselors, medical care. The works."

"You hid her in plain sight." I chuckled.

Ravin spoke, "Mama dug deeper into the message that was sent, too, the warning we'd received came from Warts computer. Charlotte was the one who sent it; she was the one who warned us of what he was doing. The bastard caught her at his computer but didn't know what she was doing. She could have sent an S.O.S message, but didn't. Cage gave her a purple heart and a medal of honor in her file."

I nodded, taking in the information that had been given.

"So far I understand why you destroyed all the evidence to the bio-weapon, why you've refused to speak on the matter. I understand the urgency of this mission. If this is the same weapon, it'll expose her and put her in a lot of danger. Not to mention the shit show that would happen if it was to be released. But, why did you go back to attack Sobek once you had Warts and the data on C.K.?"

"You went back to find her mother." Angel kept her voice soft.

Wilts gave her a soft smile.

"If Charlotte was half Pharaoh, then that meant their race wasn't gone. If we'd have known at the time about Charlotte, we would have handled the situation better, looked for others." He looked down and thought about his next words. "It took five days after we got back on Osiris before we understood what she was. We kept it quiet from the crew and told them she'd passed away."

"We decided we couldn't risk leaving a possible prisoner behind, especially if it was one of Pharaoh descent. We turned the ship around and headed back, but by that time, they knew Warts was missing. A ship of mercenaries working for him had boarded our ship in an attempt to get him and Charlotte back." He cleared his throat. "Others were waiting for us. We made the call to arm the ship, drug the crew, and storm the planet in hopes of rescuing prisoners."

"All that, and you didn't find her mother." I couldn't help but be angry. "Did you find anything or anyone?"

"No." Mills replied. "We found nothing. Not even a body. We found the skins of several Pharaohs hung up in homes. I took DNA samples of them all, no matches." I gave a dry laugh at his comment. "It's possible that the mother got away. Warts doesn't even know what happened to her," Mills continued on. "Pharaohs were peaceful and refused to fight, but their intelligence was through the roof. She could have gotten away."

"Gotten away but at the price of leaving her daughter with that monster?" I gave a sigh. "But I suppose that doesn't matter at this point in time. "General, what is our next move after this?"

"We visit Warts, try and find out if he has any idea who would know this much about the weapon he was creating."

"Would Charlotte know?"

"I haven't had the chance to ask her." Mills responded. "I'll be reaching out to her soon. See if anything Warts says rings a bell with her."

"Do you think she will? Given –"

Mills interjected, "She's intelligent and picked up on a lot more than Warts realized. Her IQ is over a hundred forty. Something she inherited from the Pharaoh race. I know she will do her best to give us all the information we need." He turned to Elba. "How far out from Warts are we?"

"A little over an hour. I kept him close." Elba gave a grin.

Ravin stood up.

"This is all very exciting, and we are all glad to be back, but I have to point out that there are a lot of people here. Now, it might be me, but I don't think we need this many." He turned to Angel. "Why don't you stay behind, you and I have the same job and –"

Angel shot up.

"What?"

"I don't want to see you get hurt, you're very pretty." He brushed his fingers across her jaw, giving a smoldering smile to her.

I laughed, catching his attention.

"I'm going." She held his eyes as he looked back to her.

"Um, no you're not."

"I'm not a *child*. Don't treat me like one." Her hand reached down between his legs and took a firm grip on his testicles. He studied her face for a moment unflinching. Honestly, I was surprised at how calm he was. Wilts and Mills stifled their laughs; they must have seen the look on her face, she would do it.

"I'm going to call your bluff here, hon…" Her hand squeezed down, curses spewing out as he tumbled down. Sweating, he reached out to the couch behind him to keep from falling all the way to the ground. Her grip tightened even more, and she gave a twist. He screamed, actually screamed. She twisted more.

"You are not my commanding officer. I don't take orders from you. If anyone is going to be left out, it's going to be you."

"Duke, help a brother out." He didn't break eye contact with her.

"She's going." At my confirmation that she was going, she finally released her grip causing him to double over.

"Ha," she taunted.

He looked at me, horror and pain etched into his face waiting for an explanation.

"She's put six men your size into the hospital in less than ten minutes."

He looked surprised, "Really?" He sized her up.

"Try and boss me around some more, and you'll find out how." She placed a kiss on his cheek and exited the room.

"I need a doctor." His breath was ragged.

"Relax." Mills stepped over to him and helped him up. "I'm sure they're still attached. I'll give you some aspirin and a bag of ice. You'll be fine."

"No, I mean a shrink. I'm a little freaked out by how much that turned me on."

"Ahh." Mills stepped back. "You'll need more than one session for that."

"Ha. Ha." Ravin wobbled out of the room, muttering with each step.

I dismissed the rest of my team, and stood next to the door waiting for them to disappear down the hallway before turning my attention to General Elba and his old team.

"Do you have something you wish to get off your chest, Sergeant Duke?" General Elba stepped towards me, an act of dominance. In any other situation, I would fall into attention, giving him the respect the General of the U.F.F.C. deserved.

"I joined the U.F.F.C. when I turned eighteen. This isn't the first thing I've seen get swept under the rug. I understand how you've planned this mission out in your mind, Ebla." My words caught the attention of everyone in the room. "You picked one of the R.R. teams that has two members without family, a member to which society would cheer to find out that he died, and one that is too naïve to understand what the hell is going on." He opened his mouth to respond but couldn't get words out. "We are disposable." I spoke toward him. "Keep in mind, people get lost in space all the time. You might have a little accident before you get home from leave." I raised an eyebrow.

"I'm glad we are at an understanding of how this mission ends... for you."

I held his gaze a bit longer before I exited the room. My team was safe for now, but once the mission was over, that would be another story. I needed to prepare, get one step ahead of Elba. Hearing what had happened on the last mission was helpful. I was beginning to see how they think, how they'd attack. I gave a dry laugh.

"Duke," Mills hollered out after me, his boots thumping against the metal floor. "Duke." I didn't bother to turn around until I felt his hand grip around my arm.

I could feel the warmth of his hand through my sleeve. I looked to his hand and back up holding his gaze, he was an inch taller than me and *very* good looking. Catching my thoughts, I mentally kicked myself. "Do you mind?"

He ignored my question. "It's not personal, we –"

"Relax, Doc." I ripped my arm from his grip. "We will do the job. Protect the girl and prevent C.K. from being released. You're welcome, by the way."

"Thank you, I –"

"After that, I'm going to put a bullet in your head, then Elba's, and everybody else on your team. I might shoot Atikins, too, but for different reasons. It's nothing personal."

"There is more to this than –"

"Save your breath. I don't care." I held his gaze.

"Confrontation?" Ravin danced his way over to us with a cigarette in hand. "What happened? Not gay? Sorry man, I thought he was."

"What?" My mind did a one eighty as I looked from Ravin back to Mills.

"Shut the fuck up, Ravin." Mills pinched the bridge of his nose. "He knows we plan to dispose of him and his team."

"Oh, well. That ain't good. No hard feelings pal." He clapped my shoulder. "It's nothing personal." He took a hit of his cigarette without a care in the world.

I looked closer at him and saw his blood shot eyes. It wasn't a cigarette; it was a joint. The bastard was high. Mills took notice, too.

"Not even an hour out and you're stoned. You've got to be fucking kidding me."

I could hear the laughter in his voice.

"I just had my nuts assaulted, sue me. Besides, I wasn't the one who told him our plan, you ass-wipe." He reached over and backhanded Mills' shoulder.

Mills tsked, "I didn't tell him you bastard." He returned the smack.

"Then how did he find out, cocksucker?" Smack.

"Because he's not an idiot, dumbass?" Smack.

"Eunuch." Smack.

"He didn't tell me. A monkey could have figured it out," I jumped in.

Ravin took a step back and eyed me from top to bottom.

"Calm down, there is no need to be hostile." I gave him a blank stare. "Well, I suppose there is. What are you going to do?" He took a drag of the joint before he offered me a hit.

"Jesus Christ." I muttered under my breath before I pulled away. I walked a few steps before I turned around and took the joint from Ravin to take a hit. "Thanks, fucker."

"Anytime, goochy." He blew me a kiss.

I scouted the ship for the next hour, starting on the first floor and working my way up. There really wasn't another soul outside of the nine of us. That was a lot of faith General Elba had in his ship and his team. No engineers, no nurses, no captain. I pushed away the thoughts of what would happen if an emergency was to arise and continued to check every wall and floor base for more compartments.

Osiris wasn't a smugglers ship, which meant they made each compartment. I found several weapons, cartons of cigarettes, coke, and busty lady magazines among little knick-knacks.

"Fuck." I didn't know what I was looking for, but it wasn't porn or cancer. I'd even double checked the compartment where Wilts hid the file on Charlotte. Nothing.

"You won't find anything." Mills' voice came from behind me. I stood up from where I was to look at him. "We really did destroy everything."

"Right."

He'd showered, trimmed his beard, and changed into uniform. He was quite the sight to see in his dark uniform, his eyes stood out against his pale face, while his – *Stop it!*

"Do forgive me, I find that to be a pile of shit."

He tsked, and I could see the frustration on his face.

"If you have a question, ask. I'll either tell you or instruct you to fuck off."

"How do you plan to kill us?"

"Fuck off."

"Where is Charlotte?"

"Fuck off."

"Is she safe?"

"I believe she is. Everyone else thinks she's in danger."

"Why do they think that?"

"Fuck off."

"Jesus. Are you going to answer every question with that?"

He debated the question before he answered, "Fuck off."

"What's the plan here then? You're out voted from the sounds of it, best be careful. I hear that'll get you chopped up."

He laughed.

"I choose what happens to her. They know that. She stays where she's at."

"Why do you have a say over what happens to her?"

"Fuck off." I saw the answer coming and said it with him.

"You know there is an old saying, 'He who does not trust enough, will not be trusted.'"

"Lao Tzu." He smiled. "He also said, 'Let it be still, and it will gradually become clear.'"

I returned his smile. "Fair enough."

"For someone who knows we plan to kill him, you don't look too worried. Why is that?"

I leaned up against the wall and gave a friendly smile.

"Fuck off."

He chuckled, "I should have seen that coming. Um, I have to ask. Why did Angel put six men in the hospital, and am I going to have to keep an eye on Ravin?"

I was still smiling, but before I could answer General Elba's voice spoke out over the speakers.

"We will be landing in five minutes. Be ready."

"As long as Ravin behaves, he will be fine. If you will excuse me." I pushed past him to meet my team in the cargo bay for when we landed. Elba kept the identity of the planet Warts was on a secret, but considering how far we traveled from Ammit, I had a couple ideas.

Cameron came running up behind me. "Sir."

"Are you doing okay, kid?" I asked, clapping him on the back. He slowed down and walked with me.

"I'm trying to wrap my head around this. I never thought I'd get a mission like this. I imagine Angel is loving it. She used to do missions like this before, right? That's what happened to her head."

"Yeah, at least we have an expert on this shit, huh?"

"Sir? She disappeared for three days and came back hungover, I'd say that's far from –"

"She had permission to be off for those three days."

"Sir, you disappeared with her for those three days, I had to pump both of your stomachs."

"You had three days without work and full pay. I don't see the issue or how that is relevant."

"It's relevant in the fact of what the mission did to her. She hardly sleeps, has drinking binges, has on more than one occasion –"

"She got the Scars team to help us, now we know what happened and what we need to do to prevent it from happening again."

"Yes, sir."

Cameron and I came up on the cargo bay, and he fell into position with Angel and Atkins. Cage was waiting with them, showered, changed, and ready to go. One by one, everyone fell in. Wilts, Ravin, and Mills.

Once grounded, we waited for Elba to meet us from the bridge. Outside the ship, the smell of sulfur filled my nose, strong enough that I hardly noticed the ground squish beneath my boots. I couldn't tell what was around us; it was too dark. The only source of light came from a small light up ahead, that revealed itself to be a porch light as we came closer.

"It smells like shit here," Atkins complained.

"Shut the fuck up, Atkins."

Wilts pushed passed everyone and took the lead with Elba.

The porch light illuminated the building that I could only guess housed Warts. Similar to the prison on Ammit, it was made from metal.

It was, however, a lot smaller and had a ramp that led up to the doorway that was guarded by two men.

I sized the two men up, not military, but they did have training based on how they handled their weapons. I looked closer… *Holy shit.*

"Sir, I think I know where the missing prisoners went," Angel spoke up as she walked next to me.

I scoffed, "Who better to torture and monitor your enemy than 'A class' felons?"

Angel's hand took hold of my wrist.

"Sam." She paused, pulling me to a stop. "I –"

"Are you always unreserved on your missions, *Duke*?" Mills had made his way next to us. "Go meet up with Wilts." He gave the order to Angel.

Angel released her grip. I wrapped my arm around her waist, pulling her closer and giving her a kiss on the thick scars that branded her head.

"Go keep an eye on Atkins. He's getting twitchy," I countered his order.

"Yes, sir."

I didn't take my eyes off Mills and waited for Angel to be out of view before I spoke.

"You lost your medical license when you went to prison, correct?"

"Yes," his tone was unamused, a sensitive topic for him. "But you already knew that."

"I did. I also know you were a really talented doctor, so when I say the words emotional dysregulation, I can assume you know what that means."

His hand pulled me to a stop outside the building.

"Angel?"

I nodded, "A side effect from her head injury."

"She shouldn't be out in the field."

"She's fine. She is not a child. If I felt at any time she was in danger I'd have her medically discharged. She needs physical touch to calm down sometimes, there is *nothing* wrong with that, and that does not suggest that she can't do her job." I took a fast grip on his arm as his eyes wandered off to Angel to gain his attention back. "Let's not forget to mention, you are not her C.O. Understood?"

"Of course."

I released my grip and motioned for us to follow after the rest of the team, making our way through the building and down the stairs to a basement. The further we went down the stairs a strong odor began to appear. Elba stopped in front of a door that was guarded by two men who gave friendly smiles to us.

"Good evening, sir, we have the bastard ready for you."

"Good work, the two of you can take a break." Elba shook their hands excusing them. "Duke, you are by definition the C.O. Get the information we need. Get creative."

"Yes, sir."

"Angel, I could use your help with arming, securing, and stocking weapons for the mission. You are the expert in that area. I want to be prepared for anything." Elba motioned for her to follow him.

"Duke?" She asked.

"Go ahead."

She smiled, before Elba turned to Cameron.

"This way. Jones, why don't you help, too."

A bit of relief shown in Cameron's eyes. He was aware of what was about to happen and didn't want to see it. I gave him a nod to go ahead. Angel's words drifted through my head. *It's personal.*

"Wilts, would you like to take the lead?" I asked.

"Yes, sir."

I gripped the ice-cold knob that would open the door to one of the worst people I'd have to encounter.

"Go ahead." I pushed open the door, the hinges creaked in protest. The smell of urine and sweat had mixed with the smell of sulfur from the planet.

In the far corner, flies buzzed over a small bucket that was overflowing with excrement. Next to the bucket bolted in the walls were chains. Under the chains, the floor appeared polished; if I had to guess it was from the years Warts was forced to sleep there.

My eyes drifted over to Warts. He was sitting at a table in the middle of the room; cuffs held his wrists together. I smiled at the sight of his bruised and swollen face and sealed the door behind me, signaling for Cage and Atkins to stand by. Cage pulled out a blade and began heating it with a lighter.

I pushed aside the thought for the reason behind that and focused on Warts again. I could still see the deep wrinkles that set their way on every inch of his face, his hair had thinned and turned gray.

He opened his mouth to give a smile, exposing the last few of his stained teeth.

"One…two…three…four…five…six… What's the occasion?" Spit dripped out over his lips with each word.

Mills walked over to the front of the room while Wilts pulled a chair out and sat across from him. Ravin came up behind him.

"Mr. Warts," I started.

"*General.* General Warts."

Grudgingly, I pushed out a smile.

"You smell like shit, Genital Warts, and that makes me want to get this over with rather quickly. I'm positive you recognize my friends." I gave a subtle smile.

He narrowed his eyes to Mills.

"The fuckers who took my daughter from me. Where is she?"

I ignored his question and motioned for Wilts to begin.

"A week ago, equipment to build a particle accelerator was stolen. That's what you needed to finish your weapon, wasn't it?"

He gave off a sinister laugh.

"I tell you what, let me see my daughter, and I'll tell you. Let me *feel* her, and I'll spill the beans."

I noticed Wilts' body shift, and I jumped in before he could move.

"Your daughter?" I gave a grin. "She's far away from here. Happily married." I lied. "She's made quite a success of herself. She doesn't even remember who you are, the U.F.F.C. cleared her memory. You're nothing but a bad dream to her."

I saw anger rush into his eyes.

"Formers law states that as the father, I am entitled to all my children until I give them away. They've taken away my rights keeping her from me. I don't adhere to *your* secular law."

"You aren't her father, you piece of shit."

Mills took five large steps and came face to face with Warts, pushing past me and Wilts.

"I am too. She has my DNA." Warts attempted to get up at the insult Mills had made, only to be forced back down.

"*I* carried her out of that prison." Mills kept his voice low. "*I* fixed every broken bone, cleaned every wound. *I* taught her how to walk, *I* soothed every night terror. That makes her *my* daughter."

Warts shot up from his chair this time, before Ravin could throw him back down.

"No!" he snarled. "She's mine."

"No. Charlotte Warts? She died thirteen years ago. My daughter, she's alive and has no memory of you. She writes me letters every week, each letter starting out 'Dear Daddy,' and ending, 'love, your daughter…' Well, you don't need to know her name." He smirked. "I carry her picture with me." He opened his left breast pocket and placed a photo face down with his hand on top. "This picture right here is the only thing you'll ever get. If you want it, you need to start talking."

Warts' eyes never left the photo that was placed in front of him.

"I tell you, and you give me that picture." Mills nodded. "What do you want to know?"

"Who stole the equipment and why?"

"Barren, he was working with me on the bioweapon. We shared the files that you erased from my computer. He is continuing our work to build the weapon." He spoke quickly.

"What else?"

"He usually works with a team of ten. You killed his last team when they boarded your ship. He would have replacements by now. More this time, I would bet, well trained." His eyes focused on the picture.

"What else."

A growl leaked from his lips.

"We terraformed a planet outside the Ra galaxy decades ago. We named it Nefertiti. Uninhabited. All testing that was done on Charlotte's Kiss was done there. That's where he will build the bioweapon. Sobek is too crowded."

"Are there any civilians there?"

"There shouldn't be, scientists and our guards. Picture." He held his hand out.

"Location." Mills pushed the picture closer, but never lifted his hand from it.

"About fifty light years northwest of Sobek."

Mills let out a smirk.

"Fuck off." He turned away and put the picture back into its pocket without exposing the image.

"That's mine!" Warts jumped up in an attempt to snag the picture. Ravin's hands pinned him to the table, he placed his knee into the middle of Warts' back to hold him down. Wilts stood, the sound of his chair scraping against the ground, making his way behind Warts to help Ravin.

Mills took a handful of Warts' hair and cranked his neck to force him to look up at him.

"When my daughter found out I would be in this room with you, she told me to 'look out for the monster. Look out for the monster, he wears the skin of a man. He doesn't have claws, he doesn't need them.'" The smell of Warts was making Mills' nose turn up. "I've had trouble sleeping knowing that you've never suffered by my hand for what you did. That's going to change."

Mills drew out an axe from his belt.

"No! No! Get off!"

Mills flung down the axe, the blade sliced through his wrist to kiss the table below in one large swing. His scream bellowed out and faded into a sob. His eyes fixated on where his hand used to be, too busy to notice the chain that slinked off. It was Ravin's turn to take a handful of Warts' hair and force him to look at the other hand.

Realizing that he was going to lose another he bucked and thrashed, but it did no good. Wilts had a solid hold on him. He wasn't going anywhere. He didn't plea this time, he only struggled to get away.

He screamed louder this time. The axe made a twin noise to what it made before. Ravin stepped aside but Wilts held his grip.

"Now, I'm not a doctor anymore, but old habits die hard."

Cage gave the knife she'd been heating up over to him. Without a thought he pressed the blade against the stumps. The sound of his flesh sizzling rang in my ears, making my skin crawl.

Wilts released Warts, who slumped to the floor sobbing. In shock, he stared at the stumps where his hands should be, mumbling words I didn't care to know. Cage took the knife from Mills and put the flame back on it. *They weren't done.*

Mills lifted Warts up off the floor and threw his body down onto the table like a ragdoll. Wilts had Warts' pants down and pinned his legs down while Ravin picked up the axe and sauntered forward. I walked over and grabbed his flailing arms to hold down. I took my free hand to lift his head up to make him watch.

Ravin took a firm grip on his genitals and cut slowly, the sound of tearing flesh drowned out over Warts' screams. Ravin stepped aside and let Mills use the tip of the knife to cauterize the wound. Simultaneously, we let go, letting him curl up in a ball.

I watched him writhe in pain but felt no regret. Justice wasn't as black and white as the worlds made it seem. He would be here for another seven years...if he made it with these wounds. It wouldn't surprise me if General Elba decided to hold off on any medical treatment.

I turned my gaze from Warts to Mills, small amounts of blood had splattered on his face leaving the tiniest evidence of what he did. It made sense now, why they dedicated themselves – gave up their lives.

I knew better than most that your team was family. I cringed at the thought of someone hurting Angel the way Warts had done to Charlotte. I gave Mills an understanding nod. Brothers in arms meant more to them than it did to most, and after all, what wouldn't you do for family?

Chapter Six

Year 5019, July 3

Staff Sergeant Samuel Ravin – Osiris

"Everyone on the bridge. Now!" Colonel Elba's voice echoed over the intercom. Wilts and I lowered our arms and exchanged glances.

"Any ideas, Boss?" I asked, the both of us jumping out of the ring to follow his orders.

"Nope."

He took the lead ahead of me, looking into every room he passed. Wilts never let his guard down, not once in all the years I've known him. Christmas shopping with the man was a nightmare. The planning started at the beginning of October. It was similar to preparing for a mission. Blueprints were handed out, all exits were known, and the building was checked every hour on the hour. All in all, he gave the best gifts.

We met Cage as she exited the kitchen looking as confused as we did.

"What's going on?"

"Not sure." Wilts nudged his head, indicating her to follow.

Colonel Elba was waiting patiently on the bridge for us. From the look on his face, this wasn't good news. We lined ourselves up in attention waiting for Mills to join us a few moments later.

"Where's Charlotte?" Elba paced back and forth in front us as he spoke.

"I put her to bed an hour ago," Mills answered. "She wasn't feeling well."

"What's wrong with her?" Wilts was the one who asked the question. A valid question, we turned to Mills waiting for an answer.

"She's fine. We are trying out different medications to combat the mercury in her blood."

"Could you get her please." Elba had stopped pacing.

"Yes, sir."

I gave a side glance to Wilts. It was clear he wasn't sure either. Standing next to Cage, he passed the glance along. I saw her shake her head. The girl was a civilian, and civilians were not brought in on operations. *Why did he need her here?*

Mills was back a little more than a minute later, his arm wrapped around Charlotte, guiding her in the room. She was still limping and most of her bruises were turning a murky green. Her face was healing but still a bit swollen, specifically around her right eye that had been swollen shut.

Her body instinctively pulled back to the exit as she saw us lined up.

"Come sit down." Colonel Elba reached out to her hand making her flinch back. He ignored it. If Mills didn't have his arm around her, I'm sure she would have fled back to her room.

He pulled out his chair and helped her sit. She refused to let go of Mills' hand until Elba had broken contact with her. Elba was the only person out of the five of us who she seemed uneasy with. Mills was the only person she wasn't truly afraid of; she never flinched when he moved around her, and she'd only sleep if he was in the same room with her.

Elba turned his attention back on us.

"I have some new information to feed you..."

I switched my gaze quickly over to Charlotte. She wasn't watching me; she was watching Elba. I did a double take when I noticed annoyance shining through her eyes. *Annoyance; was it towards Elba? Stupid question, of course it was.* She furrowed her brows, flared her nostrils, and stuck her tongue out at him. I felt a smile crawl its way on my face, and I had to stifle a laugh.

"Something funny, Sergeant Ravin?" Elba turned his sole attention to me.

I opened my mouth to respond and found another laugh trying to escape. I cleared my throat.

"Sir, you said 'feed.'" Her eyes focused on me, realizing I'd seen her.

"And?"

"Earlier today, I caught Sergeant Wilts getting spooked by a rodent and accidentally swallowed his gum. Unexpectedly, he started choking sir, and the poor bastard started to cry. It made me laugh, and your choice of words happened to remind me."

Colonel Elba's mouth dropped open for a split second.

"Lucas, are you okay?"

"Yes, sir." Wilts responded, "I usually only chew one piece at a time, but it was Hubba Bubba bubble gum, so ideally, you chew two pieces. It's delicious, but the flavor lasts only a minute. I've written several strongly worded letters to the company."

Later he was going to question me about why he covered for me. *I wonder if he will believe me?*

"Honestly, we've mastered space travel, and yet gum still loses its flavor. It's criminal," I eagerly agreed with Wilts.

"Sir," Cage spoke up before Elba could continue on. "That reminds me of an important topic. Sergeant Wilts needs to cool it on the weight lifting. I strained my back doing the Heimlich on him while he was choking."

"And why couldn't Ravin have done that?" He was up in my face, breathing down my neck. Cage was able to hold her ground in any battle, but Sergeant Wilts was easily over three hundred pounds and could squash her instantly. I was surprised how he hadn't thus far, but it was, according to Mills, an inappropriate question to ask.

"Sir, Ravin was laughing too hard to even attempt to help."

Colonel Elba slowly backed off and took his position in front of us.

"Sergeant. No more gum," he sent his order to Wilts.

"No promises, sir."

I peeked back to Charlotte, giving her a wink.

"We are crossing paths with the trading vessel we used to get onto Sobek. It is unclear if this ship is the crew heading back. There could be a possibility that Warts' men may be aboard, looking for him."

He turned around to Charlotte.

"Now, Charlotte I want to stress to you," he walked over and got on his knee before taking her hands. "If it is Warts men, they will not touch you, and you will not go back. Clear?" The fear on her face was still there but she nodded. "Good."

He stood back up and turned to us.

"I want to be prepared for the chance that it is his men. No weapons are to be fired on the ship, I do not want any damage done that could bring down Osiris, and we need to save as much ammo as possible for when we land."

"Yes, sir." we said in unison.

"They'll have to board the same way any other ship does. They will dock their ship below ours, and we won't have a choice but to let them on."

Fuck. Ideally, it wasn't bad if a ship docked with another in space. It was a safety feature for ships that were in need of restock for whatever supplies necessary.

Elba continued on, "Wilts, Mills, Cage, I want all of you at the entry site waiting. Ready to disarm and terminate. Ravin, you will take Charlotte and Warts and get them into my office, barricade yourself in there until we give you the all clear. Do not let anyone with in fifty feet of her."

"Yes, sir."

He turned and faced Charlotte.

"You will need to do everything Sergeant Ravin tells you to do. You listen to him, and he can keep you safe." Once again, she nodded her head. "Good."

"I will stand guard outside the containment bay where the rest of the crew is. Questions?"

"Sir," Mills stepped out of line to speak. "When is the ship envisioned to make contact with us if it keeps its course?"

"Two days. If they speed up, one."

My heart skipped a beat while my body jerked awake. I ignored the throbbing in my head caused by the ship's security alarm. Red and white lights flashed in unison with the alarm. I was out of bed and fully dressed in under a minute. I left my guns in their drawers and palmed a couple blades. The alarm continued to blare. Sprinting out the door, I headed down the hallway over to Mills' bunk.

His door was unlocked and the room empty. I slid open the closet door and pushed around the items. *Not there. Bed?* I got down on my knees and searched underneath. She'd pressed herself all the way to the far wall.

"Let's go." I stretched my arm out towards her. "Now." She took my hand, allowing me to drag her out from under the bed. "Eyes on me."

I didn't wait for her to acknowledge. I moved us out of the room and towards the holding cell. Passing the infirmary, Cage came sprinting toward me.

"The ship, it boarded us." She kept her direction to the bay doors. The alarm and lights were still going. Abruptly, the whole ship shook. I braced myself up against a wall catching Charlotte before she fell.

"Fuck 'em up, Mama," I called out after her.

"Fire. Fire. Exit to safety rooms. Fire. Fire." The automated system broadcasted from the overhead speakers. The sprinklers above us turned on, spewing ice-cold water. We were moving too slow. I lifted her up, wrapping her arms around my neck.

"Hold on, hun." I kept one arm free and raced the rest of the way. The water shut off before we came upon the holding cell. I set her down, "Look at me." Her eyes were full of tears. "Wait here."

I punched in the code to open the door. Warts was sitting in the far corner shackled to the floor.

"Well, well, well. Did you think no one would come for me?" He was drenched from the water pooling down on him. "Where's my daughter?"

Ignoring his comment, I closed the distance extending out my hands to his head and slammed it into my knee. That would be a nasty headache. *Too bad I didn't care.*

I slung his body over my shoulder and exited the room. Charlotte was still hunched down where I'd left her.

"He's knocked out honey, don't worry. We need to move."

I reached my free arm out and picked her up; her arms wrapped around my neck and shoulders. Her breath quickened, and I could hear soft cries that she was choking back.

I headed back the way we came, I needed to go up a flight of stairs to get to Elba's office. Problem was, the stairs were blocked. I nearly slipped on the wet metal when I stopped. I recognized him; he was one of the guards that watched over the cargo that was being unloaded. The red rash on his hands and face were still prominent.

"Ah, look who it is." His voice was crusty, carrying out each of his vowels taunting me. His hand hovered above the gun on his waist. "Hand them over, if you know what's good for you, boy."

Boy? Boy? The fuck? This 'boy' was about to kick some ass. Her arms clung tighter to me.

"Bring it."

I shifted my weight into my left leg, leaned back, and kicked him square in the chest, knocking him back. It gave me enough time to turn and get a head start. I moved quickly but didn't want to burn myself out carrying two people around the ship.

Tailing back, I headed to the training room with him right on my tail. I entered the doorway and turned left, dropping Warts without care. I spun around landing another kick on the man as he entered the doorway, sending him sliding across the floor. I settled Charlotte down next to the door frame and ordered her to wait.

I turned in the knick of time. He charged at me, throwing his arms around my waist, jamming his shoulder into my gut. I hurled my elbow down on his upper back before he could muster any strength to heft me up. He cried out in pain, loosening his grip. I seized his belt lifting him parallel to the ground, using all my strength to slung him to the floor. He bounced up before going back down. I turned as I heard a loud cry coming from the door. *Fuck*!

A large man came charging at me before I had time to move. He clashed his shoulder into my chest as we tumbled to the floor. The air pushed out of me and refused to go back in. His fist slammed down into the side of my face, retching my head to the side. Warm blood trickled down into my eye. His fist struck again.

Clenching my fists, I slammed them against his temples in an attempt to disorient him, even for a split second. It was all I needed. The bridge of my palm came up clipping the edge of his chin sending him backwards. I was up on my feet looking back toward the other man. He was still lying unconscious.

I ignored him and paid attention to the man in front of me. I got behind him and positioned my hands on his forehead and jaw. Understanding that I had the upper hand, he started to struggle. *The bastard was strong*. I planted my knee in his spine.

I almost had him when I felt a sharp pain seer through my lower back.

"I told you, boy."

A wave of pain radiated out as he twisted the knife. I loosened my grip and started to reach for the man behind me, before I could make contact, a warm spray of crimson spattered on the side of my face, and his body slumped to the floor. Unsure what happened, I kicked his body back and took hold of the other man's head again, snapping his neck.

I swung around ready to fight. He wasn't up. He wouldn't be. His eyes were still open and blood was flowing down his face. Charlotte stood over him, frozen. The heavy weight still cradled in her hands soaked in blood, bone, and hair. She looked down at the lifeless body. Crying out, she fell to her knees. The weight in her hands flew up and smashed back down crushing his face, spraying up more blood. Up. Down. Over and over. I didn't stop her. Eventually, the weight rolled from her hands.

"Come here." I knelt down to her shaking body. She jumped when my hands touched her, her skin was cool from the water. "Come here." I pulled her into me, curling her up into my torso. "It's alright." I let out a breath.

Grunting I pushed myself up from the ground and kept her close. Warts was still out, and the alarms were sounding off. My blood was pooling out, soaking my shirt. I slid the door shut and locked it. I clicked on my com.

"Targets secure. Alternate nest."

A moment passed before Wilts' radio back: "Good. Stay in the nest. Ships not clear."

"Copy."

Tearing off the side of my shirt, I stuffed it in my wound and waited.

"Are you hurt?" I asked. She shook her head. I moved her arm out and looked for blood, checking her legs and the rest of her body. Physically, she didn't have any new injuries.

Ship secure. What's your location, Ravin?"

"Training area."

"Copy that. On my way."

My head felt light, and I shook standing up. *Fuck*. Dark spots rolled in and out of my vision, making it hard to unlock the door. I still had Charlotte cradled in my arms. Wilts was down the hallway.

"Sammy are you alright?" He picked up the pace.

"I'll be alright after a date with Horace. Here, take her."

"I got her." Reaching out, he pulled her into his arms. "Sit down, brother." He used his free arm to help me down. "Mills, bring a med-kit. Look at me," He used his free hand to pull my head to face him. "You did good."

I smiled. "Go. She doesn't need to be in here."

"I got him." Cage appeared and knelt down next to me.

"Don't let him out of your sight until Mills has him." He gave his order and hurried out the room with Charlotte.

"Any fatalities?" I rested up against the wall behind me.

"None of ours. They docked and set a small explosive. Sent us falling back, that's how they got past us. It was just a handful of them." She was applying pressure to the wound as she spoke. "And what happened here?"

I smirked, "She saved my life. I don't think I'll mess with her any time soon."

"Looks like he got a good blow in first." Mills dropped his medical bag next to me. "Let's have a look." I grunted as he investigated the wound. "You'll definitely need some stitches and I'll have to cauterize the veins."

"That sounds like fun, if I don't cry, can I have some morphine?"

"Sure." He laughed. He hoisted me up and kept me balanced as we walked to the medical room. "I'll get you a lollipop, too."

"What flavor?"

"Cherry."

"Goodie." I grunted as Cage and Mills lifted me through the door and towards the stairs.

"Charlotte?" He asked.

"She's alright. Lucas is with her."

Chapter Seven

Year 5032, September 11
Dr. Horace Mills – Osiris

"I missed you, Dad." Her voice was music to my ears. It had been too long since I heard it.

I wrapped my arms around her and squeezed.

"I missed you, too, and I am so proud of you."

Her cheeks turned pink, "Thank you." She strained her neck up to look at me. "Did you see *him*?"

"I did."

"What happened? Did he want to see me?"

"Well," I motioned for her to sit down with me. "He did, but you understand that he never will?"

"I understand. I don't want to." She rushed her words out. "I used to." She looked down at her hands and began to fidget. "I always wanted to ask him why he hurt me...and why he laughed when he did." Her voice grew soft. "He didn't hurt any of you, did he?" She still wasn't looking up.

I wrapped my arm over her shoulders and pulled her close.

"There is never going to be a logical reason for what he did. Some people simply lack empathy. Unfortunately, we haven't figured out how to help those who do."

"If he hated the Pharaohs so much, why didn't he kill me when I was born?" She looked up, her green eyes searching mine for answers.

I took a breath and debated what to tell her. "A long time ago, during Earth's earlier wars –"

"Is that when they practiced the Old Traditions still?"

I pulled her in close.

"Yes honey, they were practiced until about the thirtieth century." She nodded. "During this time, a man decided to convince his army and some of his country to perform an ethnic cleansing."

She sat up, and looked at me.

"Against who? Aliens hadn't been discovered yet."

"Against his fellow man, he insisted that not everyone was born the same and strived to kill those he believed to be imperfect. He targeted those who were poor, gypsies, homosexuals, and he targeted a specific group of people who practiced an Old Tradition of Judaism. He ordered his soldiers to round these people up and imprison them.

"Or at least that was what the public was told. He hid what he was doing from the public, these prisons were camps, where mothers and their children were murdered on sight. Even the elderly were murdered.

Those who didn't die right away suffered in many ways. Doctors performed horrible experiments on many." I looked at her. "They would burn the bodies in masses to dispose of them. Family and friends never to be seen again."

"All for a cleansing? Why?"

"Short answer, the guy was an asshole. The long answer can be tedious to think about. The economy at the time was unstable, and those who were well off happened to be those of the Old Judaic Traditions. He pinned the hardship on them using the emotions of his society to blind them. His relationship with his parents was strained. His father was abusive, both physically and emotionally. Overall, honey, he did those things to gain power, and people began to praise him. He was patient and did it in phases, disguising it as propaganda."

She looked up at me.

"That's a dumb reason to hurt people." I could see the anger in her eyes.

"Yes, it is, but when does anyone use a good reason to harm another?" I could see her mulling over my words, slowly she leaned into me. "Men like him and men like Warts crave anything that will give them an illusion of power. Even hurting the ones they are supposed to protect and love."

"You wouldn't do that." She looked up at me. "You're not that kind of person."

I smiled. I was glad she knew that, that I would never hurt her. "I'm going to keep you safe. Don't worry."

I held her for a moment, keeping her close and dreading the questions I had to ask her. Who enjoyed being questioned about a past they were trying hard to forget?

"Warts mentioned someone named Barren. Does that name sound familiar?" I looked down at her. For the first time since I got out, I saw fear flash into her eyes. *She knew the name.* I pulled her into me. All I wanted to do was shield her away from everything.

"A little. Do you remember when the supply ship boarded us?" I nodded. "Those men worked for him. He hired *a lot* of mercenaries. He was the one who led a lot of the genetic testing on me."

"Warts said he was working on the bioweapon with him."

"Yes, he has a degree in chemistry and genetics."

"Did he ever take you somewhere, another planet?"

"Nefertiti?"

"Yes, you remember?"

"Not a whole lot. I didn't know it was another planet. I thought it was a town or something. He kept me in a box. It was there they did the genetic testing on me… And a few others. He kept us underground beneath a…beneath a building they made, locked in cages. I remember it being really cold at night."

"Where are the others? The ones he was testing on?"

"They didn't make it." She buried her head into my chest. "There was a man named Joseph. He was really funny and always made me laugh. I never thought I would be able to laugh. He had a tattoo of a rose on his neck. It was his favorite flower."

"I'm sorry, sweetheart."

"You would have liked him. He was like Ravin… flamboyant." She gave a nervous laugh. "I think I remember…remember the layout of the building. I'll try and make a blueprint."

"Don't worry about that –"

"It's fine. The more we know the better right? I don't want you, Sam, or anyone else to get hurt. He's really nice, isn't he?" She changed the topic, a defense she'd done before.

I nodded.

"He is," I chuckled lightly, "And too smart for his own good."

"Try playing Clue with him. Or Poker," she laughed. "Is there anything else that might be helpful? Sometimes I don't remember things until I'm reminded of it. That's normal right? For what you did."

"Absolutely. It means it worked."

Chapter Eight

YEAR 5032, SEPTEMBER 11
SERGEANT SAMUEL DUKE – OSIRIS

We were back on the ship. The coordinates to Nefertiti were already plugged into the AI that Cage had designed herself to help run the ship. It would be a three-week flight to reach our destination; time was not on our side. Hopefully, it wasn't enough time for them to finish the weapon. The thought made me uneasy that it could already be out. Luckily, Cage was able to use her skills and hack in the media databases to keep alert for anything that would be similar to C.K.

While Cage was fiddling with that, Mills was reaching out to his daughter in an attempt to find if she remembered anything about Nefertiti and the work that was done there with Warts and Barren. Mills had refused to give away how he was reaching her. I gave a brief thought about tracking all outgoing transmissions. The thought lasted a second before I knew the signals would be wiped moments after they ended. He was not that careless.

It had been more than two hours since he was supposed to have made contact with her. Wondering what he'd found out, I searched the ship and found him in the infirmary with Angel.

"Hi, Sam." Angel turned away from Mills as she spoke, giving me a smile.

"Are you hurt?"

She shook her head.

"No. I was asking Horace if he would forge an autopsy report if I poisoned Atkins. No deal." Her arms crossed her chest and popped her hip out.

He chuckled.

"I'll think about it, but no promises. Go get some rest."

She smiled at him.

"Yes, sir." She gave a small wave to Mills before brushing passed me, squeezing my hand as she did. "Goodnight, Sam."

"Goodnight, Angel." I pulled her into a hug before I let her leave.

"Did you get a chance to speak with Charlotte?" I turned to Mills who was sitting down in his chair.

"I did."

"How is she, with everything?"

"She's…well."

"You sound surprised."

"I've only been able to talk to her through letters, I've always wondered if she was telling me what I wanted to hear. That she was okay, adjusted and happy."

"She is then? Handling everything? Even when you had to ask her about what Warts said?" I walked closer to him.

His left foot pulled out a chair next to him for me to sit on.

"She got a bit uncomfortable on that topic, but she was able to go through those memories without too many issues. The therapy we did worked." The last bit he seemed to say more to himself than me.

"What was the therapy?" I rotated my body towards him. "And why didn't you…" I debated how to phrase my words.

"Why didn't I show her mercy and let her pass?"

"Yes. You're a doctor –or were a doctor. You had to know the risks of what you did, most would consider it unethical."

He looked down for a moment before he spoke.

"That is exactly what Ravin has said to me, 'unethical.' He was adamant that it was the kindest thing to do for her once we understood everything; give her peace and let her sleep."

"Are you sure it was Ravin who said that?"

He chuckled.

"You'd be surprised how intelligent that bastard is. Honestly, it's a little freaky." Clearing his throat, he continued, "Have you ever heard of the girl named Genie?"

"Can't say I have. Who is she?"

"Genie is a girl who, like Charlotte, was starved and tortured. Genie's father tied her up and locked her in a closet when she was a toddler. He kept her there until one day her mother took her out and brought her to the authorities. Genie couldn't talk, she could hardly eat and had many other health issues. She eventually learned to speak a few words here and there. She learned to play.

She never learned to talk in complete sentences like you or I, but she could tell stories with pictures. Genie was *there*, her lights were on, and she was smart; she only communicated differently, non-verbally. I thought of Genie when I had my first interaction with Charlotte; she never spoke, but I could see in her eyes that she was thinking. Putting the pieces together on what was happening around her. Charlotte was *there*, her lights were on, she was out of her prison and ready to live. It would have been unethical to take that away from her."

"Did you give the same treatment to Charlotte that they did for Genie?"

"No, Genie was research, a 'thing' to be studied until the funding ran out. I took a different approach, we all did. Charlotte was and never will be used for research. I decided to take advantage of her higher IQ and practice a therapy the Pharaohs had been studying. A therapy specifically designed to cure PTSD. The goal behind the treatment was to disassociate the events of trauma from the mind."

"You created a second personality in her?"

"In a way, Charlotte remembers everything that happened to her, but she remembers it like a nightmare. Like most dreams, the idea is for the trauma to fade away over time."

"That's incredible."

"Yes. She doesn't remember much, but she remembers Nefertiti. It was where most of the genetic testing was done on her and others."

"How many others?"

"She couldn't say for sure, that part had grown a bit fuzzy to her. She remembers there was a large building that she was taken to. I'd say if Barren is attempting to make C.K., he's doing it there, and if I had to guess, I'd say there is a possibility that there may be prisoners there we need to extract."

I nodded.

"Do you have enough equipment to treat them effectively until we can get them to a hospital?"

His jaw clenched, and he lost his smile.

"Depends on how bad their injuries are. Even with Jones helping, we only have so much."

"Shit." I rubbed my jaw. "Cameron's a good doctor, but he's not good at making tough decisions. He's still a kid."

He nodded.

"Understood. You and Angel are pretty protective of him."

I nodded.

"He's a good kid. I promised his mother I'd take care of him."

"And Angel?" He seemed hesitant. "I do apologize if I crossed a boundary with her early. I already apologized to her."

"Thank you." I gave a nervous chuckle. "Angel is the closest thing I have to family. She's advised me on many occasions, I can get a bit overprotective."

"I understand." He let out a breath of air.

"Cage?"

"Yes, she's like my little diabolic sister." He laughed at his joke.

"It must have been tough having her there on Ammit."

"It was, but we kept her safe. She didn't always make it easy. She has a tendency to edge people on." He smiled. "And Angel?" He turned the topic back to her. "What is she to you?"

I gave a moment of thought on how to explain who she was to me.

"Angel is my best friend. I would do anything for her."

"She's a sweet girl."

Laughter that echoed from the hallway spilled into the room, it belonged to Ravin and Angel.

"Ravin has…made quite the impact on her."

Mills chuckled, "You either love him or hate him."

I laughed, more to myself than to him.

"What?"

"Ravin is…in for it. Angel owns any man she goes out with. They don't even see it coming."

He was still smiling and leaned a bit closer to me.

"When we first started to be friends, Ravin told me he wanted a woman who could take him by the balls and call out his bullshit." We both laughed. "I don't think he was expecting to ever get that."

"You met Ravin when he applied for the position, correct?"

"Yes, the recruitment for his – what used to be his position. I went under as a candidate to find the best one. Observe how each person was away from authority. Wilts had a set of traits he wanted, we picked the top three soldiers after the training and went on a mission. Ravin passed with flying colors for what Wilts was looking for."

I thought about what he'd said. *Traits…what were they?* "I love the choice of words you chose. He didn't do so well in the training I take it?"

"He did great, but didn't mind telling the instructors where to shove it." He chuckled.

"Has Ravin always been…" I tried to think of a word to describe him.

"Questionable?"

"Sure, let's go with that."

"Always. His questionable personality helped Lucas adjust. He didn't know it at the time, but now he'd kill anyone who would think of hurting Sammy."

"And the drugs?" I asked. "I found enough to be a drug dealer back home."

He smiled.

"There was a kid who was struggling with the combative part of the testing, really every part of the training. When he didn't do well, everyone got punished. Ravin stood up for the kid and having experience as a combative instructor and a drill sergeant, he helped him. He helped everyone who struggled."

"One day, a candidate who was doing really well got upset at Ravin for helping everyone. He comes in and watches Ravin sparring with the kid. He sneaks up on Ravin with a hollow pipe and bashes it against the back of Ravin's head. Any other person and it would have knocked them out, but for Ravin, it sent him into a seizure and put him in a coma for a week."

"Why?"

"Ravin had a previous head injury that he kept off the record when he joined the U.F.F.C. It would have disqualified him immediately."

"A head injury? How did he get it?"

"He was living on Nile with his family when the Formers attacked the planet. They lived on the outskirts of the town. Miles away from major cities. The Formers invaded, killing everyone there. As you know, in their minds, if you're not with them, you're against them. They murdered his mother and three sisters in front of him before his father was able to grab him and run outside. His father was going to hide Ravin in a dried-up well. When he got to the well, he was shot in the back and ended up dropping Ravin. He fell over thirty feet and smashed the back of his head on a rock. He was left there for days before someone found him."

"Since then he has a pressure that has built up in his head. His brain never fully recovered from it. Any hard hits to it, sudden increases in blood pressure will knock him out. He manages to keep his blood pressure under control, it never rises fast even in the midst of battle. The nicotine gives him a short high, giving him the illusion that the pain has dissipated. Same with any other drugs."

"Jesus. They found out then, when he went into a coma?"

"The doctor who treated him kept it quiet." He shook his head.

"Who was the doctor?"

"Me." I laughed with him. "He is a good soldier, and doesn't think twice about helping anyone. Even if it means disobeying orders."

"That's what he was looking for wasn't it." It wasn't a question. "Wilts. He wanted soldiers who didn't always follow orders."

He nodded.

"That was the first thing he looked for. He's seen first-hand what happens when soldiers don't think. Shit, history has, too."

"It's a unique way to look for a team but it seems to have worked."

"Wilts was pretty impressed with you during the interview you had with him. Said you got under his skin. That's not easy to do."

"Angel helped with that. She was the one who put together that the four of you were protecting something."

"Did she now?" He snickered. "Wilts said she was also the one who told him you were…" He paused thinking of how to phrase his next words.

"Gay." I finished for him. "Why is everyone fascinated by that?" I tried to recap the events that had happened, looking for anything that would make that trivial thing so relevant.

He laughed, and scratched his head; *a nervous tick?*

"It's really not worth explaining why *they* are."

"But I get to know yours? Can I guess?"

He gave a grin. "Sure."

"I saw some of the prisoners on Ammit. Can't say I saw any that I would personally pursue. I'm going to go on a limb and say that's how you felt. Now, you're free, and you think I'm pretty."

He laughed at my explanation, "If you can last a good portion of the night and promise not to nut after three minutes –" I nudged my head toward the door.

A smile replaced his laugh, lighting up his eyes. I was intoxicated by the way his eyes seemed to resemble space, he leaned over making my heartbeat increase. *You shouldn't dip your pen in the company ink!* I could see the words pop up in my head as a warning; the thing was, it was my other head that was doing the thinking.

I leaned in and pressed my lips against his. His smell filled up my nose. Lavender mint. *Was there anything not sexy about this man?* His hands came to my face pulling me in. My blood was rushing, making me throb, I hopped onto his lap straddling him, pressing into him. His hands left my face and pulled my hips closer.

His beard tickled my face, but I didn't mind. I even slid my fingers through it. The warmth of his hands seeped through my uniform. The feel of him almost distracted me from the light rustling I heard beside us, looking up to see Ravin rummaging through a drawer across the room.

"Ravin, what are you doing?" Horace asked, his hands on my hips.

"I ran out of cigarettes, and someone who shall remain nameless. *Duke*. Tossed away my coke. That leaves me with morphine, until I can remember where I hid my acid. Don't mind me." He looked over to us, a small needle and morphine in hand. "I'm not here." A Cheshire grin creeped its way on his face. I was too stunned to move.

"There is a pack of cigarettes in the emergency candy drawer for Wilts," Horace answered.

"Oh goodie!" He set down the morphine and grabbed the carton before walking out.

I let out a sigh, his hands still holding my waist.

"I guess this isn't the best idea considering you're planning premeditated murder towards me," I said.

"To be fair, you are too." He moved his hands back to my face.

"Till then we are working together." I attempted to be the voice of reason.

"Technically yes." I snapped my head back over to the door where Ravin was. "Calm down, I forgot the morphine." He walked in to grab it. "Morally right men like you can't have sex when you are working together. It's a good thing it's after five. You're off the clock." He offered up with a smile.

"Technically," I said, looking back to Horace.

"Technically," He whispered back before kissing me, sending me down the rabbit hole. Our lips never parted as our hands moved over one another. Curiosity getting the better of me, I took him in my hand. He let out a soft laugh.

"I don't mean to be forward." He paused between a few words to give me another kiss. "It's been a long time, and foreplay is torture."

I laughed.

"Come on." I got up and motioned for him to follow me. My room wasn't far from the infirmary. Once inside, we had our lips glued together again only parting to strip away our clothes.

I stopped when I noticed the bed. Red rose petals formed a large penis, with the head facing the pillows where lots of red petals were spewed about. The nightstand had three brand new lubes each topped with a bow. It actually made me laugh.

"At least we know what they were laughing about now."

He chuckled as he wrapped me up in his large arms and lowered me down to the bed, ignoring the petals. His body was dusted in dark hair, and my eyes followed his thick, happy trail that led to his large cock that was fully erect. I smiled at the sight of it, admiring its thickness. Any other time I would love to explore his body, but it was like he said, it had been a *long* time.

He smashed his lips into mine, using his large hands to spread my legs before he pushed in. The width of him sent my eyes rolling back, I wrapped my arm around his shoulders while my other hand pulled at his hips encouraging him to keep going. He let out a groan in my ear as our bodies pressed together. He rocked his hips starting slow, warming me up, his teeth nibbling my ear.

"Harder," I whispered. He groaned in pleasure before taking heed to my words. Intertwining our fingers, he pinned my hands above my head. The thick hair from his belly tickled the tip of my cock as he worked me over and over. "Harder." I was begging now; he didn't hesitate to listen. In moments, the sound of our bodies clapping together echoed in the room.

I moaned with each thrust of his hips. If the bed wasn't built into the wall, I was positive it would be banging up against it. I freed one of my hands and interlaced my fingers in his beard to pull him closer, locking our lips. Our bodies glided together from the sweat, my hands were tingling and my toes curled; arching my back, I pressed my shoulders down tightening up from the pleasure.

"Fuck." His voice was low, he pulled up from me and secured his hands around my waist pulling me into each thrust.

I seized my cock stroking it with his rhythm. My breath quickened, and my body began to lock up, slowly my testicles pulled up, sending me over the edge; I moaned, releasing all over my chest and a bit on my cheek.

He groaned watching me, making it all the more enjoyable. His hips still moving, pressing deeper, he leaned down to lick my face clean before bringing our lips together. His pace quickened, his rhythm lost. I watched his face as his eyes rolled back before closing shut, and with a deep grunt he pulled out, spilling on my stomach.

Breathing heavily, he waited before rolling off next to me. *Damn he was good.* All I could do was to gaze up at the ceiling in a daze. His large arm swung around under my neck pulling me close. Ignoring the sticky mess we made, I leaned into him.

"Shit." His words rushed out in between his breath. A rush of heat came to my cheeks; thank goodness it was too dark to see. He kissed the side of my head. He was quiet for a moment. The only sound was our labored breathing until he spoke. "I didn't know you were a Former."

"No." I rushed out, no longer relaxed. "I was *never* a Former." I pushed up getting ready to leave. The thought that he would have been able to tell never occurred to me until now. *He was well educated.*

"I was just –" He was sitting up now. "I'm not saying *anything* about it." He pulled me in with a kiss. "Okay?" He whispered the last word to me. I nodded and exhaled air I didn't realize I was holding. "I didn't mean to ruin this. Lay back down." He fell back again, pulling me with him.

"I'm sorry. When people know, they treat me differently, either with hate or pity." I placed my head on his shoulder, my heart still beating fast.

"I understand." He was quiet for a moment before he spoke again. "Were you on Sobek when we were?"

"No, I left about ten years before you found Charlotte. My parents fled there when I was five, so I grew up there. The day we got there, they had me and my twin brother circumcised. Swear to God, that's my first memory." I snickered.

"What made you leave?" He was looking over to my face as he spoke.

"When I was eight years old, a Pharaoh who had been held captive had managed to get away and ran out on the street. I don't know what home she came from, no one claimed to be the one who had her." I shook my head, "Anyways, the town strung her up by her ankles and skinned her alive. My parents made me watch." His body shifted toward me. "While the whole town fought over her skin. I was able to hide her nearby in the junkyard that I used to play in. She was the only one I'd ever seen, and she was…calm. I can't describe how *poised* she was. To this day, I think that's what I've found the most interesting about her. She held a conversation with me as if nothing had happened. She told me I didn't have to stay there and that I could leave when I was older. She was right. Eighteen, I hitched a ride and left."

"What happened to her?"

"I left to get food for her. When I came back, she wasn't there."

He was quiet for a moment.

"Is the rest of your family still on Sobek then?" He asked.

"Yes, my parents and my two sisters still live there."

"Did your brother leave with you?"

"No, he passed away."

"I'm sorry." He waited a few seconds before he spoke again. "Can I ask how?"

My mind played the memory over. The news of what the Scars team had done wasn't announced yet to the public. It was late at night, when my C.O. woke me up from a dead sleep for an emergency phone call. It was my mother. I was happy to hear her voice again; too many years went by without it.

"Mother." I was in disbelief, "Are you alright? I miss –"

"Did you know? Did you?" She was shouting.

"Know what? What's wrong?"

"They murdered your brother! You murdered your brother!"

"Sam?" Horace's voice drew me back.

I quietly cleared my throat.

"He was shot thirteen years ago, three times. Twice in the chest and once in the head."

He sat up and looked at me, horrified. I propped myself up on my elbows and met his gaze. He opened his mouth to speak. "I don't-I remember everyone I –"

I cut him off.

"It wasn't you." From the look on his face, I could tell he wasn't satisfied. I dropped back onto the bed. "My brother was not a nice person. He beat and raped his wife and his daughters. He was twelve years old when he killed his first alien." I could still hear my brother's laughter. "After the briefing, before we questioned Warts, Ravin came to me. He wanted me to know it was him who pulled the trigger."

"I don't understand. Why are you helping us?"

"Because, if I was there… I would have pulled the trigger myself. I know first-hand, better than anyone what happens there. What they do. How they brainwash."

He watched me, studied me.

"How does the rest of your family…"

I chuckled at him.

"You don't know much about the Old Traditions, do you? When I, left I was disowned. This, right here –" I gestured between us. "Would make heads roll." I laughed at that thought.

He laid down again, sliding his arm back under me.

"I never read much on the Old Traditions until I was in prison." He rubbed his hand up and down my arm as he spoke. "I liked the overall concept of it. It was like reading a story. How someone managed to use it as a Tradition is beyond me. Even as a story, there are inconsistencies," He paused, "I'm sorry, I don't mean to degrade what you're raised in."

"No, it's true. My father broke my fingers for pointing it out. Children can be sold; women are considered property. It encourages slavery." I let out a sigh. "I wish I could say what Warts did to Charlotte wasn't typical there."

"Do they let people leave easily?"

"No, if they find out you plan to leave, they put you in a camp. I've never seen anyone come out alive. I kept quiet, left a note, and hitched a ride on a mercenary ship."

He shook his head in disbelief.

"I didn't know that." His voice was quiet, keeping the thought he had to himself.

I chuckled, looking over to him.

"Not many people do." I rolled to my side and kissed his lips. "I'll tell you more, for the right price."

"Deal." The warmth of his hands traveled up my body and pulled me closer until I was on top of him. I reached behind and took his cock, glad to feel how ready he was. I guided him in, enjoying the stretch he gave me. I gripped myself while I used my other hand to keep steady as I moved up and down his cock.

His hands came to my waist guiding me. A wicked smile appeared on his face as he watched me and I enjoyed his eyes on me. He sat up letting me lean into him, closing my eyes in the pleasure he gave me. I used his shoulders for more stability, coming down harder each time.

Lips brushing together, one of his hands took a tight grip on my cock, stroking me. The feel of his hand was too much, I grunted and released a small load. He didn't stop stroking me, and sensitive to his touch, I squirmed and cried out in pleasure.

His laugh bounced off the walls.

"Good boy." He kissed my lips again letting me push him back into the bed. His hands cuffed mine behind my back, his hips taking over. Slowly his body tensed up, softly he let out a long moan as he released himself in me.

Chapter Nine

YEAR 5032, SEPTEMBER 12

DR. HORACE MILLS – OSIRIS

A gust of radioactive wind rocked the ship. I woke, heart racing from adrenaline. I'd never been a hard sleeper, and if prison taught me one thing, you wake up to the slightest noise or movement. I let out a breath of air as I saw Sam lying next to me fast asleep on his stomach, as another small gust of wind shook the ship. He didn't move.

I smiled as I studied him. *He was delicious.* Tall and muscled to perfection, not an ounce of hair above his waist. His face was kept clean, exposing his chiseled facial features, while his light brown hair was a standard military fade, keeping the top cut short. The only imperfection on his body was a bullet wound on the back of his ribs. *Where had he gotten that?*

I leaned over to kiss his cheek while I traced my hand up and down his back.

"Let's play," I whispered in his ear. A smile crept up on his face as he opened his eyes. My blood rushed as I pressed into him. His hand gripped my wrist pulling me on top.

His body warmed mine. I kissed his neck and followed along with his spine. My hand traced the outline of his ass before pulling his hips back. I snaked my hand to the front of his waist and took hold of his hard cock. He let out a moan as my hand wrapped around him. I slid my hand up and back down.

He wasn't joking about wanting it all night, something I was eager to do. He adjusted himself on his hands and knees. The thought of being in him again almost had me spent; I pressed the tip of my cock into him, his hand reaching up to the back of my head pulling me closer, urging me in him. I closed my eyes from the pleasure. He was tight, eager. I reached for his lips with mine, rolling my tongue in his mouth letting his body adjust to me before I would thrust my hips. Slowly, softly.

It wouldn't last long; he liked it fast, and he liked it hard. His hips matched my rhythm, each embrace more forceful than the last. I kept my weight in my knees with a hand secured on his hips while my other slid up every curve of his back before I hooked it on his shoulder.

He grunted in pleasure as I pulled him in with each thrust. It made my blood boil. The sounds of our bodies meeting echoed out. I found myself grunting, holding back the pleasure he gave me. I moved harder. The tip of my head rubbing against his prostate. I pushed my weight into my hands, forcing his body down just a bit to hit his sweet spot all the more.

I grinned as his cries of pleasure grew louder. Keeping one hand down, his other stroked himself, matching my rhythm. I leaned forward until my lips could brush against his ear.

"Come on," I coached him, "Let me watch." His head leaned back into my shoulder giving me the perfect view. I kissed his neck and nibbled on his ear. "Now." I ordered him, his eyes closed, and he released with a cry of pleasure. My hips never stopped, even as his body trembled, and he fell to his forearms.

I moved faster, working him, listening to his moans. Pulling him into me, my body was warming up, the feel of my testicles crawling up got me excited. I pulled out, releasing into my palm. I groaned, running the tip of my thumb over the head to prolong the pleasure. Exhaling, I released my grip and settled onto my heels.

He pushed up, pressing his back into my chest stealing a kiss. I watched in awe as he pulled my hand to his lips, licking every drop of seed, his eyes never leaving mine. I pulled him into another kiss, rolling my tongue against his.

It was early morning when we'd finished and took a shower. I had forgotten how time almost seemed nonexistent in space; there were no suns or moons to put a body onto a cycle.

"Angel says you are an excellent tactician." I'd finished dressing and looked over to him.

"Yes." He raised his eyebrow in question.

"Come with me." I motioned for him to follow me. "Ravin has something for me I want you to look at."

"Sure." He followed me out of the room.

I wasn't sure where Ravin was, but I knew she would have given the blueprints to him. I wanted to get a head start on planning how to infiltrate the building.

"Charlotte was creating a layout to the building, at least of what she remembers. Think you can look at it and come up with something to get us in and out?" I paused to look over at him when he didn't respond. "Sam?"

He touched my arm pulling us to a stop.

"She still remembers that much? To give a detailed map of the building?"

I nodded grimly. The same thought had crossed my mind when she offered to draw the map.

"The memories should fade eventually, but the idea was still experimental at best when the Pharaohs went extinct. She does describe the memories like they are a dream, so if anything, she has that."

He looked at me with his hazel eyes. I couldn't tell what he was looking for.

"Are you okay?" he finally asked. "You've had a lot of shit thrown your way the last twenty-four hours."

No. I gave a halfhearted smile.

"I don't have any other choice but to be. This isn't about me. It never was." My heart was aching in the idea that her past life was never really gone, that it never could be. I tried to walk, but his hand pulled me back.

"You need to put the mask on yourself before you can do *anything* for her." I let out a huff air. "What?"

"You're going to be like Robyn, aren't you? Always right. It gets obnoxious." Without thinking, I pulled him in for a kiss. His left hand held my face as his soft lips brushed against mine. "Come on." I said as I pulled away. "I smell cigarette smoke coming from the cargo bay. A sure sign of a Ravin."

We followed the smell to the cargo bay to find Ravin leaned back in his chair with his eyes closed smoking a cigarette. He was sitting at one of the large metal tables, and from the looks of it, he was cleaning weapons. Off to the end of the table were several crisp, white lines from the cocaine he was taking.

"Can't sleep?" I asked walking in. His eyes shot open, and for the briefest moment, panic dashed across his face.

"Are you okay?" Duke asked, noticing the panic that was there.

Ravin looked down and back up.

"I-I'm great," he said with a smile, but his smile faded as Duke and I pulled out the chairs across from him. "Can you guys give me a minute?" he asked in a strained voice.

I ignored his question.

"I spoke to Charlotte. She was going to make blueprints of the building she was in on Nefertiti. I told her to send them to you, did she give them to you yet?" He jumped up a few inches in his chair and looked back down. "Sammy?"

He looked up with a smile.

"Hmm?"

"How much did you take?" I reached over to look at his eyes, but he pulled away.

"Um, I took…" He trailed off and leaned back in the chair. "I don't know," he said at last with a laugh.

What the fuck was wrong with him? Had he mixed the morphine and the coke? It wouldn't be the first time he's mixed drugs. I watched him; his eyes drooped shut, and his head slumped forward.

"Sammy!"

He opened his eyes again before I could shake him.

"Hmmm?"

"What did you take?"

He shrugged nonchalantly.

"Fuck if I know. Oh, blueprints. Here." He glanced down before he pushed over several papers. "She gave a sketch of Barren, too, she's quite the artist." He moaned, *from pain?* Before he collapsed on the table, making Duke and I jump back.

"Sammy!" I reached out, but before I could touch him, he was sitting back up, calm as could be.

"How much did you take?" Duke repeated my question.

"I'm dandy." He put the butt of the cigarette to his lips and sucked in.

No. I thought. *He wasn't…* I knew that look now.

"Sammy, who's-"

"Mmmm, hold that thought." He closed his eyes again and leaned back grunting.

I leaned back in my chair.

"What a-what happened there, Sammy?" Duke was leaning as far back as I was.

I knew what happened, I just didn't want to believe it. There were only three people who could be under the table, and I knew it wasn't Cage or myself.

"I don't think we want to know what happened." I said.

Angel crawled her way up from under the table and settled in on Ravin's lap. All I could do was stare at her; no words were appropriate. *How could she?* Dressed in black shorts and a matching tank, her long curly hair was down and pulled off to the side giving me an innocent look and a devilish smile.

"Hi."

"Leave." I barked at her. Giggling, she got up and hurried out the door. I turned my attention to Ravin. He didn't look too ashamed of what happened.

"You need to wipe the smile from your face." I tried to keep my voice low. "We had a *deal.*"

His hands fumbled with his belt.

"I know. I didn't break it though. Granted I didn't tell you…three hits to the nads, call it even?" I thought about that for a second before I reached out and shook his hand.

"Deal."

I ignored the confused and traumatized look on Duke's face as he stared after Angel. I laid the papers out in front of him. The top paper was labeled as the first floor of the building. All pathways contained numbers representing the number of paces it was. He instantly started studying the layout. He pushed one aside to look at the next page labeled as the second floor.

His mind was already working on a plan, I could see it in his eyes. The page that represented the basement had the most detail. *Of course, it would… That's where he kept her.*

"I'll upload these into the computer base to get a 3D model for representation." He turned to me, "Do you think she might know what was in each room? Where Barren's office was, or where the laboratories were?"

"I can ask her," I said, pulling out the basement print to look it over. *My poor girl…*

"Anything helps."

"You can have Cage run a program to take the picture of Barren and make it age appropriate." Ravin leaned over to the coke and snorted a line before sitting back up.

I picked up the picture and stared at the face of another man responsible for hurting my daughter. I clenched my jaw. What else did he do to her besides use her for experimentation?

It didn't matter, he would suffer the same fate as the others who harmed her.

Duke's hand touched my arm.

I didn't look up. "The bastard's mine."

Chapter Ten

YEAR 5032, SEPTEMBER 16
DR. HORACE MILLS – OSIRIS

"Horace, do you have a minute?" Ravin's voice came from behind me. I was in the kitchen chopping vegetables for supper. He was standing in the doorway, debating on entering. "About a couple days ago, with Angel." He took each step slowly until he was next to me. "I didn't mean-I'm sorry. It's not what it looks like."

"That's why you have been avoiding me." It wasn't a question; I knew that was why I couldn't find him when I went looking for him.

"This isn't a conversation I want to have."

"You shouldn't be getting involved with her –"

"Pot," he motioned to me and then to himself, "meet kettle."

"That's different." I snapped my words out. "He knows what will happen at the end of this. Angel does not."

"Oh, in that case, I'll tell her. Then it's the same."

"It's not your place to tell her, it's mine or Sam's."

His eyes got wide, and he cocked his head back.

“First name basis with the fuck-boy are we?” My knuckles turned white from gripping the knife in my hand. His eyes didn’t miss it. “He must be *good* if you’re willing to stab a friend over him.”

“Friend? Would a friend do what you did? We had a deal.” I couldn’t help but draw out the last word. I found myself standing nose to nose with him, knife still in my hand. My chest ached, and hasn’t stopped since I saw the two of them.

“I’ve kept the *deal*… I was honest with you from the beginning on how I feel.” His legs had taken a larger stance while he spoke. He had been honest, but I was still pissed. Something I was honest about from the beginning. I lowered my hand.

“You swear?”

“Of course,” Ravin’s eyes didn’t lose contact with mine. “I wouldn’t risk our friendship.” This was three years after we were sent to Ammit. The air was cold enough to sting my face, the prison was quiet with all the prisoners sleeping. Not even Lucas or Robyn were awake. *“Is that something you can accept?”*

“I’ll try.” My mind drifted back to the kitchen I was in. “You’re right.” I let out a sigh. “This shit got a bit too complicated.”

“It’s not complicated. *You’re* the only one overthinking this…besides Elba, but that’s what we love about him. You both instantly decided the only way for this to be a success is to kill everyone.”

“*You* agreed to that plan, that no one would know about her and live.”

“That was before.”

“Before? Before what? Nothing’s changed.”

He looked dumbfounded.

“How is it that me, the one with brain damage, isn’t the dumb shit right now? Put two and two together. One, Duke is someone who can be trusted. Even Lucas likes him, and he does not like easily. Two, you are ready to gut me over a guy you met less than a week ago. Don’t you think that should have an impact on your decision?”

He was right, and that pissed me off all the more.

"I'd gut you for less and you know it."

He didn't care.

"If you want to make it work, we can find a way. She wants to make it work."

"Fuck you." It was just over a whisper. I backed away and set the knife down. "For a stone-cold killer, you're too soft. We can't let feelings get in the way of what we need to do."

"Bullshit. Feelings got us into this. I don't want to kill Angel. Not with everything that's been done. You don't want to kill Duke, and *she* doesn't want you to either. You won't ask Sam for help. You have too much pride."

"We can't trust him. We can't trust anyone."

"The one person we can trust is Sam, you would know that if you actually spoke to him instead of fucking him. He's from Sobek, and he knows first-hand the fucked up shit they do. Do you really think he would do anything remotely close to helping them? If that doesn't sell it for you, then trust in her when she tells you he can be trusted. She's known him for a long time." He pulled out a piece of paper. "Take a look." He shoved into my chest. "A letter she wrote to me, about the vacation she went on with Sam. Her words, 'He's my best friend.' Are you really going to murder your daughter's best friend? Better yet, have you told *your* daughter that you're fucking her bestie?"

I slammed my fist into his jaw, knocking him down.

"I'll take that as a 'no'." He rubbed his jaw but didn't bother to get up. I shouldn't have hit him in the head; he would be fine, but I knew I gave him a major migraine that won't go away anytime soon. "I came here to apologize to you. I'm sorry." He pushed his way to his feet. He turned and walked out, but paused to look over his shoulder. "Oh, and I mean it. Like I said I did years ago." He almost spat the words out.

My fist bounced off the cabinet that I swung at. I swung a few more hits cursing under my breath. *Fuck.* He was right. *I hated that.* I couldn't take any chances… I needed her to be safe no matter what.

I pulled out the photo I had of her in my pocket. She was standing with Sam outside my parents' restaurant on Earth. It was during winter, and both were bundled up. She'd taken him there for the seasonal soups my mother would make. I'd made her quite a few on the ship all those years ago. She went there every year to get some. I couldn't help but smile at the picture, she looked incredibly happy, not a hint of sadness was on her face. Even now, I didn't see one.

I let out a breath. I hadn't told her yet, but she knew. I'd grown to know Sam through her letters, or at least that is what it felt like. It made it easy to be with him, but in many ways, it made it wrong.

I placed the picture back in my pocket. My parents were dead now, and their restaurant ended up closing. They never knew who Charlotte was, or probably even recognized their yearly customers. They never knew why I did what I did, but they never stopped being parents. I received letters once a month from them.

My mind went back to the bitter morning when I got the letter that my father passed away, followed by the one two years later for my mother. That was five years ago, almost six. I shook the memories away and finished up.

Cage was the first one in.

"Is it all done?"

"It is, dig in."

She already had a plate in hand. She was usually the first one to eat; she loved her food hot and refused to eat if it wasn't.

"Thank you. I've missed your cooking. No more questionable oatmeal." Her plate was full, and she was eating in less than a minute. I clicked on the overhead speaker to inform everyone that chow was ready.

Wilts' large footsteps raced down the hallway before he nearly missed the door, sliding on the metal floor.

"Steaks?" he asked, charging in.

"Yes, and don't forget to chew." I fixed two plates before thinking better and made a couple more before I sat down next to Cage, who was already halfway done. "There is a meringue pie in the fridge," I whispered to her. Her eyes bulged as she jumped up darting to the fridge. Wilts, noticing the pie, instantly fought her for it. It was beginning to feel like it used to be.

"What the hell are they fighting over?" Duke asked as he came in with Atkins, instantly their eyes were drawn to the two adults struggling in the corner.

"Meringue pie. It's the only thing they fight over." General Elba slipped past them to get a plate. "Well, that, and if the dress was gold or blue."

"It's gold."

"Don't tell that to Wilts."

"Bet you three hundred credits Robyn gets the first piece." Ravin walked in with Angel clinging to his arm. As always, she had a large smile on her face. It was a peaceful sight to see after years of pissed off inmates and guards trying to murder you.

"Come on!" Angel let go of Ravin's arm and pulled on Sam's. "Homemade food!"

"I fixed some plates." I gave her a smile while Ravin eyed me suspiciously. I walked over to Ravin. "I'm sorry, brother," I whispered in his ear as I pulled him into a hug.

"I am too. I didn't expect this to be easy for you." He gave me a wet kiss on the cheek before I pushed him away. One by one, the rest came in.

"Thank you for cooking us dinner, Mills." Jones was already stuffing his face. I was surprised to see such a young member on an R.R. team. "Where did you learn to cook like this?"

"I grew up in a restaurant and helped my parents out."

"It reminds me of my mother's cooking."

I gave him a friendly smile, *poor kid.*

"Horace," Cage whispered under her breath, getting my attention. "Why did you hit Ravin in the head? He could have had a seizure."

"He's fine. I hit his jaw, not his head."

"Why? Because he told you what we are *all* thinking?"

"You agree with him?" I stopped eating to look at her.

She looked from me to Sam before speaking. "Yes."

"And when did the two of you get together and gossip about this?"

"A few nights ago, we also think –"

"You bastard!" Ravin shouted, jumping up he knocked his chair over and ran out the door gathering our attention.

Angel stared after him and turned to me.

"What happened? Is he okay?" she asked.

"I put laxatives in his food." I shoveled a spoon full of potatoes in my mouth.

"For what? You already hit him. Are you jealous?" Cage asked.

"Yes." She watched me.

"The kicker is," Wilts chimed in. "He stole my Laffy Taffy earlier, so I put a starved rat in his toilet."

I nearly choked on my food trying not to laugh.

"That was me, not Sammy."

"Shit." He started laughing.

"Did you put laxatives in anyone else's food?" Angel asked, giving me a bit of a glare.

"Just his." I gave an innocent grin. I could tell by the look on her face she wasn't satisfied. "Eat *your* food before it gets cold."

Reluctantly she obeyed.

"That wasn't nice," she added under her breath.

"He'll be fine."

"Mills," Elba's voice boasted out across the table. "How many times do I have to tell you to stop poisoning Ravin? You're not children."

"I don't know, Ravin's pretty childish. I bet he retaliates within the hour." Wilts grinned.

"Oh, I plan too." Ravin walked back in. "That was a good one, Papi. It's a good thing your room had the closest bathroom." Lifting up his chair, he casually sat back down.

"It is not."

"Oh, don't worry I didn't turn on a fan, light a match, or keep the door open." He leaned back and wrapped his arm around Angel's shoulders. I clenched my jaw to the point that it popped. Angel on the other hand didn't seem to mind, in fact she coughed to hide her laugh. He didn't take his eyes off of me. "Let's dance."

"Your move."

"No, it's my turn." Angel butted in. She'd finished eating. "Come rub my feet Ravin." She hopped up from her chair holding her hand out.

"Of course, Mon Cheri." He followed her out the kitchen never breaking eye contact.

"Huh," Sam pondered looking after the two. "How are you guys considered the most dangerous team?"

"We're mighty." Wilts piled a spoonful of pie in his mouth.

Chapter Eleven

YEAR 5032, SEPTEMBER 22
MAJOR ROBYN CAGE – OSIRIS

"Hey sweetheart, what are you doing?" I looked up to see her green eyes watching me.

"I was ordered to hide," She walked over and sat across from me. "Do you need any help?"

"Sure, can you clean the .50 cals?"

"Yes, ma'am."

I watched her for a moment; I was truly amazed to see the treatment Horace had done worked. Wilts had taught her how to clean and fire weapons before we'd landed back at the U.F.F.C. space station years ago. It was in that time period that Ravin had taught her how to defend herself with hand to hand combat. "Who are we hiding from?"

"Atkins, he bothers me."

I chuckled at her.

"He is a bit obnoxious. He spat on me when I corrected his calculation mistake. I about broke his nose right there." I smiled as she laughed.

"Was the calculation for the waves that are hitting us?"

"Yes, we should be able to avoid it coming back if we circle out far enough."

She nodded, her weapon disassembled and ready to be cleaned.

"May I ask you something Charl –" I stopped myself. "I'm sorry, I know you don't go by that name anymore."

She didn't seem upset and gave a smile.

"It's okay, Ravin accidently calls me by it sometimes. What's your question?"

"Promise to tell me the truth?" She nodded, but didn't speak. "You understand what's going to happen once we get back? What's going to happen with Duke and the rest of his team? You haven't said a word about it…"

She looked down and started to clean the weapon, "Promise not to tell Dad?"

"Our secret."

"I won't let you kill Sam." She kept her eyes fixed on her work.

"By asking me to not tell your dad, I am assuming you haven't brought this up to him."

"No."

"Why not?"

"I don't want him to be mad at me." Her voice was soft and her eyes watered.

I pushed up from the table and walked over to the mic.

"Horace, can you come to the cargo bay." I hadn't even sat down before she spoke.

"You promised."

"I promised I wouldn't tell him, you, however, will." I lifted her chin to get her to look at me. "He can't fix something if he doesn't know about it."

"I don't want him to be mad."

"Mad about what?" Mills was already here and walking up to sit beside her.

"Go on."

He wrapped an arm around her.

"Are you hurt, honey?"

She shook her head, "No. I know you plan to kill Sam after this, and I'm not going to let you." She looked up at him, her eyes fixed, and not a trace of leniency in her words. "I'm sorry, Daddy."

He was quiet, looking at her eyes, seeing what I saw. "Honey, we have to think of what could happen if –"

"Then I'll deal with it. I'd rather it be that way."

"Okay. I'm sure we can convince Ray to leave Sam alone or find a bargain to make with him. That way he won't get hurt."

"That was easy." I looked at him with surprise, every time Ravin or I brought the subject up he rejected it. I suppose it wasn't easy for him to reject what she wanted.

"Too easy." She agreed with me. "Do you think it's because they are crossing keys?" She asked me with a grin.

"It has to be." I didn't hide my laugh as the horror creeped its way up on his face.

"What?" She asked, "You thought I didn't know?"

For once, he was speechless.

"Robyn, could you give us a moment?"

"And miss this? I don't think so."

He pinched the bridge of his nose and closed his eyes.

"I don't think this is an appropriate time right now, Robyn."

"I don't think it's appropriate to be bumping uglies with Sam." I grinned at how wide his eyes went.

"I don't mind," she chimed in. "I think you are cute together." She whispered the last part to Mills.

"Okay, Sam lives, and I'm thoroughly embarrassed."

He moved to get up; I reached out and took his wrist.

"Horace, this was hard for her to tell you." He sat back down, "Let her know you are not mad, and I'll go talk to Ray." I pushed up to my feet, his hand squeezing mine as I walked past. I smiled hearing him reassure her he wasn't mad. Of course, he wouldn't be, but I understood where she was coming from. The person you love the most you don't want to disappoint.

I dragged the tips of my fingers across the wall of the ship as I made my way to Elba's old office on the top floor. I'd missed this ship. I always dreamed of dying here, there in the infirmary. After all, who didn't want to die at home peacefully?

I stopped and took a few steps back to look in Duke's room. Ravin stood balanced on the corner of the chair taping everything from clothes to pencils to the ceiling. "What are you doing?"

"Shit!" Distracted he struggled to catch his balance before crashing into the floor. "Damn Mama, I am getting you a bell." He pushed himself up, peeling the tape from his face.

"What are you doing?"

"What am I doing? *What am I doing?* Oh, I'll tell you. Revenge." He was back balancing on the chair, the sound of tape pulling from the roll followed his words.

"So, you're taping everything to the ceiling?"

"I have my reasons. Hand me the pencils."

I smiled.

"You're a child." I handed him the pencils.

"I am not."

"Listen, I am on my way to speak with Elba. I was talking with –"

"I know, I told her I'd make sure Sam lives. The pillow please."

"You knew?"

"Thank you. She told me the first night and asked me not to say anything. The little spitfire had a plan already, taking one from our book on faking deaths."

"She was going to fake Sam's death?"

"Yup, well we – me and her."

"Well, she won't have to do that now. Horace can't say no to her, and Lucas will eventually side with us. Elba will be the tough one."

"He'll come around." He hopped down, "Spread your legs." He got behind me ducking low and lifted me up on his shoulders. "Tape the chair." I shifted unsteady on his shoulders, holding onto his head for support as he lifted the chair up to me. "Elba has a soft spot for her, he shows love a little tougher than most. It's why she took so long to warm up to him." His hands moved to my torso giving me more support as I taped the chair.

"Say Elba agrees, what do we do if Duke doesn't take the news so well? Especially with the relationship he has with Horace. It was stupid of Horace to get involved with him. He *knows* better." I muttered the last bit to myself. I'd been trying to figure out what he'd been thinking.

"He meets the man who's been taking care of his daughter, a man she praises, a man who is a hottie with a body. If you think about it, he's already met Sam and holds him to a high light, it's not that stupid if you really think about it. You done?"

"Yes."

He squatted down and helped me off his shoulders.

"From what I hear, Sam's got quite the liking for Horace. It's not one sided. I also hear he's a bit of a slut." He wiggled his eyebrows. "Come on, let's dethrone Elba's authority. My work is complete." He blew a kiss at the room.

I looked back at the room before he shut the door and shook my head. *How long had it taken him to do all that?* I wrapped my arm around his as we walked.

"I suppose that's a way to look at it. He seems to find Horace's quirks cute. But that might go away, once he knows."

"Nah," I gave him a questioning look. "He doesn't know *it*, but he does love her, and there is no way he's going to hurt or expose her. Honestly, he might be more motivated if he knew, just my two cents. He might never look at her as a daughter, but the love is there."

"You make it sound like they are going to be together forever."

"What's wrong with happily ever after?"

We rounded the corner coming up onto Elba's office.

"Nothing, as long as she gets it too. I just don't know if I trust him. He's from Sobek."

"I don't think that should be a factor. Horace trusts him, she trusts him, and I trust him." I passed him a side glance. Horace had put his trust in Lucas and in Ravin when he first met him, and he wasn't wrong about them.

"I trust all of you."

He gave me a kiss on the side of my head as we rounded the corner into Elba's office. I tsked when I saw Duke with him going over several papers.

"Can I help you?" Elba eyed us, along with Duke.

"In the words of Elisabeth Swann, we feel it is necessary to disincline to acquiesce to your request, about that one thing." Ravin nudged his thumb in the direction of Duke. Duke's eyes shifted from side to side as his lips repeated Ravin's words.

"I'm sorry, you what?" Elba placed his hands on his desk and stood, the legs of his chair grazed the ground.

"In the words of Stanly Hudson, 'did I stutter?'" He snapped his fingers, but jumped behind me as Elba moved to the side of his desk.

"You should have."

I stepped around and behind Ravin, pushing him forward. He stumbled but quickly regained his composure. "I'm out of witty quotes," he whispered to me but kept his eyes forward.

"Braveheart," Duke tossed the suggestion over. "Try Braveheart."

Ravin snapped his fingers, "You the man." Switching to an old accent, he continued. "All men betray sir, and all lose heart." He placed the palm of his hand over his heart and bowed his head, I hid a smile as I saw Duke do the same motion.

Elba's tight lips and boring eyes didn't flinch, "And who is we?"

"Everyone, sir," I stood on my tiptoes to look over Ravin's shoulder.

"And where is everyone else?"

"Well, Horace is reaching out to Charlotte for some more information, and Lucas doesn't know yet."

"Yet? You sound sure he's going to agree with you on the topic."

"Does he ever disagree with her?" Ravin cut in. "All she's got to do is show some titty, and boom," He clapped his hands imitating an explosion. "He's on board."

"It doesn't work like that. We will continue as planned. Understood." It wasn't a question. He moved to sit down but paused midway when Ravin spoke.

"I didn't want to play this card, but we don't work for you anymore. So, you can try to order us around all you want…" He waved his hand in the air as he spoke. "But we don't work for you." He repeated again finishing with a pop of the hip.

Elba's mouth hung open as he stared at him.

"You may not work for me, but I can still kick your ass and drag you outside. In case you haven't noticed it's a bit cold out." He walked out from behind his desk and came nose to nose with Ravin.

Ravin licked his lips, eyes dancing, then he spoke.

"You'd have to catch me first, old man." He ducked and pushed me to the side as Elba reached his fist out. "Too slow!" He turned and charged down the hallway Elba on his heels.

I laughed, turning to Duke who was smiling at the interaction.

"I bet you three grand Ravin is still running at chow time."

He chuckled, "I don't gamble."

"It's not gambling if you know you're going to win."

"So what order is Ravin disobeying that has led him to being chased around the ship?"

I gave him a light smile, "You'll see." I walked away going to find Wilts. He wasn't far, and was using the powdered room in our bunk. As always, he never shut the door; one of the few things he did that bothered me. I was used to relieving myself in front of others due to the military and prison, as was he, but that doesn't mean never use a fucking a door.

I leaned up against the doorframe for a few seconds, "Boo!" I screamed.

Unaware of my presence he jumped at the sound of my voice, missing the bowl and pissing on himself. I hunched over laughing.

"Why?" He didn't bother to put himself away as he turned toward me, I laughed harder.

"Getting a little rusty, are we?"

"No, it never occurred to me I'd be assaulted while using the john in my own home." He paused, "By my lady."

The flatness of his face kept the smile on my face.

"I didn't assault you."

He let out a huff of air, "May I finish?"

"No one is stopping you."

He turned back around and began to relieve himself again, and knowing it would make him uncomfortable, I walked over and stood next to him. My shoulder touched him just enough to stop his stream.

Taking a deep breath, "Why?" He asked again.

"It brings me joy."

Unamused by my comment, he went back to concentrating.

"In need of a prostate exam?" Mills laughed behind us.

"Really? You too." Lucas zipped up his pants and turned around. "I just want to pee."

We both laughed, "Elba still needs convincing. I'm sure –"

"Robyn," Horace cut me off. "I was just telling her what she needed to hear."

"You lied to her!" I shouted at him. He tried to speak, but I cut him off. "What happens when she finds out?"

"Hold on." Lucas bumped in. "What is going on?"

"She asked Horace not to kill Sam, and he lied about it. Said he wouldn't do it."

"Robyn, he is right." Lucas touched my arm.

I pulled my arm away, "No, he's not." I knew in their minds they only wanted to keep her safe; it is what we all wanted. But ultimately, it was her choice… Why couldn't they see that?

"Sam is going to be K.I.A." Horace kept his voice low and lowered his eyes. "It's why I was able to lie to her. She can't know, Robyn."

I smiled.

"I suppose you are right. He will be killed in action. Excuse me." I pushed passed Horace. *Where the hell was Sammy?* We had work to do.

Chapter Twelve

Year 5032, September 31
Sergeant Samuel Duke – Osiris

"According to our A.I., Nefertiti is about a day's flight away. Let's go over the plan." I looked over to General Elba sitting a few chairs down from me. "If this is going to work, we need to keep our heads out of our asses and do exactly as I say." I waited for him to nod in understanding, before I continued.

"There are only nine of us, and we have no idea how many men are on Nefertiti. I'd like to avoid blowing up half a planet this time." I directed my comment over to Wilts, ignoring the glare he gave to me. "If everything goes right, we can be back on the ship in a few hours."

"This isn't the first time we've done this. In fact, I've been doing this since before you were born. What's the plan?" Wilts kicked back in his chair clearly irritated.

"Well, Toots," I clicked on the stimulator. "We are going to orbit jump down. Once we –"

"Nope. No, not going to happen." Wilts was sitting straight up, shaking his head, rushing his words out. "I vote bomb? Who's with me?" He raised his hand high followed by Ravin.

"Lucas," Horace interjected. "You'll have to excuse him. It's been a while since he's jumped. He's tad nervous." A grin followed his tease, edging up Wilts.

"No one will know. What's the issue?" He was speaking to Ravin, the only one on his side.

"We orbit jump," I repeated, taunting him a bit. "That's the best way to get on to the world without anyone detecting us. General Elba, you will be flying the ship. Find a secure location to land, away from us, away from them. Send us your location, and we will come to you. Considering how we've all graduated kindergarten, I'm assuming you all know how to avoid being seen and to hide all the marks you take care of."

"Assuming we don't die during the jump, what's the plan once we get to the ground?" Cage asked.

"Our target is this building." I swiped my hand against the hologram that transformed to the image Charlotte had constructed for Horace. "This here is the building as Charlotte remembers it. Eight floors and a basement. Cage, I want you to go out on foot. Scout ahead. I want you in the building before anyone else, take a peek at their systems. Grab anything that is beneficial; wipe it clean. Atkins, you will be with Wilts. Wilts, if I can't kill him, neither can you. Cameron, you're with Horace. Ravin, you will be with me. Angel, be our eyes. Questions?"

"Yes, sir." Angel spoke. "What about Barren?"

"Unfortunately, we don't know where he will be. Only what he looks like." I swiped the simulator again to reveal the image of Barren. "Luckily, the area they are in is small. Whoever comes across Barren: do not kill. We need him alive. We can't have another mishap of not gathering all the information."

"Once we have C.K. and Barren, we will correspond to the basement."

"What's in the basement?" Cameron asked.

"The basement is where they've been known to keep their test subjects."

"Are you telling me that this is a rescue mission now?" Atkins, who was silent, finally had an opinion to share.

"If there are prisoners still alive, yes."

"Bullshit. The mission was to retrieve the bioweapon, not rescue poor shmucks that were too stupid and got kidnapped."

"Were you not loved enough as a child?" Angel asked with disgust in her voice. "We can't leave *anyone* behind."

"Bullshit, we aren't even here. Remember?" He pushed his way to his feet. "Shit, are we even getting paid for this?"

"I wasn't loved enough as a child," Ravin said, pulling the attention of everyone to him. I'd been distracted by Atkins and didn't notice that he had lined up three lines of coke. "I've got daddy and mommy issues. That's why I've always been an independent slut. Won't see any pimp owning this." He snuffed lines in between words before he leaned back in his chair.

"You were a prostitute?" The words slipped out of my mouth.

"Twelve to eighteen." He grinned, clearly proud of himself.

"That's not necessarily true. Do you remember the Victoria's Secret Party, the one where you were being passed around like a cigarette?" Horace pointed out.

He laughed.

"That was a good night."

"You made me over five thousand credits that night."

"Wait, is that why you gave me money the next day? And didn't you take a drag of *this?*" He motioned his hands down his body.

"Excuse me," General Elba nearly shouted.

"Oh, sir." Horace apologized as he straightened up in his chair. "It's not what it sounds like. He was on acid and thought that penises were straws."

"To be fair," Ravin butted in. "Everyone else was sucking on them."

Horace eagerly agreed.

"We were sharing a pair of fraternal twins. He mixed the brother and I up. Honest mistake."

"An honest mistake, you didn't correct," Cage pointed out. Horace flashed her a devilish smile.

"Why wasn't I invited to this party?" Wilts' voice sounded offended.

"We have a mission to do in the next twenty four hours. Pay attention!" Elba's voice bellowed out capturing everyone's attention. "Atkins, we will be rescuing all prisoners that we find. You will not receive a penny for your work. Ravin, you lied about your head injury and your drug habit. Now, I find out you have a history of prostitution, how the fuck did you make into the U.F.F.C.? Mills, stop selling Ravin. Wilts, you were there. Ravin roofied you." He turned to each one as he spoke. "Continue Sergeant Duke." He rubbed the side of his head.

I stood dumbfounded. *Holy hell this group of people are way too close.*

"Once we have any prisoners in hand, we will make our way to the ship. Toots, you'll be in charge of handling C.K. Keep it safe."

"Questions?" I looked around. Slowly, Cameron's hand raised up. "Yes."

He turned to Ravin. "Why would you roofie Wilts?"

"I don't remember," Ravin passed the question to Horace. "Why did I?"

"He found out it was you stealing his Skittles. The obvious solution was to roofie him."

"I knew it was you." Wilts stood up. "Your ass is grass." He lunged across the table in an attempt to grab Ravin.

For someone high on drugs, he managed to get out of the way rather quickly. He picked up his chair and used it to keep distance between him and Wilts.

"If you have a problem with me, take it up with my pimp."

"Mills, your pathetic hooker stole from me."

"Beat his ass?" Horace suggested.

"What?" Ravin shrieked before he dropped the chair and hightailed it out of the room, with Wilts right on his tail.

"Was that a necessary question, Jones?" Elba asked.

"I was really curious, sir," replied Cameron.

"If you didn't ask, I was going to," Angel whispered over to him.

I shook my head.

"Get some rest and be ready to go at 0600 for the orbit jump. Dismissed... I guess."

I clicked off the computer while everyone but Horace filed out.

"Sam, can I talk to you?" I passed him a quick look and ignored the rush I got even though we'd spent every night together so far.

"What's on your mind?"

"I wanted to thank you."

"Don't." I didn't look up from my work.

"I mean it. There is more to this than her being my daughter." His voice lowered.

Catching his tone, I looked up.

"What are you talking about?"

"I joined the U.F.F.C. when I was eighteen. For over fifty years, I've seen things, done things that have ripped away parts of me. Parts that make me human." I watched his eyes as he spoke. "The worst part is, you don't even know it's happening. It's a nightmare you can't wake up from. I can see it happening to you already."

"Becoming numb is something that comes with the job."

"It goes beyond numb. *You're* gone. Who *you* were."

"You're not gone, you can wake up. The problem is once you wake up, what you did is still there, what you had to witness is still there. It's always easier to remain asleep because how else are you going to make it to tomorrow?" Charlotte woke you up, trust me I understand," I stated the fact.

He gave a loving smile at the sound of her name.

"She did. She made it possible to be awake without the burden. I would put her in the room next to mine at night, and I would wake up every morning with her glued to my side." From the look on his face, he was re-living the memories. "It's perplexing how something so simple can heal you. It's one of the reasons I love her so much."

I smiled at his words.

"We forget that not everything is cured with medicine. A hug can do more wonders to stop the pain than morphine can. Trust me, I understand." I squeezed his arm. "Charlotte will be kept safe."

He smiled at me, "Thank you." He spoke quietly, leaning in to pull my face to his and gave me a kiss. It was a slow kiss that made my blood boil.

I reached for him, enjoying the bulge that met my hand between his legs. His arms tightened around me, pressing our bodies together. Enjoying his taste, his smell, the way he felt. I got lost in it.

His hands reached for my belt. I caught myself on the table and did my best to stabilize him as a large gust of wind pushed up against the ship, distracting us. The force of it knocked over all the unsecure objects to the floor.

"Are you alright?" I asked.

"Yeah. Those waves are getting stronger each day." He straightened up, still alert. I knew why: Nothing good came from winds out in the middle of space. "Are you okay?" He asked in return.

I nodded.

"I'm fine." I looked out the front of the ship. Nothing but the dark, star filled void met my eyes. "Have you ever been caught in one?"

"No, Cage has been tracking it. Hopefully we can avoid it before it grows."

Another large wave hit the ship, this one knocking us to the ground. I caught him, his large body pushing the wind from my lungs.

"I'm going to feel that later." I sputtered out my words between breaths.

"Let me make up for it." He pushed himself on his arms but didn't get off. His face had the same devilish smile from earlier, giving me goosebumps.

"Get off of me." I shoved him off, in an attempt to get up. It didn't work, still unbalanced from the previous gust of wind the next one knocked me back down to the ground, well, onto him.

I fell face down on his crotch, his laugh was as devilish as his smile. Heat flushed into my cheeks as I felt him start to grow once more. Without thinking I looked up to see that the smile never left his face.

"That's mature," I said eyeing him as I pushed myself up on my feet, hiding my smile.

He laughed as he pushed himself up. "The big bad putty tat blushes. Come here." He pulled me in with a kiss. *God, he was tasty*, and who am I kidding? In his words, *I wanted to play*. I didn't kiss him back, instead I pushed him away causing him to stumble. I couldn't hide my smile now.

He reached for me, but I stepped to the side out of his way.

"I have work to do, if you don't mind." I turned back around to the table to reach for the files that spilled out from the waves, leaning over a smidge.

"Come on, let's play," He whispered before he nibbled on my ear as he pressed up against me. The moment his teeth touched me, goose-bumps erected up all over me.

"No," I pushed him off without turning around. "I *don't* want to."

"Please." He drew out the word, already pressed back against me. His hands slid around my waist to the front of my belt and with a flick of his wrist, it was undone.

"No," I responded a bit sterner. His fingers already had my first button undone. I elbowed his side, knocking the air from him. "I mean it." I felt my blood pumping, making me swell.

"Why not?" He wrapped his arms around me and forced himself against me this time, preventing me from pushing him away.

He was rubbing himself against me before he pushed me down into the table the sound echoing out when I hit. He used his body weight to keep me bent over as he pulled my hands behind my back. Holding my wrists with his one hand, the other yanked my pants down. I attempted to get away, but each time he pushed me down again. His foot kicked mine farther apart.

Pushing up, I twisted my head to steal a kiss before he pushed me flat against the table one more time. I throbbed when the sound of his belt unbuckling filled my ears. I couldn't help but moan when he forced himself on me.

Dr. Horace Mills – Osiris

"Horace," Ravin's voice came over my shoulder. "Can you do that thing I love so much?" He gave a grin as he spoke. I was hunched over Angel's file in the infirmary. I'd spent so much time here, it was home. The one place I could really think, so far I still couldn't decide what to do. As the time grew nearer, I found myself hesitating. I did not want to kill Sam.

I turned around to him covered in sweat.

"Did you just now get away from Luke?" I couldn't help but laugh.

He looked around uncomfortably.

"Sure, let's go with that." He walked over and hopped up on one of the beds.

It had been a while since the last time we did this. Stop his heart, let him rest, and start it back up again. Even his resting heart rate would give him pain, the pressure never stopping as long as his heart beat. This unethical and highly unrecommended procedure let him be pain free for the next twelve hours.

"Are you ready for tomorrow?" I gathered the medicines to inject him with as I spoke.

"I am. Are you?" He held my gaze. "You still plan on gunning down Sam and saying it was a Former?" I could hear the disdain in his voice.

"What else am I supposed to do? I can't even handle the thought of someone hurting her."

"I know she's asked you not to kill him. I know you lied about that. Why?"

I didn't respond as I began sanitizing his arm and prepping the needle.

"What are you going to do? Kill everyone who knows about her? Keep her isolated from everyone? Take her from one box and put her in one that has a few extra inches for her to move in?"

"No," I rushed out. "Only those who will jeopardize her secret."

"Did you catch that?"

"What?"

"It's her secret. If she wants to tell someone, then she has every right to. She's been wanting to talk to Sam about it for years, and *you* are the reason she hasn't. You have no idea how much she loves you, how much faith she's put in you. You are the only person in all the galaxies that she wants to make proud. She can't stand the thought of you being mad or disappointed in her, but she can't let you or anyone else take away the only other person who's mattered as much as you have to her."

He leaned back in the bed before he continued, "That is beside the point. It's her decision, and as her father, your *only* job is to support her and be there even if it blows up in her face."

"And Cameron? He could easily turn tail and alert the authorities. Sam? Say he gets mad, who is he going to take it out on? Her? Me? Say he feels betrayal, exposes her out of spite? What then? Leave him alive, so he can go and spread rumors of a half breed Pharaoh child? Good idea."

"Enough," He turned his voice hard, something he had only done on a few occasions with me. It was the only time he was ever serious and demanded direct attention. "You don't own her. You don't have this right you are trying to have with her. Stop."

I took a deep breath and sat down on the stool next to him.

"You're right, I don't." I rubbed my hand down my face. "What do I do?"

"Accept it. She doesn't have to know you lied. I'll be with Sam tomorrow; it'll piss Wilts off when I don't pull the trigger, but he won't make a scene in front of everyone. When the two of you are alone, let him know it's over. He will listen to you as her father."

I nodded my head. He was right.

He shook his head in disbelief. "Shit, when he finds out she's been on the ship with us, hiding about… Can I be there for that when you tell him?" His voice was back to its playful tone.

"Sure, it'll save me from reliving the embarrassment. Bring yourself a date while you're at it." I gave a small laugh. Looking at the medicine I stood back up to finish.

"Do you like him?"

I sighed.

"Yes. I do."

"Then this should be easy for you. You can't lose by doing this, you will have your daughter, and I have my money that you will have Sam, too."

"He's not wrong."

My head snapped over to the door where Sam stood. *Fuck! How long had he been there?* I glared down at Ravin, who cringed. He was in clear view of the door. *Sneaky son of a bitch.*

"She asked me to talk to you. In her words, and not that I don't disagree: 'Will you talk to him? He's being stupid.' Now…" He took the syringe of medicine. "I'll give you two some alone time." He stuck the needle into his IV and relaxed into the bed. "Wake me when you're done."

The heart monitor slowed down with each passing second as Sam's footsteps came closer. He was standing next to me as the monitor went flat. Six minutes.

"How much did you hear?" I asked.

"Oh, is the big, bad putty tat mad?" He used my words from merely hours ago.

"Hardly." I turned toward him. "I only need to know if you are going to have an accident walking to your bunk tonight."

He was smiling, unaffected by my empty threat.

"You mean did I hear you have a crush on me and that Charlotte is actually on the ship with us? Nah, I missed that part."

"I'm sorry, I told you this wasn't personal."

"Enough, I told you already, your daughter comes first."

"I don't understand."

"Understand what?"

"*You.* You're from Sobek, you should be angry. Hunting any alien around you. Seeking revenge for what we did. Ravin killed your brother. You know I planned to kill you and everyone else on your team. Yet, you are still helping."

He leaned up against the bed and looked at Ravin. His arms crossed over his chest; it was the first time I'd ever seen him do that. His whole face tightened. I'd struck a nerve from the looks of it. *But with what? That was supposed to be a compliment.*

"I suppose the answers to that aren't important." Even his voice seemed to have walls built in. He straightened up. "Make sure the infirmary is ready for any possible prisoners we take aboard. I'll see you at the jump in the morning." He didn't look at me as he walked out.

I wanted to chase after him. I didn't strike a nerve; I pried a door that shouldn't have been touched. I looked over at the timer, I had another minute and a half before I had to bring Ravin back. Hopefully that would be enough space for him before I could apologize.

I pulled over a chair and waited for the timer to go off before I picked up and added another medication to his IV and charged the defibrillator. He woke on the fourth shock, his body seized up as he struggled to breathe. I turned on the oxygen mask next to him and helped him put it on to breathe. After a few breaths, he sat up but didn't give up the mask quite yet. Looking around, he opened his mouth.

"How did you fuck it up this time?"

"What makes you think I fucked it up?"

"I was dead, not stupid."

"I opened my mouth. How are you feeling?" I had my stethoscope out, listening to his heart.

"That's usually how you do it. I feel fucking fantastic."

"You need to rest for the rest of the night." I helped him to his feet and started to walk him to his bunk.

"You should apologize."

"Shut up Sammy, and be sure to tell her that you spoke to me."

"Apologize. She's going to be in danger as long as she's alive. You can't isolate yourself, why not have someone who holds her to the same value you do?"

I opened the door to his bunk to see Angel waiting. She was still in her uniform with her hair pulled back in a bun. Jumping up from the bed she rushed over to help get Ravin in the bed.

"Do you feel better?" she asked nervously.

"Yes, works every time." He placed a kiss on her forehead before he laid down.

She gave me a smile.

"He will be okay?"

"He will be fine. Keep him hydrated, and make sure he rests."

She pressed into me.

"Okay." Her voice came out muffled. She buried her head in my chest, choking back tears.

I hugged her.

"He's not going anywhere."

A sob left her but she nodded her head, I held her close. Poor girl, why she took a liking to Ravin out of all the people, I couldn't answer.

"He was in a lot of pain. You'll see the difference when he wakes up."

She looked up but didn't pull away, her green eyes wet with tears.

"Promise?"

"Swear." I gave her a kiss. "Would it make you feel better if I came back in an hour?"

"Please."

"Okay." I smiled. "Don't cry." I wiped away her tears. She slowly pulled away and curled up on the bed next to Ravin who was already fast asleep. Her right hand rested on his chest. "Strong heart beat?" I asked as I laid a blanket over her.

"Yes." She sniffled but gave a smile. I was halfway to the door when she spoke again.

"Are you going to be okay with the new plan?"

Her question made me stop.

"Yes, now get some rest," I said before I walked out.

I headed for Sam's room only to find it empty, his uniform on the bed. He'd changed. I cursed under my breath. I searched the ship to find him in the training area going rounds with the punching bag.

He was dressed in standard military workout sweats, shirt off exposing his muscled body that was covered in sweat. I called out his name over the blows, he passed me a glance but continued on.

"Sam," I called again getting up in the ring with him. "Can we talk?"

He paused.

"Is it about the mission?" He asked.

"No."

"There's your answer." He went back to punching.

"Alright, listen then. I don't know what I said to upset you, it wasn't meant to. I'm sorry."

"I'm not upset. You made a great point, a point I guess we both didn't take seriously. One of us isn't making it out alive, right? It's smarter to end the night time benefits now." He didn't pause his blows and spoke between each hit.

I let out a breath of air.

"We aren't going to kill you or your team anymore. The weeks leading to now let us think we can trust you. You heard how I feel towards you. Whether that's something you want or not is irrelevant to the decision made. But if you feel the same –"

He gave a solid punch to the bag making it fly back before he turned to look at me.

"That's cute."

"Excuse me?"

"No ass before bed, and you turn into a real Romeo. Grow a fucking pair."

I was shocked, looking around pretending to look for the person he was talking to.

"Oh, I know you are not talking to me. I will beat your ass." He pretended to shake in fear. I didn't expect to laugh. That was one of the many things that made me enjoy his company, his sense of humor was similar to hers. "Please, go back to listening."

"Go on, Romeo." He started to remove his wrist wraps. I stepped in and took over, taking advantage of being able to have his hand in mine.

"Do you feel the same way?"

"Does it matter?" He pulled his hand away; his face went tight like before.

"It matters to me." I reached for his hand again.

"Yes." He left his hand in mine this time. "Still, it doesn't matter."

I set his hand down and picked up the other to remove the wrap on it.

"I would say differently." I searched for his gaze that was unreadable. Taking his free hand, he pulled my face to his and pressed his lips to mine. Slowly, he kissed me before he backed away, leaving an arm's width between us, only because I refused to let go of his hand.

"You hate The Formers, but you don't hate me. Can you even explain that?"

"You said it yourself, you were never one of them. You're not like them."

"How would you know? You don't know anything about me. I was fourteen when I murdered my first alien. It's a right of passage on Sobek, the way to become a man. Mercenaries bring shipments of aliens who are released into the woods. Fathers take their sons out and teach them how to hunt."

"My first kill was a child who begged me for his life. I couldn't pull the trigger by myself, my father came behind me and helped. The next year, I learned to pull the trigger myself along with the next two years before I could leave." He looked at me with each word he spoke. "I murder children while you save them." His voice cracking on the last word. "Do you still want more of a man who's murdered children?" His eyes filled with tears. "I'm exactly like them. No matter how much I try to not to be."

"No," I said pulling him in. "You're not. You did what you had to, to survive. We are all guilty of that." His hands held my arms and pressed his head into mine. "That takes a lot of strength. Something I've admired about you from the moment I knew you."

"The only thing I've ever prayed for is for forgiveness. I don't think I have been."

"That's because there is nothing that needs to be forgiven. It's wrong to kill a child, yes, it's wrong to force your children to partake in insane rituals. It's not wrong to be a victim." Still holding his face, I had him look at me. "To answer your question, yes, I still want more of you. I need the strength that you have, and not just for the rest of the mission." I kissed him between my words. "For everything else that might come my way while keeping my daughter safe."

He relaxed, and I saw a hint of a smile on his lips. I would go as far to say that he looked relaxed for the first time ever. Truly relaxed. *Has no one told him it wasn't his fault?* The years of abuse he'd given to himself wasn't necessary, *No wonder he knew about being asleep.*

"Thank you," he said in a soft voice.

"Once we have the prisoners and everything is settled, we will tell you everything. All I ask is you take any anger out on me and no one else."

"You're doing what you think is best for her. That's nothing to be angry about."

Chapter Thirteen

YEAR 5019, JULY 15

CHARLOTTE WARTS – OSIRIS

"What are you doing up this late?" Wilts' voice came from behind me, making me jump up from the chair. "I'm sorry, I didn't mean to scare you." He chuckled. "I'm still not used to seeing anyone up at this time." As always, he gave me a friendly smile.

"I couldn't sleep again." I held the book I'd been reading close to my chest.

"Me either." He wheeled over a chair to sit next to me. Every few nights, he'd sit with me, almost never sleeping himself. "It's nice to finally have some company." He gazed out into space getting lost in his thoughts.

It was easy to do, getting lost in thought, staring out into space. It was beautiful; vast. It was welcoming. Space offered to take you anywhere. I'd never imagined I could go anywhere. Every chance I could, I'd open the blinds and look out.

I sat back down but didn't open my book.

"I still get nervous," I whispered.

He looked over to me and gave a softer smile.

"Me too sometimes. It'll get easier, I promise." I returned his smile. He was always so kind; they all were. "What are you reading now?"

I shifted in my seat to face him.

"*Of Mice and Men*. Horace said it was his favorite book. He helped me read it the first time."

"The first time? How many times have you read it?"

I counted on my fingers before answering.

"Three. I'm confused about the ending. Why George kills Lenny. He took care of him and kept him safe, then it was like he got tired of him." I looked down and fanned the pages out. The thought frightened me. *Would Horace grow tired of me? Would the others? Am I a burden much like Lenny?*

"Remember when Candy let the other man kill his dog because he couldn't do it?" I nodded. "He then regrets not doing it himself moments later, wishing he was the one that did. Candy was responsible for his dog and should have been the one to help the dog to peace. Do you follow?"

"Yes. If-if you are responsible for something, you need to take care of it."

He nodded.

"The gentle spirit that Lenny was, he is unable to understand what is right or wrong, and it gets him into a lot of trouble."

"Like when he didn't mean to kill Curly's wife?"

"Right. Curly doesn't care; he wants revenge and isn't going to stop. George knows this, knows that if Curly gets his hands on Lenny, he's going to make it as painful as possible. He also knows that he can't keep running. It's mercy that George shows Lenny."

"Mercy. That's like compassion?"

"It is. It's why Horace loves that book. As a doctor, his world is ruled by showing compassion for everyone he treats. Sometimes, it's hard to give."

I thought about what he said. *Mercy.* My eyes wandered to his scars. *See my scars? He helped me get better, he's going to do the same for you.* His scars covered him from head to toe, I'd often wondered how he got them and if that was how he, too, met Horace.

He caught my eyes.

"Horace showed me a lot of compassion helping me. He still does." His fingertips brushed up against the scar on his arm. "Many doctors wouldn't have bothered to help me."

"Why?"

"The same reason they wouldn't have helped you. They'd have believed our quality of life was gone. The physical and mental pain is not considered to be worth the quality we received. Horace gave me a choice once I woke up, for the option of a dignified death if I thought it wasn't worth it."

"Who was it who hurt you?"

"I was given a mission to protect a family. They were like your mother, Pharaohs." I smiled. I didn't know much about my mother, but I loved to hear any mention of her. "It was a family of five, three kids all under the age of twelve. They were one of the last known families of Pharaohs, and I had to find a place where they would be safe. I got so close to the family the kids called me Uncle Luke." He was staring out into the black. "I kept them safe for over a month until my old team and I were heading back to base when our vehicle hit an IED. I woke up chained to a table."

As he spoke his voice got deeper and he lost himself as he looked out into space.

"The people who set up the IED wanted to know where I hid the family, so they could kill them. When I wouldn't tell them, they did this to me." His hand brushed over several scars. "When I wouldn't tell them what they wanted, they brought in one of my team members. I can't even remember his name, but I can see his face. He told them everything, where they were, how to get in."

"They let him go with the rest of my team, but kept me. I was an obstacle that needed to be eliminated. So, they continued to torture me. I died twice before Horace saved me."

"What happened to the family?"

"They were murdered." The words pushed through his teeth.

"And your old team?"

"I killed them."

I looked at him, up and down. He was large and towered over everything, I tried to imagine him doing such an act. I'd never seen him aggressive; he was quiet and kept to himself unless Ravin was around. He was more childish then.

"I'm sorry they hurt you."

"I'm sorry your father hurt you. I won't let him do it again." His hand came over and squeezed mine. "Go get some rest."

I smiled getting up, *I won't let him do it again…* Those words repeated through my mind. I took a few steps before I turned around and gave Lucas a hug. "Thank you."

He returned my hug and gave me a kiss on the cheek, "You're welcome."

I gave him a final squeeze before I headed to bed. I wrapped my arms around myself as I walked. The ship was always on the chilly side, the temperature kept low to preserve energy. Horace had given me my own room that was next to his, but I couldn't sleep in there.

I headed to Horace's bunk and opened the door. He was already asleep. I slid into the bed next to him. My weight woke him, and he looked over to me and gave a smile.

"Can I sleep with you again?"

"Of course." He moved over a few inches to make room before he pulled me close, so I could rest my head on his shoulder. I pressed into him, the warmth of his body driving away the cold.

Chapter Fourteen

YEAR 5032, OCTOBER 1

SERGEANT SAMUEL DUKE – OSIRIS

The sound of my alarm woke me from a dead sleep. Searching blindly for a few moments, I was able to turn it off. Horace, who was usually easily, woken was still asleep. His arm was draped over my waist, and his body was pressed up against mine. Any other time, I'd ignore the clock and enjoy this, but in less than an hour, we'd be making the jump to Nefertiti.

"Wake up." I kept my voice above a whisper while rubbing his arm that was wrapped around me.

"Hmmmm?" It came out groggy, and it made his chest vibrate.

"Come on." I couldn't help laughing. I moved to get up but his arm pulled me back.

"Let's bomb the planet and call it a day." He ran kisses on and down my neck. "No one will know this time."

I flipped over, his eyes still closed. He looked peaceful even in the dark. Using my arms, I drew him closer and gave him a kiss.

"I think it's best to keep the explosives away from you for the rest of the trip."

His laugh echoed off the walls.

I gave him another kiss before I got up to shower, with him not far behind. Once showered and dressed, we strapped our vests full of knives, guns, and ammo and made our way to the cargo bay where we'd make our jump.

Angel and Ravin were already there, ready to go. Ravin's arms wrapped around her pulling her in and showering her with kisses. I took in how his skin seemed brighter, healthier, and from what I could tell his energy was up… *which was an odd thing to even think about.* He wasn't exactly one to be burned out.

Wilts, dressed and ready for the jump, was pacing around the cargo bay. He gave us a quick glance but ignored us after that.

"Good morning, sir," Cameron said as he came in.

"Morning. You ready, kid?"

"Yes, sir, I'll admit I'm a little nervous. I've never done a non-orbital jump out of basic."

"You'll love it," Horace advised. "Just be sure to bend your knees, and you'll have a blast."

"Yes, sir." The smile on his face said how happy he was to receive the advice.

"Ravin!" Wilts' voice bellowed out from his diaphragm followed by Angel's laughter. "Leave her alone, this is not a vacation." Ravin didn't look an ounce surprised at the large man who yelled at him.

He released Angel from his arms.

"Don't worry." Ravin sprinted over to Wilts. "I have love for you, too." His arms wound around Wilts, pulling him into a hug, showering him with twice as many kisses as he did Angel.

"Get off of me." He attempted to push him off, but Ravin stuck like glue. "Get off!" Wilts shouted again, but I could hear the laughter he tried to keep away and the smile on his face.

I watched their endeavor.

"Wilts really doesn't like jumps, does he?" I muttered to Horace.

"Not one bit. It's never been this bad though. Must have been the time away from it." Ravin had his legs wrapped around Wilts now.

"How long have the love birds been at it?" Cage asked, walking up to Horace.

"Few minutes," he replied, pulling her into a side hug.

For the first time since I'd met her, she gave me a smile. Most days, she kept quiet and focused on cleaning weapons with Angel. Other days, I'd go all day without seeing her.

"As squad leader, it's your job to handle *that*." She motioned with her head over to Ravin and Wilts.

"Let me love you." Ravin cried out.

"How often does *that* happen?" I asked.

"Couple times a month." Her smile widened. "Ravin has no boundaries."

"So I've noticed." I gave her a smile. "I'm honestly surprised he hasn't been shot yet."

"He grows on you," Horace interjected with a smile as big as Cage's. "Do you remember when Wilts wanted to kill him?"

"Yes." Cage began laughing, a bit too hard to where she snorted. The more she snorted the more she laughed. It was a cycle that had Horace laughing.

She opened her mouth to continue, but General Elba's voice came over the loudspeaker, catching our attention. Well, most of ours. Acting as captain, he was flying the ship.

"Prepare for the jump. Two minutes." Atkins hurried in as Elba spoke, taking his place next to Cameron and Angel while Ravin and Wilts didn't pay any heed to the announcement.

Catching her breath, Cage, still in Horace's arms, was using him to hold herself up.

"It's a good plan, Sergeant Duke."

I smiled at her compliment as she walked over to the port next to the others. One by one, everyone but the 'children' put on their helmets and prepared for the jump. "Toots, Molly, enough dicking around. Ninety seconds to jump."

"Happily, get this fucker off of me." Wilts was laughing now. He gave a hard shove to send Ravin ass first on the ground.

Lining up with the rest of us, we waited.

"Sixty seconds." Elba's voice came over the loudspeaker again.

"Mic, check." One by one, we sounded off, coming in clear.

Our magnets kept us glued to the ground as the doors opened, revealing Nefertiti below. It had been a few years since my last drop like this; the landing always hurt like a bitch. I gazed out taking in the brown planet. As we grew closer, the image of a small green area came into view.

"Angel. You're up." I called out to her. Helmet on, along with her skintight drop suit and a weapon in hand, she was out of the ship within a second.

"What the fuck! Why would you let her jump first?" Wilts yelled into his mic. "She's crazy! It could be dangerous down th –" I leaned over and clicked off his magnet. The force of the gravity sucking him out. "You asshole!" His voice faded out as he fell from the ship.

"My love." Ravin shouted, jumping out after him.

"Cameron, Atkins, Cage, Horace." Taking a deep breath Cameron jumped, followed by Atkins and Cage. Horace took my hand in his and gave a tight squeeze before he jumped. Clicking off my magnet, I took up the end.

Adrenaline running through me, the first thing I felt was the intense heat. The fall lasted little over two minutes. My eyes glued to the ground below me, I watched the rest of my team hit the ground and take position. Preparing for the land, I kept my body loose even as the force of the hit vibrated up into my legs, settling into my knees.

"Cage, how are the oxygen levels?" I looked around. The planet was hot and dry, similar to Sobek. Desert. We'd jumped five miles away from the Former's Base. There was no cover around until we reached the vegetation.

"It's normal, sir."

I unsealed my helmet, letting the hot air fill my lungs. Already sweating from the drop, the dust began sticking to my face.

"This place is a dump," Ravin remarked, taking off his helmet.

"There is really nothing here." Angel was looking around. "How did they terraform this whole planet to support them?"

"Stolen money and child labor. All they need to do is build the generator to produce the oxygen. Let's move and fan out a half a mile. Ravin, take the lead, Cameron front right, Atkins front left. Mills, Angel take the rear." Wilts, Cage, and I took to the center.

"We have about a mile before we hit the verdure." Ravin led us on, his weapon at the ready. "Then it's only four more miles."

"Verdure?" Wilts commented.

"Mills?" He used his comm. to speak. We were distancing ourselves out for the walk.

"Verdure. It means vegetation. A noun, dating back as far as the fourteenth century. Origins have it traced to the Latin word '*virere*,' which means 'to be green.' Now, in the sixteenth century the word was used to describe a tapestry with plants on it. In Old Italy –"

I laughed at Horace's expanded lecture on "verdure."

As we marched towards the base, the suns moved higher in the sky. The sight of it reminded me much of home. I smiled, thinking back on old memories. As young kids, Derrick and I were almost inseparable. Every night, we came home to a belt for staying out too late.

As glad as I was to leave Sobek, there was a lot that I did miss. Even as the weather there hit one hundred and ten, my brother and I still enjoyed running outside. It wasn't uncommon for one of us to get a heat stroke.

Wilts continued to curse under his breath about the heat.

"We should have bombed this planet, too." Wilts' voice broke in through the comm. "It's not on the radar, and no one would fucking know."

"I recommend the same thing. We'd be done by now if we did it," Horace answered him.

"Is that your answer for everything?" I asked clicking onto the comm. "Bomb here? Bomb there?"

"Everywhere a bomb-bomb," Ravin sang. Hints of laughter filled my helmet. Soon the sight of the vegetation came into view. The closer we got, we fell back into a straight line for the dense patch of greenery.

"Keep yourselves covered, and don't touch anything. We don't know if anything here is poisonous." I looked around as I spoke. This small patch of forest here was miles long, and according to Warts, their base was located here.

"It is pretty here." Angel turned her head from left to right.

She was right, it was; the density of the trees and plants reminded me of a rainforest, compacted in. The ground squished with each boot that came down. The trees reached high into the sky, coming together to block out the sun, giving us a break from the intense heat. Moss and ivy stemmed their way up the trunks, hiding the bark. Ferns bushed out along with other plants I couldn't identify. White and purple flowers covered the forest floor.

"I don't get it. This place has a lot of diversity. Why is there no life? I don't even see insects." Cage was the one who asked the question. "Shouldn't there be something?"

"There probably is," Cameron clicked in. "Many people forget that plants are considered to be alive. I would bet that at a cellular level, there is something more complex evolving. The Formers wouldn't care to look for life that small."

"Does that mean this is a new planet?"

"Life takes years to appear; it always starts as a complex cell that divides and evolves with its environment. They evolve to survive, which is why life on every planet varies from one to the next. The only similarity that has been found is that all are carbon-based life forms. Carbon seems to be the key."

"Not bad, kid," Horace complimented.

"Thank you, sir. I've always loved science. As a kid, I always had to connect the dots. Everything had to be explained."

Wilts chuckled at Cameron's comment.

"Were you that annoying kid in class that asked 'why?' to every question."

"Yes, sir."

"I would have stolen your lunch money."

"I brought my own lunches, sir. I have a gluten allergy."

"Alright, daily wedgie until you brought me money."

"Wouldn't it be easier to steal his lunch than extort the kid?" Ravin asked.

"No. I like gluten."

Cage laughed.

"You're lying. I bet the nerds hired you for muscle to keep the bullies away. I actually have a peanut allergy myself," she continued. "Didn't really matter. They were too expensive to fly in. It was my wedding day when I found out. Blew up like a balloon."

"We are in unknown territory. Perhaps we should shut the fuck up and pay attention?" Atkins' voice was raised and caused my ears to ring.

"What? Can't walk and talk at the same time?" Angel taunted him.

"Play nice, Angel. Atkins, shut the fuck up, and keep walking." I directed my orders to each of them.

Keeping our formation, we walked on. No hostiles were visible yet, and no IEDs. As of right now, everything was going according to plan. There would, however, be hostiles at the building; the question was how many would be there.

"I got visual on the building," Ravin radioed in. "Quarter of a mile ahead."

"Hostiles?" Wilts and I asked in unison.

"At least forty that I see."

"Fall back to my position." The rest of the team moved forward as Ravin and I switched spots.

The Formers had thinned out the forest around their large base and built small buildings surrounding the edges. Old trucks that I would bet still run on fossil fuels seemed to be left out for anyone to use. *Helpful.* The building we were looking for was in the far back towards the other end of the clearing. Guards armed with guns walked around. *Not helpful.* They didn't seem too worried about an incoming attack, so non-military. Most likely mercenaries.

"Cage, first priority for you is shutting down their systems. No alarms, gather all intel. I don't care how you do it, but get it done. Atkins, Toots, go left and loop around behind the base. Clear as you go, set up an escape vehicle for any prisoners. Disable other vehicles. I want a clean getaway. Cameron, Mills, go right, same goes for you. Clear as you go. The less people who know we are here the better. Angel, go high, give us cover. Ravin, you are with me. Everyone meet at the basement."

I waited in place with Ravin while the others followed my orders. Ravin's hand made contact with my ass.

"And what are going to do?" Overly eager to know.

I directed my eyes to his hand that was still gripping my ass. He grinned and gave a squeeze, turning to face him, I lined up our noses. My right hand came down and gripped his front. We stood in silence staring at each other. His groin grew harder the longer my hand lingered on him.

"Wow, Angel is lucky." My hand was overflowing with him now. "I thought she was kidding about you."

The smile that was on his face faded.

"Angel-Angel and you talked about me?"

I grinned, "Yes."

"Just size?"

"If it makes you feel better. Sure."

"Lots of men get leg cramps when having sex." His voice got high, and he jumped back from me.

"Do they?"

"Yes, as a matter of fact."

"I guess I'm lucky."

"Indeed, you are, Papi is very talented." He gave a crooked grin.

Curiosity finally got to me.

"Have you and Horace been together?"

"I am a gentleman. I don't suck and tell."

I looked at him.

"Any other time I'd beat it out of you. However, we have to get going. Charlotte gave me a message."

The smile on his face faded, and he looked worried.

"Horace, he told –"

"Told me what?" I took a step closer to him. *What did he almost spill?*

"What did Horace tell you?"

"Nothing, what did you think he told me?"

"Who?"

"Horace."

"What about him?"

"Horace, told me what?"

"I have no idea. Can I have a clue?"

"I changed my mind; I will give away our position to beat the shit out of you."

"Whip me, beat me, hurt me, baby."

"For the love of God." I pinched the bridge of my nose. "Seriously, how has no one shot you yet?"

"People love me."

"Debatable." I pulled out a folded piece of paper that Charlotte had stuck into my pocket. "I don't know when, but Charlotte put this in my pocket. Probably when I was sleeping. I'm guessing you or Horace told her I knew where she was." He opened the note to read it.

"Barren has his own housing? I don't understand. Why wouldn't she tell us this?"

"You'll have to ask her that yourself. She didn't want everyone to know, clearly, only you and I know. Let's get him, knock him out, find the bioweapon, and rescue the prisoners."

"Why didn't you ask Horace for help with this? She's his daughter, don't you think he'd like to know?"

"He's too close, and I am too close to him."

"Fair enough, I'll have your six."

I nodded, before shouldering my weapon and moving on. We kept ourselves about a quarter of a mile away from the base as we walked.

Eventually, Ravin spoke.

"I've never seen Horace get caught up on anyone before." I smiled but kept walking. "He seems to really like you. This whole situation has been hard for him." I gave a dry laugh to his comment "What? You don't believe me?"

"I like Horace, but he's acting like an idiot. You all are."

"Um, ouch."

I stepped over a large log and ducked under a branch.

"What makes you all think that I don't understand? You act as if I'm not capable of it."

Ravin snickered before side stepping to the left behind a tree for a split second before he stepped back out, dragging a lifeless body with him. Hiding the body under leaves as he answered me. "You're telling me that you are one hundred percent 'okay' with the whole situation?"

I walked on, not waiting for him.

"If I wasn't, why would I have agreed to help?"

"Because you're a good boy who does what he's told?"

"Ha, ha." I veered to the right where I heard a twig snap. A man was turned, taking a leak. I came up behind him, hand over his mouth to muffle his scream. My other hand held the knife that slit his throat. I drug his lifeless body over and hid him beneath plants.

"Is it because I'm from Sobek? I'm not capable of understanding sympathy?" I stepped back on the path where Ravin was leaning up against a tree waiting for me.

"No, that's irrelevant to us."

"Why then?"

"There is *one* more secret."

That made me pause. *Was he serious*? I turned around to look at Ravin. I opened my mouth to speak but had trouble finding the words.

"Is there even a point in asking what it is?"

Ravin looked down, he seemed to be mulling over his thoughts before he looked up.

"When he tells you, depending on how you handle it will make or break you and Horace. Horace knows this, it's why he's afraid to even try with you. It's not something he could keep from you."

I pondered his words for a split second before turning around and marching forward. *What is it..?* "Is it…a secret that's dangerous in any way?" I didn't turn around.

"If you want it to be, or it can be something that benefits you."

"Thanks for the riddle. Barren's base is up ahead." I moved closer to the edge of the forest to get a look. According to Charlotte's note, it was the house with the cross on it. He took shelter here after Warts disappeared thirteen years ago.

His house was an easy find; much like anyone with power on Sobek, his home was well taken care of. It was surrounded by a five foot wall, making it impossible to see what was happening around it. The gate leading to the house was composed of wrought iron, exposing the white cross on the front, but it also gave limited insight of the door to the house. From what I could see, the front was guarded by two men.

The first man was armed, ready, and alert. His legs had a large stance, indicating he was ready for a fight. The second man had the same demeanor. I turned toward Ravin, who was next to me.

"Let's go in the back."

He nodded.

Keeping low, we moved parallel to the wall, I kept watch as Ravin peeked his head over for a split second.

"Six guards on the inside of the wall. They are behind the back of the house. We are clear to go over."

"Any of them Barren?"

"No, sir."

"I'll go over first, cover me."

"No, no. After me." Holding his weapon in his left hand he hoisted himself up with his right followed with his legs, keeping himself flat he rolled over the wall. I heard a soft thud of his body hitting the ground on the other side.

"Fuck!" he whispered, loud enough for me to hear.

Shit! I was up and over the wall, fearing the worst. I crouched on one knee weapon ready. No guards near us, they were around the other corner of the house. I looked down to see Ravin flat on his back looking up at the sky.

Innocently he looked over to me.

"I think I fucked up my back."

"How the hell are you a trained killer?"

"Sue me, I got excited."

I offered out my hand.

"Let's go."

Keeping low, we walked by the wall of the house, avoiding all windows. The guards were gathered in a circle, talking among themselves, their weapons leaned up against the wall of the house or on the small table nearby.

"I'll take the redhead, the fatty, and the hipster."

"Fuck you," I kicked him. "You're not getting all the big ones. I'll take the hipster and the redhead along with the sissy looking guy."

"Trade you the fatty for the redhead."

"Fine." I was up with a knife in my hand, angling the knife, I tossed it, planting it in the throat of the heavier weighted man. As soon as I let the knife fly, I had my hands around the hipster's neck, snapping it. I eyed my next target, a younger guy who was still processing what was happening.

Ravin used an elbow to the throat on the red headed man, crumpling him to the ground. Palming a knife, Ravin engrained it into the temple of the man next to him. I reached out for the last one, before a bullet went through his eye, splattering blood. I looked over to the other man, a bullet had gone through his head too.

I gave a smile, as I heard Angel's voice echo in my helmet. "Miss me?"

"Thanks, Babe."

"Damn, baby. Where in the worlds are you?" Ravin spun in different directions looking for her sniper's den.

"Close enough for comfort. I count another five inside. All armed," she responded.

"What are their locations?" I asked.

"Three men in the front. Two in the back."

"Barren?"

"One of the men in the back, sir."

I signaled Ravin and moved back to the front. There wasn't a back door for us to infiltrate. "Angel, can you get the guards?"

"Already taken care of, sir."

Ravin and I headed to enter the home. I noticed a few other bodies lying on the ground. Angel had been busy. The door was open; the three men inside didn't hear us enter. The suppressor on our weapons hid our presence from the men in the back.

Keeping our weapons shouldered, we moved through the house. From all appearances, the house seemed normal. Photos decorated the walls, a dining table, furniture. It gave an eerie energy knowing what truly happened here years ago. Peeking through the last doorway, I caught sight of the two men hunched over a desk near a window. *Barren.* I swallowed my anger.

I lined up my scope, ready to take out the other man in the room. A loud buzz whizzed passed my head and the man next to Barren brushed a hand around his as if to swat away a bee. He turned around and spotted us. I fired my weapon as Ravin charged Barren.

"Don't move." Ravin's voice turned deep.

Barren's eyes went wide as he threw his hands up in the air. His eyes were deep seated in his sunken face and, much like Warts, his hair was thinning exposing his scalp.

"Don't shoot." His voice shook on each syllable.

Ravin's finger danced on the trigger, debating on pulling it and ending the life of a monster. I understood his anger, but we couldn't kill him.

"We need him alive, Ravin." I placed my hand on his shoulder trying to get him to come back to reality. Barren relaxed hearing my words. "For now." I looked directly at him as I spoke, enjoying that his relief didn't last long.

Without a blink Ravin fired his weapon. The force of the bullet shattered Barren's shoulder, making him cry out in pain. I kept my weapon ready as Ravin lowered his and began to search him for weapons and to get a pair of cuffs on him.

"He's clean."

I kneeled down in front of Barren. His skin sweating and turning pale.

"Charlotte's Kiss. Is it finished?"

He looked away.

"No."

Liar.

"Where is it?" I pulled a knife from my waist pocket and pressed the blade into his wound. He opened his mouth to scream, only to have it muffled from the cover of Ravin's hand.

I gave him a minute to calm down.

"How-how do you know about this planet?"

"Irrelevant. Where is it?"

"We are…trying to protect everyone. We can't trust these unnatural vermin. They will kill us all if we don't do something." His words came between deep breaths. "You don't understand. It's for the best."

That's what made these men incredibly dangerous; they believed. I signaled Ravin to cover Barren's mouth once more as I dug the knife deeper into his shoulder wound.

"Last chance to answer. Where is it?"

"You have to understand –"

"Hold his hand." I directed my comment to Ravin who secured Barren's hand down on the desk.

"No!" Ravin's other hand wound its way back around Barren's mouth.

"I'm thinking of a number, one through five." I hovered the knife above Barren's hand.

"Four?" Ravin asked.

"Try again." I pressed the blade down into Barren's fourth finger. It easily cut through his flesh, it was the bone where I had to use more strength. *Crunch.* "Guess again."

"One?"

I brought the blade over to his thumb. "Nope."

Barren shook his head and his muffled cries called out for us to wait.

"Are you going to tell us where it is?" Ravin asked this time.

He nodded his head. Tentatively, Ravin removed his hand.

"It's in the lab." He spoke heavily on each breath.

"Motherfucker do you think we are stupid? We know it's there. What room?" Ravin smacked the side of Barren's head.

"Third floor. Chemical Room."

I clicked on my comm. to radio Cage. I paused for a minute and held Barren's gaze.

"If you're lying, I'll inject you myself with Charlotte's Kiss, and watch you rot.

"I'm not. I swear."

"Cage, come in."

"Yes, sir?"

"Charlotte's Kiss is on the third floor. Chemical sector."

"Copy, sir."

I flipped the butt of my gun and slammed it into the side of Barren's head.

"You're fun to work with." Ravin grinned at me before flicking Barren's dismembered finger at me.

"Let's go." I holstered my weapon and reached for Barren's unconscious body.

"No. No." Ravin snaked the body from me and hefted it on his shoulder. "You're already doing it wrong."

I scoffed at him and shouldered my weapon again.

"Let's move, Molly."

We exited the home and through the front gate. More bodies that Angel had dropped littered the ground.

"Sir, clear passage to the lab. Head west." Angel's voice filled my helmet.

"Copy."

We kept low and followed the directions Angel gave us. The lab itself was large and kept decent compared to the other dusted and broken down buildings.

Cage had disconnected the alarms and cleared her floors along with everyone else. The inside of the building reminded me of an old hospital back on Sobek. Old artwork hung on the walls, crosses… Even the smell was similar.

Our timing couldn't have been more perfect. We met up with the rest of the team as we made our way to the basement where Cameron and Wilts were waiting.

"Sir," Cameron was standing outside the basement door with Wilts. "We need a key to get in."

The rest of the team came in behind me, each one checking in. All here. The door to the basement was covered in dried blood, dust, and rust. Large chains secured the door handles together. I lowered my weapon and approached the door. The chain was easily ten kilos, the lock itself, however, was new.

"What's the hold up?" Ravin pushed his way up from the group leaving Barren's body behind on the ground. He wasn't even sweating;

the only give away that he didn't get up from a chair was the fresh specks of blood on his hands. "Ah, I see. I got this." He pushed his weapon into my hands.

"Hold up there, Molly, I got this," Wilts cut in and used his hand to keep Ravin from approaching the door.

"Did you not listen?" Ravin pulled on his ear. "I got this."

"Compared to me, you are an Oompa Loompa. Oompa Loompa." He gestured out to Ravin, before gesturing to himself. "Ironman. I got this."

"If anyone is Ironman it's Robyn. Oompa Loompa. Ironman. Sad little man."

"Fuck you."

"Fuck me? Fuck you."

"I'll beat your ass." Wilts took a step forward and became nose to nose with Ravin.

"Joke's on you, I'd like that."

"Ladies, put a tampon in it, and get back to work." I turned around to Angel who held the supply bag. "Got anything that will cut through this?"

"Yes, sir." She already had the bolt cutters in her hand.

"No." Ravin and Wilts shouted in unison. "I got this."

"Jesus. We don't have time for this." I was losing my patience.

"Odds," Ravin called.

"Fine. One, two, three shoot. Yes!" Wilts shouted for joy as Ravin cursed.

"Two out of three."

"One, two, three, shoot. Ha! Suck it muffin and stand aside while *I* got this."

"Damn, I never win."

"Because you always do the same number." Horace gave Ravin a pat on the back for comfort.

"Weapons ready. Angel, take up the back." I gave out the order.

Wilts turned parallel to the door before adjusting his weight into his back leg and kicked the door handle off with his other. The noise of it scraping against the stone filled the space we were in. Wilts counted to three before opening the door.

The room inside had a few lights, making it difficult to see inside without straining the eyes. The smell of rotting flesh, was sour, pungent, and overwhelming. It stormed at us with the breach of the sealed door.

I took the first steps inside, giving time for my eyes to adjust to the dark. The floor was dirt and the walls stone. An estimated twenty cages lined the walls from floor up to the ceiling. Unable to comprehend what I was seeing, my feet guided me to the middle of the room.

"Shit," Horace whispered behind me. He looked around, taking time to look at each cage "We can't help them." He turned to me, his face was stricken with horror, it was written clearly in his eyes. I imagined mine was similar. His chest rose and fell quickly, but he managed to clear all emotion from his face.

The rest of the team whispered among each other, but that wasn't enough to draw my attention away from what was around me. The cage next to me had two rotting bodies left inside, insects of every kind eating the flesh. Clear impressions of human teeth from hungry prisoners lingered in the flesh.

The loud clink of a chain falling to the ground behind me caught my attention. It was Angel, trying to open one of the cells to free the unmoving woman inside. She wasn't dead, her eyes were wide open, watching us. From the way she looked, she'd been here far too long.

"Angel." Wilts tried to pull her away, but she wasn't having it. His playful energy from before was gone, like Ravin's.

"Open the door." She dragged him closer to the cell door.

"I'm not going to." Was his response.

The reality of what would happen set in on her.

"Open, the door." She spoke calmly. He shook his head. The spark that lived inside her shot out. "Open the door!" Not only did she shout, she shoved him into it.

"Get her out of here," I barked my order. *She needed to calm down.* Wilts didn't bother to drag her from the room he threw her over his shoulder and had her out the door. They didn't need to have her energy around them. "Ravin, keep an eye out. I don't want any surprises. Cage, you and Cameron go back to the infirmary you know what we need. Atkins, find a vehicle. Move. Mills, calm her. Dope her if you have too."

Everyone kicked into gear, I was the last one out and shut the door behind me. Angel was squaring off with Wilts, doing her best to get back into the room.

"Get out of my way. Now!"

"Angel, you need to calm down." I attempted to reach for her.

"No," She nearly screamed at me. "You can't let them kill everyone. You said it yourself. We would be rescuing the prisoners."

"Angel," Ravin was back. "A rescue isn't always that simple."

She ignored him and tried to push passed us again.

"Move." We didn't. "Now." She pulled her gun out and pointed it at Wilts. He put his hands up but not in surrender, it was to order us to stand down while he handled Angel.

"There is no quality of life, for anyone in there."

"You don't know that."

"I do."

"Bullshit. We are going to rescue everyone. That's what we do. We don't murder innocent people."

"We give out mercy. Mercy is one of the hardest things to give out, it comes in many forms. It's what makes it hard sometimes. This isn't about you, it's about them and what they *need*," Wilts kept his voice calm.

"What about Charlotte? You saved her. How is she different from them? You said it yourself, she was down here in those cages. Are you regretting saving her now? Wishing you gave her mercy?" Her eyes were overflowing with tears. Her hand was shaking, something I've never seen her do in the field.

"Charlotte is a fighter. Lots of variables came into play with her."

She didn't believe his words; she pulled back the chamber on the gun loading the bullet.

"One more chance to move."

I put my hand on Wilts' shoulder.

"Angel, he is right, there is no quality of life. You saw what they did." I was standing next to Wilts now, trying to take her attention away from him and onto me. It worked. "The uproar of the civilians if we brought these people back alive would cause an investigation. Any other time, that wouldn't be a bad thing."

"No!" She shouted. "Charlotte had none. I read the file; she was treated far worse than them. Stop making excuses."

"Charlotte didn't know a different world existed. She didn't know there was a place outside of this. A place with true unconditional love. She is able to see the blessing, they won't. It'll be a nightmare for them. Charlotte embraced what we gave her. They won't." Wilts continued on. "They will be scared of their shadows, scared to sleep, scared to move. How is that a life? The experiments forced on them, that will leave them in physical pain for the rest of their life, *if* they can still move after it. We know what that's like."

"Last chance." She focused her attention away from me to Wilts.

"Angel," Ravin took two steps closer to her, putting the barrel straight to his chest. "He's right. The right thing isn't always easy. Take in account the people who found me, they took the easy road instead of doing the right thing and killing me."

"Wh-why would you say that?" Her whole body was shaking.

"Look what I do to keep the pain away. Drugs, alcohol. I willingly die to get peace from it. Everyone was willing to save me, but they didn't want anything to do with me once they did. No one did. It's why I was never adopted; no one could love the damage I was given. I wish someone was there to make the right choice and used a bullet. You have to take all of that into account with these prisoners.

"I love you." She backed up to give an inch between the barrel of the gun and him.

"I love you, too." He reached out to take her hands. "Trust me when I tell you that this is the right choice. The variable of Charlotte not even taken into account."

"How do you know it's the right choice?"

"Experience. We've *all* had it. Even you know it's right. It's just a little too close for home for you at the moment."

"I want to help them." She broke at the last word and started to cry. Ravin had the gun out of her hands and into mine while embracing her in a hug.

"I know." He placed a kiss on her forehead.

"Mills, help Ravin get her upstairs, and make sure Atkins is ready."

"No." She pulled away. "I'm sorry. I don't want to go. It's my responsibility."

"And you are ours. Go. It'll be done right. I promise." Wilts' voice had turned that of a father.

She looked at me for the final order, I nodded. "Go." I waited until I heard their footsteps fade away, I double checked my weapon. "Get the left, I'll get the right. Load up the bodies as soon as possible. I want us back on the ship in an hour."

"Yes, sir." Wilts reopened the door with his weapon at the ready. I still wasn't prepared for what I had to do. I'd never had to do it on this scale before.

I used a bullet to open the lock on the cage cells, starting with the first one. It was an older man, naked. Dirty. His hair had grown white from age, and his beard was long and unkempt. In his arms was the rotting body of an older woman, my guess: his wife. He was staring down at her face before he looked at me. His eyes were dead and didn't leave mine, understanding my intentions, he gave me a smile. My mind wanted to go on autopilot, but I couldn't. For every kill, I made sure I was there when I pulled the trigger.

I raised my weapon and fired. His body slumped over on his wife's. I heard Wilts' weapon fire behind me. It was the woman who Angel was trying to free. I moved on to the next cell, three dead bodies and an unconscious woman. I fired.

On to the next… Two men as dirty as the old man in the first cell. The first one closed his eyes, but his smile didn't leave; the second much like an older man watched. Peace etched into his eyes. I fired.

The next, a dead body with missing limbs. Next. A man holding his motionless child. His face burned and blistered. The experimentation done to his child left the spinous processes growing out her spine right before my eyes. The man held his hand out but didn't speak. He didn't need to. I pulled out my handgun and turned off the safety before placing it in his hand. From the look of stature, he was a form of military, understanding what we'd explained to Angel moments ago.

He whispered to his little girl and gave her several kisses, lining up her head with his he pulled the trigger. The bullet went through hers and then his. The blood splattered out on the floor. I reached down to retrieve the gun; the little girl's eyes were still open. Slowly, I closed them.

One after the other. These images would be stuck in my mind for the rest of my life. One after the other, I thought that it couldn't get worse. Each time it did. The last cell was filled with two little girls. The dresses that they had on were torn and tattered. I couldn't understand it; I didn't want to understand it. Why these men did what they did; they'd sewed them together at the ribcage. One of the girl's legs was broken and twisted around.

A young boy was lying on the floor next to them, he couldn't have been older than ten. His limbs had been removed, switched and sewn back on. None of them moved, he had no control. He was trying to get up, to move. Nothing but his torso could move. No tears, from any of them.

The image of the boy when I was fourteen flashed into my mind. He was laying down on the forest floor, crying, begging me for his life.

Too scared to move. His last words were him crying out for his mother. To this day, I had no idea if his mother was brought to the planet with him or if he was taken from her.

"Sam," Horace's hand touched my shoulder. I was too focused; I didn't even hear him come back in. "Cage and Jones are back if you want to help them."

I shook my head.

"Let me help you." He whispered the words in my ear before stepping forward, talking to the little children, his weapon ready. Wilts came in and began to comfort the other child before he too would pull the trigger. I nodded before stepping out of the cell. They waited until my back was turned to fire their weapons. The suppressor on the guns, did nothing to muffle the sound that rang in my ears.

Chapter Fifteen

YEAR 5024, MAY 15

SERGEANT SAMUEL DUKE – DUKE'S OFFICE

"As you are. I found you a new member for your team." Colonel Siks was an older man, standing in front of my desk in his well decorated uniform. His once blonde hair had grayed, and his large eyebrows grew out in every direction. It was usually the only thing I could focus on when I saw him.

I looked up from the report of my next mission. It had only been a day since I lost Sergeant Gore. He was a good soldier and was ready to settle down and have a family. Unfortunately, he wasn't able to do that with his current job; his new desk job started today. Out of the field for good.

"That was fast. Who is he?"

"*She* actually."

"Sir, permission to speak?"

"Proceed."

"I run a tactical team, not a Girl Scouts club. I don't need a soldier who can't pull their own weight. If one of my men goes down, he *won't* be left behind."

He let out a smirk and dropped a file down on my desk. "Why don't you take a look at her."

Might as well humor the man, I flipped it open. Angel Mills.

"Is she related to Doctor Horace Mills?" I couldn't help but ask.

"Not sure."

She was in her forties but her picture gave the impression of someone in their mid-twenties. Caucasian, brown hair except for a quarter on the left side of her head, that was shaved clean due to large scars. First page down, I was already impressed. She was overqualified for this job, a medal of honor and a purple heart. She graduated top of her training group, excelled in hand to hand combat and weaponry, and her IQ was above average.

"Who the hell is she? How is she still a Sergeant?"

"She turns down promotions."

"You're kidding." Who in their right mind would do that?

"Keep reading."

Born on Earth. No living mother or father.

"Sir, there is no history here about how she got her medals, her mental health, physicals, more than half of her childhood is blacked out. I need to see those."

"Not going to happen. All you need to know is a higher up cleared her. I called about those myself. I was instructed to 'fuck off,' her involvement in a classified mission is no one's business. Her file was wiped to keep her safe. The scars on her head were part of the casualties of the mission."

"How was she wounded."

"Classified."

"Classified? Bullshit."

"She's a good soldier. She will fit right into your team, I think. What do you say?"

Honestly, I was impressed.

"When will she be here?"

"Tonight, after dinner. She'll be in Gore's old bunk." He got up without another word.

I looked at her file a bit longer before turning to my mission report. My team and I were to leave for our next mission in a day. She'd better be ready. I sent a wave to Romeo and Phillips of the new member who was joining our team.

I spent the rest of the evening examining and devising a plan for our mission. An unknown group of Formers had managed to lock down a town. Within six hours, a wall was up, sealing in the community. I'd seen this done before. All adults are driven into a building to be slaughtered like animals. The children were then conditioned to The Formers beliefs. Sermons were preached over loudspeakers every minute of every day. The Old Traditions Book was given to every child who was forced to read it through every night.

It was believed the Formers group responsible had a total of one hundred armed men. There was one opening at the entrance of the town guarded by two men at the gate and three snipers on the top of the buildings nearby.

Night would be the ideal time to attack, before their shift changes. It would be then they'd be tired and unaware. Once the town was clear, a shuttle of troops would be flown in to take care of the children. Find them new homes, new parents. New families. It made me sick.

These types of attacks from The Formers started three years ago. It was unknown if they were becoming desperate for more followers, or that they simply had the extra men to spare in these frivolous attempts.

The loss of their leader, General Warts, who was murdered a little over nine years ago, didn't seem to slow them down. Every alien they came across was murdered.

It was 2200 when I'd finished planning out our assault. Mills should be here by now. I filed away the paper work on my desk before making my way to her bunk.

I had worked with a woman twice before this; each time was the same story. They couldn't make the cut. Unlike other team leaders, my standards for my team were higher. Any slip up from them resulted in leaving my team.

A. Mills. The name on the door already changed. I knocked on the door and waited a second for the door to open.

Mills was smaller in person, standing a little over five feet. Her hair had pulled to the side for the night and dark green eyes locked onto me. She saluted and transitioned into attention.

"At ease." She stepped aside, inviting me in. Her things were already packed away, the only thing left out was the book that she must have been reading. *Of Mice and Men*, an old copy and well-read by the looks of it. "We have a mission in a day. Tomorrow you'll be briefed at 0800 given an hour to be ready to go before we head out."

She nodded.

"Yes, sir."

"I hope you're as authentic as your file claims. One strike is all you get before you are out. Understood?"

"Yes, sir."

"Any questions?"

"No, sir."

I nodded. My hand hovered above the door handle.

"Are you related to Horace Mills?" I asked, half turned.

She gave me the kindest smile.

"I have no blood relation to him, sir."

I returned her smile.

"Get some rest. I'll see you tomorrow."

Chapter Sixteen

Year 5032, October 1

Sergeant Samuel Duke – Osiris

"Duke!" Wilts' voice boomed off the walls of the ship, his heavy boot steps thudding behind me.

"Not now." I kept my speed. "Finish loading the bodies to the infirmary."

"No." His hand took a death grip on my arm. "We need to talk about what happened. Angel –"

I tore my arm from his grip.

"I do not have to explain my orders to you or how I handle my team. She is not your soldier and," I gripped his vest and yanked him out of the way as Cage and Cameron carried the body past us. "You are not the leader of this team. Understand?"

"You *knew* Angel was unstable, yet you continue to allow her in the field. You willingly put her in danger." He kept his voice low but the aggression was clear, knocking my hand away.

"I *never* put her in danger."

"You did."

I was nose to nose with him.

"You know nothing about Angel to be having this response to what happened. I love Angel more than anyone, if for a second I thought she was unfit..." I lowered my voice as Ravin and Atkins brought the next body by. Ravin gave me a death stare as he walked. "She feels things deeper than others. That does not make her unfit. With what we saw, we are all allowed to react. If you need to take five, go."

"She should never have been allowed to see that."

"No, she shouldn't have. None of us should have. None of that should have even happened. But the worlds turn, and shit happens. It's why we took this job. It's why Angel took this job. She did her job, and she kept *you* safe. That's more than you did for your team over a decade ago."

His eyes burned and his fists curled up.

"We kept Charlotte safe. It is what we do; we keep others safe. That's not what you did for her."

My jaw popped. My words stuck in my throat. I turned on my heel; he called after me, right on my tail. I'd ordered Angel to go to her bunk, to have her calm down, while everyone else was to unload the bodies.

My fist pounded on the door.

"Angel." I turned to face Wilts, his face angry.

"What the fuck is wrong with you?" He was back in my face. "Give her –"

Her door opened, her eyes puffed out with her nose running.

"Yes, sir?"

I held Wilts' eyes.

"Disarm Wilts. That's an order."

I stepped back, giving her room.

Wilts' eyes turned from anger to confusion. He passed his confused look to her. Angel's fist struck his face, knocking him back a step, while her left foot extended out behind his, causing him to fall over. Knife in hand, she jumped on his chest, using her knees in his shoulders to pin him down, the tip of her knife pressed against his throat.

He laid flat, watching her. He slowly moved his eyes to me to see my gun drawn. I fired at his chest, the suppressor hiding the shot. The bullet embedded in his vest, Angel's knife never moved. I move the gun up, lining the sights up with his face.

"Angel can take care of herself. If she can't," I knelt down keeping my gun aimed. "That's where I come in. I would shoot Charlotte in the head, without a second thought, if it would protect Angel from even getting a scratch." I holstered my weapon. "Understand." It wasn't a question. "Now, take five or help the others take the bodies to the infirmary. I want Mills to begin the autopsies and running their DNA to find their families." I wrapped my arm around Angel's waist, helping her to her feet.

"Come on, let's take a minute."

She let out a shaky breath and lowered her opal knife.

"I win," she said playfully to Wilts, wiping away her tears. The anger was gone from his eyes, and it was replaced with something else…*pride*? I pulled her into her room, closing the door behind us, leaving Wilts on the floor.

"I'm sorry. I shouldn't have done what I did. I wanted to save them and make sure they could go home."

I pulled her into my arms as she buried her head into me.

"I know."

"Are you mad at me?"

I gave her a kiss before pulling her to the bed.

"No. I am hurt though."

She straightened up, her eyes filling with tears and overflowing.

She opened her mouth to speak; I could hear the sounds fighting to get their way out. I watched her eyes fill with panic then fear.

"I'm sorry. I wasn't trying to show any disrespect to you."

"Take a deep breath." I unclipped her hair pin letting her hair fall out, I pulled it off to the side and ran my fingers through her hair. "Calm down." I smiled at her. Her rapid breaths caused her body to tremble. Slowly, her shaking dwindled.

"I would never hurt you intentionally."

"I know." I leaned in to kiss her forehead, before I started to wipe away her tears. "I don't expect you to be okay with what we saw, but why didn't you trust me? You've always trusted me. I would never give you an order that is morally wrong, even if I am appointed to."

The words clawed their way out, while her hands took a secure hold on my wrists.

"I'm sorry." She broke into a sob. "I can't even tell you why."

I pulled her into a hug, squeezing her tight, I turned her chin up, so I could continue to look into her eyes before I stole a kiss from her. "I love you, Angel."

"I love you, too."

"What we do isn't easy; it wears you down over the years."

She pulled away, the panic setting back in her eyes.

"I can do my job, I made one mistake. Don't take this from me. I *need* this job." Her chest began to heave once again. She loved this job; it was what she'd formed her world around.

"Angel, breathe. Look at me." I searched for her eyes. "This isn't an official mission. I won't take this into account." I pulled her into a hug. "Besides, I couldn't do my job as well without you."

Sergeant Major Lucas Wilts – Osiris

I pushed myself to my feet, stunned at how flawless Angel's attack was, even with her emotions running though her. Her eyes didn't lie that she would have slit my throat if Duke told her to. I pressed my ear against the door, straining to hear. Muffled voices before Angel's sobs took over. *Poor girl.*

I paused, resisting the urge to open the door. Deciding better, I stormed down the hallway to the infirmary. The others had laid the bodies out of the way. The body of a woman was already disrobed as

Horace began to clean the dirt from her. Cameron was setting up the utensils for the autopsy.

"Cameron, beat it." My voice caught their attention. "Now."

"Yes, sir." He sprang out the door.

"What is wrong with you? You should be pissed at what happened."

Horace turned his attention to me.

"What is that going to accomplish, besides making her dismayed? You made it worse with your temper tantrum."

I sighed. He was right… I'd been upset and done what Angel had done. It was too close to home. I walked closer and started to help him clean the body.

"He calmed her down. Even under the pressure she was feeling, she could have pulled the trigger, I have no doubt about that now. Duke made sure of that." I paused and watched him contemplate my words.

"What do you mean?"

"I mean I got my ass kicked." I looked down at the woman's bruised face, *Charlotte.*

"He told me he'd kill Charlotte to keep Angel safe." My words caught his attention. "I am sorry I didn't listen before. Sam lives, yes?"

"Yes."

"I'll talk to Elba."

Dr. Horace Mills – Osiris

"Horace." Sam's voice floated in through the doorway.

"In here. I'm on the fifth body. Sexual assault on each one so far, male and female. I have a tox screen running for drugs and any other chemicals. Cameron is in with Barren treating his wounds." I kept my attention on the body in front of me; I'd finished up with her organs and was moving on to examining the brain. I heard his footsteps approach behind me.

"Do you think any of the chemicals used are related to C.K.?"

"I would bet on it." I set down my tool and turned to him. He looked tired, worn down. He looked how I felt. "How is Angel?"

His body went rigid as his eyes narrowed.

"She's fine." I knew Angel meant a lot to him, I didn't know how much until now.

"I'm not asking to get at another angle. How is she?"

He watched me for a moment.

"She was a POW, a little over a decade ago, similar setting. That would set off anyone."

"Is she resting?"

"Yes."

"Good." I let out a sigh before taking off my gloves. "I'll go check on her in a bit." I turned towards him. "I'm going to talk to Charlotte tonight. Let her know everything."

I could see him mulling this over.

"I don't need to know who she is. I know the thought of anyone discovering her is petrifying. All I need to know to know is Angel and Cameron will not be harmed. Can you promise me that?"

"Yes."

"Tell Charlotte what?"

Angel's voice came from behind Sam. I looked over his shoulder to see her. Her eyes were puffy, but she had a smile on her face now. I returned her smile. She moved in slowly.

"I'm sorry for how I acted earlier. I'm level headed now." Her eyes moved to the body beside us. "Can I help with the autopsies?"

"Could you clean the next body for me while I finish up with this one?"

She nodded and moved to pick up the next body, to set on the table; one of the little girls. I paused when I heard Barren's voice, I couldn't make it out.

"Jesus." Sam muttered under his breath.

"What is he screaming about?"

"Formers don't believe in medical treatment, believe it or not. I bet he's screaming at the antiseptic. Finish up with the bodies as soon as you can." His hand gave mine a gentle squeeze. "I'll be checking the weapons if either of you need me." He passed Angel a wink.

I kept my grip on his hand as he tried to walk away; I kept my voice low enough so Angel wouldn't be able to hear over the running water she was using on the body. "She'll be glad that you know *who* she is."

Chapter Seventeen

Year 5032, October 1
Sergeant Samuel Duke – Osiris

I tried my best not to have the idiotic grin I knew I had painted on my face. He said *who*, as if I already knew her. My mind floated from each person I knew to the next...*who? Who* was on the ship, that much I knew. Where? That I didn't know.

I could still hear Barren's voice echoing out in the ship. I could only imagine what Cameron was dealing with in there. Receiving treatment from anything but prayer wasn't acceptable. Poor kid, he should dope the son of a bitch.

Barren's shouting grew louder as I approached the door.

"What the hell is going on?" I walked into the holding cell where Barren was.

Barren's head wound was bandaged up, but blood was seeping through.

"Interrogation," Horace said, standing up, his fists a deep red and covered in blood. He must have seen my confused look; he was supposed to be in the infirmary.

"The bastard won't say anything related to the weapon," Wilts answered from the side.

"I got him to talk in less than five, should I take over and show you how it's done?"

He gave me a grin and gave a side glance to Barren's missing finger.

"One, I am having fun. Don't rush me. Two, *I* haven't even started."

"Fair enough, but stop messin' with him. Get the answers we need. We need to know if more than one vial of C.K. was made." I looked over to Horace. "How the hell did you get here before me?"

"This ship is my home. I know all the short cuts. Besides, I thought you were going to be checking the weapons?"

"I will. I thought you were going to be working in the infirmary?"

"I will. Cameron, get me something that'll make him talk."

"Yes, sir." Cameron, who was pushed away in the far corner, was a white as a sheet. He'd been that color since we opened the basement door. Poor kid.

I took a grip on his shoulder before he could leave the room.

"Have Angel bring the medicine and anything else, take a beat."

"Thank you, sir." His whole body seemed to relax with his next breath.

Horace wrapped his hand around my arm, pulling me toward the door. I stood still, *Why did he want me to leave?*

"What's going on?" I searched his eyes and face for any tell.

"Nothing." He leaned in and gave me a kiss. "I need to –"

"Disgusting –" Barren's voice boomed out to us. He was cut off with Wilts' large fist striking his face.

"Last warning to keep your fucking mouth shut." Wilts turned toward him, daring him to continue. Barren glared up at Wilts but didn't say another word.

"Come on." Horace urged me to the door again, but was met by Angel, who was looking down at the medicine in her hands.

"Here is that medicine you need…" She stopped dead and looked at me. She looked worried. Her eyes moved from me to Mills.

"Charlotte? Is that you? Charlotte!" Barren shouted. My head snapped to his direction. He was staring at Angel. "Is that? My God you are beautif –"

Wilts slammed Barren's head into his knee, splitting open his nose before he fell unconscious.

Everything after that slowed down allowing me to catch every detail. Menacingly Wilts turned to me. His face...his face was sharp; it was the look he had when we pinned Warts down. His hand already had a blade ready to find its home in me. He closed the distance between us in two steps.

Horace's hands touched my arm, before he could get a grip to pin me down or *maybe* even push me out of the way; I sent my elbow back and cracked it into his face, simultaneously I kicked his feet out from under him.

Wilts swung his knife low. I'd seen him fight; I knew what to expect. I blocked it and gave him head-butt to knock him back. It didn't phase him; his massive fist swung into my ribcage. I pushed past the pain and sent an elbow into his back. He dropped his knife. Having the upper hand on me, he wrapped his arms around my waist and plowed me into the wall behind me. His fist slammed into my side again. I used my knee smashing it into his side while using the force behind my arms to push his upper body down.

I went to put his head into a lock before Horace tackled him to the ground, both rolling on the floor, fighting for dominance. Horace managed to pin him down and get a good few blows in before Wilts wrapped his legs up and around his neck.

I ran over to get Horace free; Ravin who must have heard the commotion ran in and had the same idea. Together we managed to pry them apart. Horace was in my arms while we fell to the floor. Ravin was wrestling on the floor now with Wilts.

"Calm the fuck down!" Ravin shouted while pummeling Wilts.

"Get the fuck off of me! We need to deal with this!" Wilts was shouting over Ravin.

"I don't give a shit! It's not your decision." Those words seemed to calm Wilts, still on the floor they looked to me and Horace.

"He *knows*." Wilts' words leaked out between his clenched teeth.

"I don't give a shit." Ravin had won. "He was going to know by the end of the day. You know that."

I kept my arms around Horace, who was straining his neck to look at me. *Angel.* I looked back to the door where she still was. Her hands covered her mouth, frozen. I couldn't comprehend what must have been going through her mind.

"He attacked first, what the fuck does that say?"

Ravin's chest heaved.

"What happened, Duke?"

"Barren wouldn't shut the fuck up. Preaching about his bullshit, tired of hearing it, Wilts knocked him out. That's all."

"Is that what happened Horace?" Ravin asked.

"That's what happened." Horace's words came in heaves. He was putting his trust in me.

"Angel, is that what happened?" He asked her.

She nodded, unable to get her words out. Ravin let go of Wilts and had Angel in his arms in seconds. She watched me, words unable to come out.

I stood up helping Horace up with me. Coming down from the adrenaline, I felt the pain in my ribs where Wilts struck me. I walked out pausing only for a moment to squeeze Angel's arm.

I'm not mad, I mouthed to her.

Atkins was headed down the hallway and stopped to look at me.

"What the fuck is going on?"

"Nothing. Everything is taken care of. Go back to your duties." I didn't stop to talk. I pushed past him to my bunk.

Once inside my bunk, I yanked off my shirt and looked down to see a large bruise already taking shape. I was positive some of my ribs were cracked. *Fuck, he hit hard.* I opened up a small medical drawer that was full of Band-Aids, wraps, and disinfectants. I pulled out the wrap.

"Sam." I looked over to see Horace standing in the doorframe, lip bleeding. I looked away and started to wrap my ribs.

His hand took the wrap, pulling it tighter before continuing.

"We were going to tell you tonight. Please, don't be mad."

"Mad." It wasn't a question. I looked up at him. "Don't be mad? Why would I be mad?" I was shouting. "How would you feel if you learned that the only person in the world who matters the most to you was raped and tortured? Don't be mad? Fuck you!" He looked bewildered. I didn't care, I shoved him back. If I wasn't mad before, I was mad now. "What I am feeling isn't anger, I can promise you that." I was hurt, hurt that I couldn't stop it. Perhaps if I'd stayed on Sobek I could have found her, could have helped her. The 'could haves' filled my head.

"She wanted to tell you, the year she met you. I told her not to."

"She's the only family I have, and I go and fuck her father. Did you ever think of how that would make her feel?"

He leaned down to pick up the wrap from the floor.

"She always spoke about you in her letters, every single one. I feel like I know everything about you. Your favorite color, your favorite dishes." He sighed. "I know that at least once a week you wake up with Angel curled up in your bed. Every time, you'd make her French toast and hazelnut coffee. You hate hazelnut, but you keep it there for her."

He smiled.

"I apologized to her; I was afraid she'd be upset, but I've felt like I knew you for years when I met you. She wasn't upset, I'd go as far to say she wasn't even surprised."

My heartbeat slowed, and the tightness in my chest faded. *She wasn't mad, of course not. I'd told her how I'd felt about him already.* The thought drifted through my mind.

"I need to talk to her." I'd been too upset, too confused to even have words for her. Horace's hands held me from moving to the door.

"Sit down. Let me get this on." He urged me to the chair, his hands were warm to the touch. "Ravin is with her. She'll be okay."

He sealed the wrap.

"Your original plan was to kill us, but you were going to kill her on paper. Angel. Wasn't it?"

He nodded.

"Create a new identity for her, like we did before. She doesn't want to do that. She spoke of her life through her letters, we didn't know how much she loved it until now. She swore to me she'd do anything to make sure you went unharmed at the end of all this."

"Us aside, there is no way I'd let her secret out. She's not my daughter, but she is my family. I have as much to lose if it was to leak out." I slid my fingers across his beard as a smile drifted across his face. "I hope you can trust that."

"I do." His fingers interlocked with mine as our lips pressed together, before he rested his forehead on mine. His breath warmed my face.

"I wanted her to tell you. I'm sorry you found out that way."

"I know." I pulled his lips back to mine, breathing him in.

His hands traced across my chest.

"You need to –"

I captured his lips again, pulling him closer by taking fistfuls of his shirt. "In a minute." Keeping his lips to mine he dropped to his knees pulling our lips apart. His hands were already cradling me, stroking me.

The warmth from his hands made my body tingle, I could feel my heart pump faster. His eyes danced with excitement as his lips parted before sliding over my head and all the way down, I closed my eyes, moaning. I slid my fingers through his hair, cradling his head. The warmth of his hands swirled around my hips and up my stomach. *God, he knew how to make a man quiver.*

Releasing me, he came up and captured my lips. I lifted the hem of his shirt, exposing the thick black hair. Pausing for our kiss, I lifted his shirt off. His body was thick with muscle that my fingers loved to dance over. We kicked off the rest of our clothes, I wrapped my hands around his waist, enjoying the feel of his body.

He hefted me up in his arms and pressed me against the wall, his lips never leaving mine. My fingers tangled through his hair and traced down his back, around his waist… A deep moan escaped his throat as I wrapped my hand around him. His hands urged my legs open, lifting me up he balanced me by pressing his hips into me. He caught the surprise and excitement that grew onto my face. He pressed his face to mine, keeping his eyes glued to mine as he pressed himself all the way into me, going slow.

I trembled in pleasure; his slow thrusts warmed me up for what was to come. I steadied myself on him. His hips never missed a beat to the pattern of thrusts, teasing me with a deep thrust in between. Sweat was dripping from his face, leaving his lips salted.

"More," I breathed the word out to him before dropping my head back against the wall.

His teeth came down on the side of my neck, nibbling. Pressure started to build, my palms tingling. I gripped him tighter, my breath quickening. I freed one hand, wrapping it around me only to have his hips stop.

He tossed me onto the bed like a ragdoll and crawled on top of me.

"Not yet." His lips brushed against my ear as he spoke, giving rise to the pins and needles that broke out down my spine. I wrapped my arms around him and pulled him close. I trailed my hands down his arms and his back, memorizing each curve. Turning over I pressed into him, taking him in again.

His lips kissed down my spine, hands holding my hips. I could feel his body heat radiating onto me. His hands rested on my ass and guided me with each of his strokes. Over and over again. I gripped myself, stroking with his rhythm. The heat building up again.

He leaned down to my ear again.

"Not, yet." His voice was husky.

I nodded listening to his words. *Not yet.*

I glanced over to Horace, he was covered in sweat and chest heaving. "That was a good use of a break, but we should really get back to work." I smiled as I spoke.

He chuckled, leaning over to kiss me.

"I don't think my C.O. will mind."

I pushed him over, crawling on top parting my lips letting his tongue intertwined with mine.

"I don't think so either." I rubbed my hips against him, his hands encouraging each movement. We laid quiet for a while breathing each other in until three knocks vibrated against the door.

"Sam?" Angel's voice drifted through.

"Usually this isn't as awkward." I pushed up from Horace, catching a smile. I wrapped a towel around my waist before opening the door. She was still dressed in her uniform, her eyes seemed less red, but I could see the lines of worry on her forehead.

"Hi." She kept her voice soft.

"Hey." I kept the door cracked stepping out. "I was going to talk to you, I got –"

I saw a smile creep up on her face.

"You got distracted." She finished the sentence for me.

"Yes. I shouldn't have… I'm sorry. Can you give me five minutes? I'll get dressed and apologize properly."

"I actually came here to apologize. I did want to tell you." She looked at the ground.

"Don't apologize." I lifted her chin up. "I feel like a shitty friend. Are you mad at me?"

"No." She shook her head, her smile back. "I see your stupid smile when you hear his name. You're such a girl." She balled her fist and lightly punched my shoulder. "Besides, everyone here is really important to me, I'm glad you're at least getting along." She gave a friendly smile.

"I don't want to cross any boundaries… I say as I just had sex with your dad…again." I couldn't help but cringe. *God, I am a shitty friend!*

"No, you're not. Dad is an amazing person, and so are you. It makes sense that you both would want to be together. And I kind of took over while you were busy. I am doing the autopsies with Cameron. Ravin is running the DNA, Robyn is searching through the files from Nefertiti. Lucas is interrogating Barren. Atkins is doing busy work. Elba is working on the file for Cameron. He's going to die skiing; it is very sad. Basically, you and Dad will get in the way." She gave a nonchalant shrug.

"I love you, Angel."

"I love you, too. I'd hug you, but you're all sticky."

Chapter Eighteen

YEAR 5032, OCTOBER 5

GENERAL RAYMOND ELBA – OSIRIS

"What do we know?" I asked standing over a deceased woman's body. Jones and Angel had done a respectful job completing the autopsies. She'd been cleaned, groomed, and handled with care. I didn't take my eyes off of the woman who couldn't have been more than forty years of age. *So young.*

"Jones identified her as Amanda Rice, mother of two. She went missing three years ago, presumed dead." Mills sighed. "She was on vacation."

"Are any of the children here hers?"

"No." He steadied himself as the ship rocked. He glanced around. *We were crossing back through the waves.* "We were only able to identify one of the children." He motioned for me to follow over to the far table that was pushed up against another; one table held a small girl the other an older man. "This is the only child that could be identified, which means the other children came from Sobek."

"Who is she?" I studied the girl's face, my eyes fixated on the hole on the side of her head.

"Nancy Fields, and this is her father Quila Fields. They went missing nine months ago. In that short time, they seemed to do a lot of damage to them. She's the only one without sexual assault wounds; her father had the most."

I closed my eyes. *How could all this have happened without us knowing?* I truly was failing as the General.

"Have we figured out why they were experimenting this time?"

"Honestly, I don't think this was about experimentation, at least not all of it. The findings in their exams crossed with the files Robyn has searched through; this was partly for entertainment."

I let out a heavy breath. To think how far the human race had advanced, yet there were still those who refused progression. Crime rates have dropped to almost nonexistent on several planets; others had higher rates, but those dropped with each decade. It's humbling to look at the numbers, to see the progress. Seeing this, was a gut punch that almost dropped me to my knees.

Mills continued, pulling me from my thoughts.

"He was a soldier of the U.F.F.C., five years from retirement."

"Embalm the bodies, fix what needs fixed, and freeze them. Create files for those without. Everyone here died in a group ski trip on Bardaen. Even those who've been missing for years. They were stuck in the snow. I'll have Ravin hide their bodies there, and let the civilians discover them over time."

"Yes, sir."

A large wave hit the ship causing the tables to shift a few inches.

"Get started, you've got a lot of paperwork to do."

"Yes, sir."

"One more thing. Barren. You agree with keeping him alive? He confessed to there being no other knowledge of C.K."

"I do agree. Warts said the same thing. I'll have him polygraphed when we dock, triple check. I don't want to have to cover up another mistake."

He nodded, eyes fixed on the father and daughter.

"I never asked, but what made you decide to take this role with Angel? I've never heard you mention once about kids or a family."

"I've always had a family. Cage is my little sister, Lucas and Sammy are my brothers. You, a father." He pulled a sheet over the little girl. "When I was carrying Angel out of there, I swore to her I would get her out. I swore no one would hurt her again. The relief…the trust that she put in me, is something that I can't explain. When she woke and understood what was happening, she looked at me like I was the only thing that mattered. I guess the simple answer is I took the role because she trusted me to do it."

I smiled.

"You're a big softy."

He chuckled.

"Yo –"

The metal of the ship creaked with the large wave that struck the ship, I lost my balance, falling to my knees with Mills. This wasn't good. I pushed to my feet, only to be sent flying into the table behind me as another wave hit the ship. I cursed under my breath coming to my knees as the pain waved up and down my spine.

"You alright?" he asked, helping me to my feet.

"Yes, get a medical bag and head to the shuttle."

Chapter Nineteen

Year 5032, October 5

Staff Sergeant Samuel Ravin – Osiris

I woke to my body being thrown from the bed, hitting the wall on the other side of the room. *What a fun way to wake up.* The whole ship tilted to its side; everything that wasn't secured came flying towards me, including the mattress. I managed to roll to the side and cover my head.

Sirens screamed across the loudspeaker; red lights began to flash. *What in the galaxy was going on?* I scanned the room, *Where's Angel?* I fished my clothes out from the mess and was out the door. I ran down the hallways jumping over doors as necessary.

The metal shell of the ship creaked loudly due to rapid heat waves. I threw my hands over my ears to drown out the sound, part of me began to wonder if the ship was going to break in half.

Turning down the next hallway, I collided with Duke. A cut above his eye was dripping blood down his head.

"Other shuttle." He shouted while pushing me around.

"Angel?" I shouted back.

"I checked the whole area and locked the sectors. Check the top level, I'll check this one." He was shouting but the creaking of the ship made it almost impossible to hear him.

"Barren?" I asked running back down the hallway.

"Wilts has him."

I nodded and headed to the top level of Osiris, checking every room along the way. *She's not here*... The ship never felt this big. I made my way to the bridge, checking under each desk. *Not here*, I turned to leave when I caught a glimpse out the front of the ship. Bright oranges and reds flared out-flickering; at its center, a pitch-black grave.

I pushed on the intercom to override the siren.

"I would like to confirm the black hole we are about to be sucked into. If you would like not to die a horrible death or travel down an unknown worm hole, I do suggest you get your ass to shuttle number two. We need to evacuate before we enter the Event Horizon. And as always thank you for flying Osiris Air." I didn't bother to click off the speakers before I turned back around and booted out the door, securing it behind me.

Angel wasn't on this level, perhaps she was at the shuttle already? I sprinted back down the stairs to the second level. I breathed a sigh of relief as Duke came around the corner, Angel at his side with a briefcase in hand. My guess, it contained C.K. and all records of it.

"Have you seen Dad?" she asked, steadying herself as another wave rocked the ship.

"Not yet."

Another wave from the black hole knocked against the ship sending it spiraling. I caught Angel, holding her tight as we rolled, Duke landing next to us. The ship was upside down now and slowly tipping. Gravity was increasing, pulling down on us in every direction. *We were getting closer*... "I'll find him. Go with Sam."

A small wave tipped the ship further; I wrapped my arm around Angel's waist and gripped the wall with my other.

Sam reached for Angel.

"We've checked the whole ship." I could hear the worry in his voice.

He was right, but Osiris was more than three stories. Over the years we carved out cargo holds within walls, the ceilings, even in the floors. Weapons, medical supplies, and emergency supplies had been stored in each one. Sam had found several, but not nearly all of them. Horace probably went to a specific one he hid himself.

"I'll find him." I squeezed his shoulder. "Get to the shuttle."

He nodded, taking Angel in his arms. We sprinted down the hallway that would soon split off to another. The ship shook, creaking before tipping further up. I took a fast hold on the door frame, legs dangling down. I looked toward Angel and Sam dangling above me. My heart raced as Angel started to slip, using his leg Sam caught her, pulling her back up.

Crawling up his body, she moved into the second hallway that would take her to the shuttle.

"Get to the shuttle," he ordered her as she turned back around. She glanced from him to me.

"Move," I shouted up at her. Reluctance was in her eyes, but she listened and grabbed the briefcase containing C.K., disappearing. The force of the gravity made it near impossible for me to pull myself up. My body was beginning to feel stretched out, elongated. Sam landed in the room of the doorframe I was clinging to. He gripped my wrists as yet another wave struck the ship forcing Sam to lose his balance and fall.

I watched in horror as his hand missed mine by a fraction of an inch as I reached for him.

"Duke!" Hoping somehow that if I called out his name it would stop him from falling. His body bounced up from the floor after he hit.

I followed after him, jumping from door frame to door frame.

"Sam." I jumped the last six feet, ignoring the pain that stemmed from my ankles. He was struggling to get his breath, but he was alive. "Can you move?" I asked.

"Let's go with that." He struggled to sit up. I put his arm over my shoulder and hefted him to his feet.

I dragged him over to the wall, kicking out tiles making a questionable ladder, looking up at the ground we had to cover, a pinch of worry sprouted in my chest.

"Go." I pushed him up, holding his back to stabilize him. He climbed his way up, wobbling with each movement. He had a good four-foot jump to make to get to the door.

"Sammy! Sam!" Wilts' voice bounced off the walls.

"Down here." I called out. I heard loud thunks as he hopped down. Covered in sweat, he reached down for Sam's hand. Together, we climbed back up.

"Was Horace in the shuttle?" I yelled over the noise.

"No."

"I'm here." Horace shouted running down the hall to meet us. "Move your fucking asses!" He jumped across the hall hauling a huge bag strapped to his back. "Angel?"

"Shuttle." Wilts hollered, pushing us in front, before taking the bag from Horace, to help me with Sam.

"Let's go," Elba shouted standing at the front of the shuttle. Past him, I could see the others, Atkins, Jones, Angel, and Cage all strapped down in their seats.

Each shuttle held four people, which meant the rest of us would have to stand. Barren was chained to the wall next to them, unconscious. I stumbled in, the shuttle door sealed, Elba punched in the coordinates to evacuate the ship. Tesla had created a system in each shuttle for U.F.F.C. ships designed to escape black holes as long as they are within the accelerated disk; once past that, there was no way to get out. The system activated to take the shuttle back to the nearest planet...Nefertiti. The amount of power and fuel used to escape uses all the backup supplies. Most of the time, we could avoid black holes; our technology was able to predict when a star was about to collapse.

The problem was, this part of space was uncharted to the U.F.F.C. This was unpredictable.

Another substantial wave hit us, sending us piling to the floor. The metal on the shuttle began to creak, echoing in the tiny space.

I struggled to get up; the force from the black hole increasing by the second.

"Get us out of here!" I called out to Elba who was struggling to stay upright at the control panels.

Propulsion from the fuel jets began to push us outwards. The force of the black hole lightened up as I secured myself in front of Angel. I placed my knee between her legs and pushed it up against her along with my thigh to give her more security, while I used the metal wall behind her to hold on, her hands wrapped around my waist pulling me closer. The matter outside the shuttle was hitting us, forcing us sideways while the thrust from the engine was pushing us out.

The adrenaline pumped through my body, *when it died down…if we didn't die I dreaded what my head would feel like.* Only a few have survived black holes and lived; others were lost.

"Is everyone okay?" Horace asked.

My muscles didn't want to let go of beams I was holding onto. I looked down to Angel who had her arms glued around me and her head buried in my stomach. I could still feel the force of gravity on the ship, but it was almost imperceptible as we traveled farther out.

Lucas had braced himself on the bars above Robyn, securing her in the same way I had with Angel. Jones, the poor kid was white as a ghost and could easily be in shock. His hands still had a death grip on the metal straps used to buckle him in.

Atkins, the bastard, was still alive, and a tinge of disappointment went through me. His hair was hanging down in his face hiding his eyes. His hands had the same death grip that Jones had. Even Elba who didn't get startled by anything looked taken aback. His dark skin looked pale, and his eyes were three times their normal size. Horace and Duke took haven on the floor, holding each other while using the metal grate floor to keep from flying about. Duke looked the calmest out of all of us, *did nothing throw this guy through a loop?*

"I'm…alive," Angel breathed out poking her head up. The force behind the black hole undid her chignon letting her hair fall.

"Same," Robyn said a few seconds after. The rest of us sounded off.

"Wha-what happened? Is it safe now?" Jones asked. He managed to peel his hands away from straps.

"I believe we are safe now, but there could be some waves that will hit us." Horace grunted as he lifted himself up to look at the control panels. "The black hole ripped us from our course. Osiris is gone by now. The shuttle is programmed to head to the nearest planet. Nefertiti."

I helped Angel unstrap.

"Barren stays out."

Horace nodded and was already searching for a sedative in the med bag he threw together before boarding the shuttle.

"Mills." Elba's voice shook along with his legs as he stood up from his seat. "Check everyone out, women first, the kid next."

Doping Barren, Horace moved to us. I stepped out of the way and walked to Duke. "Are you okay?" I asked crouching down in front of him.

"I'm fine." He wiped away the sweat on his head and pushed himself up, wobbling a bit. I gave him a hand, before his legs buckled from his weight.

Wilts took five big steps to join us.

"You alright, brother?"

He nodded.

"I'm fine. We were heading back to an enemy planet with no means of fire power. We need to think of something fast. Find out what we have."

"Gather everyone's weapons." Duke turned to me while he spoke. "Ammo, too. They have guns there we can use. We only need to get to them." I nodded.

"Robyn." I helped her up from her seat. "You okay, Mama?"

"I'm okay." She let out a heavy breath. "What's the plan?"

"I need all the supplies you managed to get. We need to see what we got."

"Of course." She pulled out what she'd grabbed "It's not much, I was sleeping when it hit. Sorry." Her weapon, three knives, and a med-kit.

"It's better than nothing." I gave her a kiss on the cheek.

"Jones." I called out to him and gave Robyn a final squeeze on her hand. "What did you bring us?"

"I was able to grab a bit, sir." He pulled out his weapon, two packs of ammo, three knives and two med-kits.

"Good job, kid."

He gave a smile.

"Thank you, sir."

"Go give Robyn a quick once over. Make sure she's okay."

He nodded. I turned over to Atkins.

"I need your weapons." I'd noticed he'd been eyeing me the second I'd started gathering everyone's supplies. He'd gone as far as to position himself in the far corner away from me.

"I don't need to give you shit." He spat each word at me. He seemed to have regrouped since the shuttle settled.

"Give. Me. Your. Shit." My head was pounding and my stomach was twisting. I wasn't going to ask again.

"Go. Fuck. Yourself." His hand pushed me away at the end of his words. I balled up my fist and decked the side of his head, knocking him to the ground. I'd have to give him some credit, he was still conscious. The chatter between Duke and Wilts halted, as did Mills and Angel.

"Give Ravin your weapons, Atkins." Duke spoke up from behind me, whether he overheard the conversation or not, he was able to guess what was going on.

"Why should I?" Atkins stumbled to get up.

"It's a fucking order. That's why." Duke sounded a bit closer than he did before.

"What does it matter? We are fucked!" He was yelling. "We are headed right back to Nefertiti, we have no weapons, and our ship is gone! There is no way we are going to make it out."

"I won't ask again." Duke kept his voice the same pitch but the force behind the words said he wasn't intimidated.

"No, I'm done taking orders from a faggit!"

I jumped on him. He was still weak on his feet from the first blow. He crumbled down, but I lifted him up with one hand and used my other to pummel him. His face covered in blood, his whines stopped after the second punch. It didn't matter; I kept going. No one stopped me either.

When I was satisfied, I let him fall to the ground and searched his body for weapons. He had five ammo cases, two knives, and a small pistol on his ankle. I disassembled the weapon and put it with the others by the panel. Elba, Duke, Wilts, Angel, and Horace already set theirs down. It wasn't much, but at least we all had our weapons, knives, ammo, and med-kits. The bag that Horace had ran after had more medical supplies and MREs.

"What can we do with this?" I stared down at the weapons with Duke.

He sighed and shook his head.

"Ever pray before?"

"What in the world is that?"

He chuckled.

"Here." He pulled out a pack of cigarettes. *Cigarettes!* "Take a beat."

I gave him a kiss – "I love you." I sat down in one of the seats closest to me.

Angel waited a minute before sitting next to me.

"Don't put it out." She smiled. "Can I do anything?"

"I'll be alright." I stole a kiss from her before taking another drag. She kept quiet while Duke and the others kept their voices light. The pain dimmed a bit, and I pulled out another cigarette.

"Are you alright?" I couldn't believe I hadn't asked her yet. "Where were you?"

"Yes. I was on the ship. *Looking* for you. Didn't your mama ever tell you to stay put when you're lost?"

I laughed and pulled her close.

"No, as a matter of fact she did not."

She tittered and leaned into me.

"Mine either."

"That's not funny." I looked down at her to see a smile on her face.

"It is a little."

"No, it's not." Mills knelt down in front of me. She tsked at him, causing us both to smile. "How about some morphine?" He was filling up the needle.

"Give me the drugs." I held my arm out for him, tapping it. "How are you holding up?" I asked. He looked tired and simply worn down. "No offense, but you look like shit."

"I was having a *really* good night." A smile crept up on his face.

I looked over to Duke who was working with Elba and Wilts. He looked tired but nowhere near as bad as Mills.

"I bet." I gave him a grin.

"Uh-huh," Angel giggled as she jumped up from her seat. "I'm going to check on Cameron. He looks like he's going to puke." She pulled Cameron off into the far corner.

"You talked to him about Angel?" I kept my voice low. He was done with administering the morphine and taking my vitals.

"Yeah." His voice matched mine. He was grinning.

"I'm glad he was okay with everything."

"Me too." He seemed to be in disbelief. "It's like he already decided to be before he even knew."

"I could have told you that." I couldn't help but taunt him.

"Shut up."

"How is he?" I raised an eyebrow. "Better than Steve?"

His smile grew, before speaking he looked back to see if he was listening. He was still engaged working on a plan.

"Absolutely. He can go all night."

"His poor ass." We both burst into laughter. The attention of the shuttle turned to us for a moment.

"You'll be alright, just take it easy for the next hour."

I finished my cigarette just as the morphine started to kick in. The pressure in my head was fading, the only evidence was mild migraine.

"Do you feel better?" Angel sat back down next to me.

"Much." I gave her a kiss.

She nodded and leaned her head into me.

"Please don't leave me alone there." Her voice was hardly a whisper. "I can't…" She trailed off.

"I won't. I'll keep you safe."

"Thank you."

I pulled her in close, enjoying the warmth of her body.

"It'll be okay." I whispered to her.

General Elba gathered our attention to the front of the shuttle.

"We have six days until we reach Nefertiti." Wilts was distributing the weapons back, the ammo, medkits, and comms. evenly out to us. He left Atkins on the ground.

"We have limited firearms on the shuttle. Until we can get any from the Formers, we will have to rely on hand to hand combat and make what we have count. There are several ships on the planet we can commandeer. We need to get to one without being detected. Above all, keep C.K. away from the Formers. Cage, you will be the one holding on to it. Jones, you will cover her, don't let her out of your sight. We move together. Mills, you take the six of the team. Ravin you and Wilts will lead. Duke, Angel, you will take the sides. I'll scout ahead."

"What about Atkins?" Jones asked.

"Atkins?" Wilts walked to his body and gave a shake, waking him up. His face was still bleeding. He tried to escape from Wilts' grip who was standing behind him.

"Get off of me you bastard." Atkins words were slurred.

"Atkins, is no longer going to be with us." Wilts removed a blade that he had strapped to his leg, holding it in front of Atkins throat. Understanding what was going to happen, he began to fight. Without a word, Wilts slit his throat, blood began pooling on the floor.

"Wilts, you really need to think before you start killing people in tiny ass shuttles. He's going to start to smell and the blood is all over the floor. What are we going to do about the body? And Jones is going to be sick!" I got the words out before he upchucked up in the corner.

Wilts looked at the blood coating the floor.

"Jones, clean up this mess."

"And the body?" I reminded him again.

"Anyone hungry?" Wilts offered with a grin, Cameron turned pale and turned back around to the corner.

Chapter Twenty

YEAR 5032, OCTOBER 6

SERGEANT SAMUEL DUKE – OSIRIS SHUTTLE

"Are you hanging in there?" Cage sat down next to me as she spoke.

"Yeah." I gave her a smile. "I thought you were sleeping?" Bags had formed under her eyes. She shook her head and looked around. Everyone was else fast asleep, her eyes drifted to Wilts, then to Horace, who was leaning up against me.

Wilts, Elba, and I spent the day devising a plan, finding the best possible way to make any situation work when we land. Everyone's adrenaline was coming down, making us all tired. The only person relieved of what happened was Barren, who would remain sedated on the floor.

Having to move Atikins' body out of the way, we laid the poor bastard beneath the floor. It wouldn't hide the smell, but he was out of the way.

"I was. I've never been that close to death before." Her hands were shaking. "I understand why Wilts doesn't sleep much now."

I scoffed.

"It does make it a bit harder. At least he's sleeping now, huh?"

"Like a baby." She laughed lightly. "The one time I actually want him to be awake at night." Her eyes were still on him. "Do you mind?"

"Not at all."

She was quiet for a moment.

"I know we didn't talk much but I've been very curious about something..."

"What's that?"

"Horace said you're from Sobek." I nodded. "I've met people who come from Sobek, but none who became a soldier. No offense, but I trust you about as far as I could throw you, and that ain't far."

I laughed.

"You seem pretty calm for someone who doesn't trust me."

"I trust Horace, and he trusts you. He's a really good judge of character."

"My grandfather was a soldier for the U.F.F.C. on my mother's side. I never met him. He died when his team discovered Babi. His body was never found"

"They ate him." She filled in the blank.

"They did. It's why my mother hates other races as much as she does. She won't take into account all the variables of what happened. Anyways, I found a picture of him in his uniform when I was fifteen. She kept it hidden from my father. Three years later, I joined the U.F.F.C. in honor of my grandfather."

"Was it hard for you to leave home?"

"No."

She took a deep breath.

"It wasn't hard for me either. It was actually going home that was hard. My husband used to beat me every night before I joined. My mother would hide the bruises and would ask me what I did to provoke him. When I ended up in the hospital, she would help him make a cover story, so he wouldn't get questioned by the authorities." Her eyes wandered over to Wilts again. "I joined the U.F.F.C. when I couldn't take it anymore. Somehow that made me the bad guy.

"When I would go home," she continued. "He would still beat me, and my mother still hid the bruises. It's as if I failed as a wife and daughter. Now," she let out a heavy sigh, "I've failed at being a soldier; I should have been able to calculate the black hole, my numbers were off, and I don't know how."

"I'm going to stop you there." I wrapped my arm around her. "One, a husband should never put his hands on his wife. He failed. Two, a mother should never allow her child to be in that situation, let alone enable it. She failed. Third, you can't calculate something you have no control over. Especially something we still don't fully understand. Nothing to fail at there."

"You sound like Horace."

I pulled her closer.

"He seems like a smart man."

She gave a soft chuckle as her eyes drifted off into space.

"Thank you."

I gave her a kiss on the side of her head.

"You're welcome."

She smiled, and intertwined her arm with mine.

"I was going to marry Lucas before everything that happened. I think I still might." She leaned her head against my shoulder now.

"What kind of wedding?"

"June. On a beach, Ravin is going to be my maid of honor. He even promised me he'd wear a dress. Peach."

I laughed.

"Do I get to come?"

"Yes." It was Wilts who spoke, his eyes still closed.

"I can't wait," I chucked. Lowering my voice, I spoke to her. "Can I ask you a question?"

"Yes."

"I've got to know, have Horace and Ravin been together?"

She sat up.

"I've been trying to figure that out for years! I mean, Sammy will do anything with legs, and, well, Horace has a pair." She erupted with laughter, snorting uncontrollably. Finding it contagious, I laughed with her waking everyone up.

"Care to share what's so funny?" General Elba asked, he was on the opposite wall from us, glaring.

"Nothing, sir," Cage answered, a huge smile on her face that lit up her eyes. My heart warmed seeing such a sight. "I was about to head to bed." She hopped up and moved to sit next to Wilts. He looked groggy but slid over, giving her room. She was still laughing as Wilts wrapped an emergency blanket around her.

Slowly, everyone fell back asleep, one by one. I leaned my head back; I was still on watch for the next couple hours.

"What were you two giggling at?" Horace whispered. I looked down, his eyes closed.

"Girl stuff," I chortled.

He let out snicker, "About?"

I draped my arm around his shoulder pulling him closer.

"The only two worth gossiping about on this shuttle."

"I deny everything." He opened his eyes and flashed his devilish smile at me. His devilish smile changed to a soft smile as he sat up. "You look like shit. I have next on watch, rest."

"It's only a couple more hours. I'll be alright."

He leaned in and pressed his lips against mine, breathing me in. His hand rubbed across my chest. "You're right, only a couple hours. It won't kill me."

I smiled at him, "Okay." I shifted my weight, the fall I took early made it nearly impossible to move without my body aching.

Shifting his body toward me, his arms guided me back against him.

I was only asleep for a few hours before I woke up to General Elba shaking me. His hand held me down from getting up too quickly. His finger rested over his mouth. I looked around, everyone was asleep. I slowly sat up, being careful not to wake Horace. The sudden movement made my body ache.

"We have another problem."

"No," I responded, getting a bit of joy at his confused face. "I refuse to acknowledge any more problems."

He rolled his eyes.

"Alright, we have a situation that isn't worth smiling about."

"That I can work with." He pulled me to my feet and led me over to the control panels, and went to wake up Wilts.

"The shuttle was damaged. We are losing oxygen, heat, and fuel. At our current speed we will die before we reach Nefertiti." Elba kept his voice down.

"Put us into hyperspace. That puts us a day and a half out."

Wilts clicked around on the panel to measure the distance.

"We won't make it through the morning if we do that. It takes up too much energy." Elba shook his head, clearly already considering that option.

"What about inducing comas, have only one person awake until we arrive?" Wilts fired out another option. "We could lower the temperature too... That might work."

"Do we even have the medicine here to do that?" I interjected. We all exchanged glances.

"Wake Mills," Wilts ordered.

I nodded. Moving over I crouched down in front of Horace, gently shaking him awake and signaling for him to be quiet.

He eyed me, then Wilts and Elba. Pushing up, we walked back over. "We are about to be dead in the water. Oxygen is dropping. Can we put everyone in a coma?"

He rubbed his beard and analyzed the data from the panel. "It might work. But..."

"But?" Elba questioned.

"I don't have enough medicine. I packed for body injuries. I have enough to keep one, maybe two people asleep. It still won't give us enough oxygen."

"But it'll buy us time," Wilts confirmed. "It'll give us time to come up with something else. Dope the kid and Angel."

Horace reached for the medic bag.

"Hold on." I rested my hand on his arm. "Elba, did you ever upgrade Osiris?"

He looked a bit confused.

"No."

"What does that matter? It's in bum fuck Egypt by now." Horace watched me.

"Osiris, was one of the first models built. Before the U.F.F.C. transferred completely to nuclear power."

"What are you getting at Sergeant?" Elba crossed his arms.

Horace grinned.

"A second engine."

"What do you mean a second engine?" Wilts glanced between us.

"The Tesla agency, built a backup engine in the older models. An engine that runs off of carbon-based fuel. In case, the nuclear-powered engine got damaged. The ship could switch over to the spare engine." I kept my voice down.

"That's great and all, but we don't have any carbon-based fuel to put into that engine." Elba gestured around. "Fresh out of fossils."

"Actually, sir," Horace's words drifted cautiously. "We do." He looked at me.

"Where?"

"Atkins, sir."

Elba's jaw dropped and turned toward me. Speechless.

"I don't have an issue with it. I'll toss the bastard in."

I jumped hearing Ravin behind us. *How long was he standing there?*

"Jesus, anyone else awake?" I hissed out. One by one Angel, Robyn, and Cameron raised their hands, but stayed lying down. "Great. Well,

Ravin. It's not that simple as tossing him in. We need to calculate the right amount..."

"Oh, okay. No problem." Ravin turned to Horace. "Want to dumb that down for me?"

"We need to make the fuel last. Put in the right amount of fuel at a given time."

"Oh, okay. No problem." He looked over to Wilts. "Want to dumb that down for me?"

"We cut the bastard up and throw him in piece by piece."

"I love it. I'm in. As always, you guys do the...whatever it is you do and, I'll do the slice and dump."

"No, no. I slice and dump." Wilts' backhanded Ravin's shoulder.

"No, no, honey. You *were* sliced and diced," Ravin reciprocated the slap.

The remark made Wilts laugh.

"Ladies, please," I sighed, the deep breath sent a huge wave of discomfort through me. "The engine is on the outside of the ship. One of you guys will suit up. Horace, can you calculate how we can make this work?"

Chapter Twenty-One

YEAR 5032, OCTOBER 6

DR. HORACE MILLS – OSIRIS SHUTTLE

The air was already getting thinner; I had encouraged everyone to sit and do their best to relax with the dwindling oxygen. The heat was turned down to the lowest setting that we could survive at without freezing. I'd spent most of the morning crunching the numbers.

"I have gone over the statistics, there is one way we can all make it to Nefertiti."

"That should be a happy thing, why do you sound upset?" Wilts leaned in to get a better look at what I'd scribbled down on the walls of the shuttle.

"We go into hyperspace. The first twelve hours will be covered by the regular engine of the shuttle. When it dies, we switch over to the carbon engine. We fuel the engine every hour. If we keep the temperature down and turn the oxygen to level one, and keep down, we can reach Nefertiti."

"Reach, not land?" Sam pointed out.

"Yes." I sighed. "It'll be a rough…landing."

"That's crashing, not landing," Ravin squibbled.

"I can manually control the wings of the shuttle, give us a softer landing." Elba looked at Ravin. He could; Elba grew up flying ships with his father. It was how he was able to pilot Osiris with only himself. "It won't be easy, but it can be done. Wilts." He paused, realizing what his next words would be. "Get Atkins body, be respectful. Mills, adjust the controls. I'll switch us into hyperspace."

The shuttle lurched forward as it increased speed. Clicking in the new stats, my breath was visible now, and my fingers grew stiff. *Crack!* I twisted my head around. Wilts was crouched over Atkins body, cleaver in hand. His eyes hard, his face was tense to the point it reminded me of stone.

My mind drifted to when I first saw him. I'd been assigned to retrieve the team that had gone MIA, and when the family they had been required to protect was murdered, I'd found him strapped to a table and filleted like a fish. He'd withstood the torture the Formers did, and he didn't break. I'd never respected anyone as much as I respected him at that moment.

His body had grown too weak to even beat it's own heart. No arrhythmia to defibrillate; CPR was a fail. There was only one way, we'd strapped him down to the gurney, my team laid down cover fire.

I'd never done an open cardiac massage until then, in fact it was the only time. Any other person, I would have left alone, let them have peace, but much like Angel, Wilts was a fighter. The trauma that the body went through, it didn't go away. I watched him suffer to this day, his heart never fully recovered. I swore, in that moment I'd keep watch over him. Be there to help him through at every point.

He woke angry, heartbroken when he learned the family he'd die for – did die for was murdered. Murdered because his previous team couldn't handle doing what was right. They broke, snapped, and gave away the position of the family.

I remember that day, too, vividly. His wounds had scabbed over, left eye still missing. He cried a single tear and went silent. Spoke when spoken to, passed his psychological test. I knew he wasn't stable, far from it, but I let him walk out of the hospital.

What he didn't know, and still doesn't, was that I followed him. Watched as he tracked down his team, secure them in a warehouse and butcher them. I waited outside. Ignoring the screams, the cries for help.

I covered up the mess; hid the DNA. He wasn't able to be charged. He became my brother after that. I joined his team and saw what had become of this great soldier. He couldn't sleep; nightmares every night of what happened to him and of what he did. Mentally and physically, he suffered, but much like Ravin he fought against the pain. Insisting that he was glad I saved his life, it didn't matter; I felt guilty. It was because of me he was in pain.

I watched Wilts swing his blade up again, dismembering the arm.

Chapter Twenty-Two

YEAR 5032, OCTOBER 8

SERGEANT SAMUEL DUKE – OSIRIS SHUTTLE

"Everybody, strap in." Elba braced himself against the control panels.

Our shuttle was coming in fast to orbit, already the temperature inside the shuttle was rising, and it was going to get a lot warmer before we landed. We'd suited up, helmets on. Barren remained chained and blind folded on the floor, while Angel, Robyn, Cameron, and Horace strapped themselves into the seats. Ravin took the spare straps from the emergency bags and tied them above the seats for those of us who would have to stand.

I secured my hand around the strap above Horace; his hands took a hold of my belt, steading me against the shaking shuttle. I shoved my knee on the seat and pushed my thigh up against him to return the favor.

I looked around to make sure everyone else was secure for the landing. Ravin, Angel, check. Wilts, Robyn, check. Cameron, check. C.K. was secure near Elba, check. The force increasing by the second made my stomach churn and my body sweat. My shoulders ached, fighting against the force of the ship rattling side to side.

If it wasn't for Horace's grip, I would have started to tumble as the shuttle rolled in every direction. I was glad I hadn't eaten much; I would have tossed it up. I ducked my head and used my biceps for cover.

"Hold on!" Elba shouted, but it was almost nonexistent. "Prepare for impact."

The speed of our fall continued to increase; the rapid change in gravity caused my blood pressure to rise and made my head spin, fighting against the forces that would make me lose consciousness.

"Sam!" I felt Horace's arms shake me as he shouted.

My mind went black. Only to regain consciousness from the pain my body felt. Now, even breathing felt intolerable. I was lying on my back next to Ravin and Wilts, the rise and fall of Ravin's chest told me he was alive. Wilts was face down; I couldn't see any movement. I reached over and checked for a pulse. *Alive*. I let out a sigh of relief before attempting to sit up.

"Are you okay?" Angel's voice came from behind me her hair had come undone and a large bruise was forming on her head.

"I'm fine. Are you hurt?" I pushed myself to my feet and helped her unstrap from her seat.

"I'm okay." She wrapped her arms around me, taking a breath in. "Where's Elba?" She was looking around.

I followed her gaze to the controls that had been destroyed in the crash; the side of the ship was ripped open. *Could he have been sucked out?* As bad as Elba missing was, what was worse was Barren was gone too.

"There is no blood." I gave her a kiss on the head hoping to reassure her. "Wake Ravin."

"Yes, sir."

I moved over to Cameron, who was out cold. "Cameron. Wake up." I took a hold of his shoulder to give him a firm shake. "Cameron." His eyes twitched open.

Dazed he looked around.

"Sir?"

"Look at me." I took his head in my hands. "Are you hurt?"

He looked around; I could still see he wasn't all the way back.

"Cameron." I gave him another jolt.

"I'm fine, sir."

I unclicked his straps.

"Check Angel."

"Yes, sir."

I turned to Wilts, who was sitting up, scanning the shuttle. Noticing who and what was missing.

"Wilts, are you good?" I placed a hand on his shoulder to get his attention.

"I'm good."

"Good. Wake up Cage."

"Horace." I knelt in front of him and gave him a shake. "Wake up." His eyes flickered open, looking around. "Are you alright?"

His hands wrapped around my wrists.

"Angel?" He looked around me.

"She's fine. Cameron's checking her now. Are you sure you're alright?"

He nodded, unclicking his belts.

"You?"

"I'm fine."

He moved his hands to mine. "Squeeze. Follow my finger." He gave me a quick check smiling when I passed.

"Hurry, let's get everyone checked. Elba and Barren are missing. Wilts," I turned around to him. He had a few cuts on his head that Cameron was patching up. "The bioweapon?" He pulled away and checked in the compartment he stored it in.

"Shit!" He shouted. His voice echoed off the walls. "It's gone." He kicked the wall leaving a large booted imprint.

"Barren could have it." Cage double-checked the compartment.

"Elba could have retrieved it from him by now." I wasn't sure if I believed these words. "We need to move. We can't leave without the weapon; this is unknown territory. Be alert. Gather your weapons."

Wilts pulled me off to the side.

"We need a ship."

"The people on this planet got here on one, I'm positive there is at least a shuttle here. Anything larger will be away from the lab they built. The problem is, we don't need the ship."

He agreed.

"Let's break. Cage and Ravin can find us a ride out of here. Whatever the system is, she will be able to access it. I want Ravin to cover her."

"That'll work. Barren is a priority; there aren't a lot of places to hide here, but that doesn't mean this'll be easy. This is his backyard."

"We should stick together until we reach their town. We've been here, too, so we aren't completely blindsided."

I signaled for everyone else to join.

"Cage and Ravin, go on ahead, look for a ship. The rest of us can sweep the place. We need to find the weapon, Elba, and Barren. This place is a giant circle. Let's hit it from five points. Horace, sprint to the far end, dispatch anyone, those who get away; push forward. Wilts, go to the far-left point, Cameron the right. Same goes, push them out. Angel and I will start at the front. Search every home. Every room."

"If Elba did go after him, he would leave us some breadcrumbs to follow. Keep an eye out for anything," Wilts added in.

"Sir." Cameron looked nervously at me and Wilts. "The black hole that sucked in Osiris will still be out there. When we get aboard another ship, will it be sucked in too?"

"We'll have to go around," Horace jumped in. "It'll use a lot of our fuel, but we can send out a beacon to a U.F.F.C. rescue squad."

He looked satisfied with Horace's answer and shouldered his weapon. I eyed everyone, ensuring they were ready. "Same formation as last time."

We loaded our weapons and set out under the suns. I wasn't sure how long we'd been out; the smoke from the fall was visible in the sky.

Anyone on the planet who was paying attention could be heading our way. I looked around, all desert.

"Cage, which direction?"

"This way sir." She pointed towards an arrow drawn in blood on the desert floor. "Elba's got our backs." She said with a grin.

"Alright. Keep alert. We may have company coming soon. Everyone, keep your trackers on, Elba could turn his on at any point."

It must have been mid-day, as the heat increased and the suns beat down directly on us. Wilts instantly started cursing the heat, I on the other hand couldn't have been more pleased with it. The warmth from the suns was warming up my body, dulling some of the pain.

"I don't want to say 'I told you so,' but I told you so. We should have blown up this dump." Wilts commented, wiping the sweat from his brow.

"Trust me, I won't question you next time." I chuckled.

"I don't know about anyone else but I will be glad when this mission is over." Angel's frustration was heard in every word. "I've never had a mission be this tedious before."

"Not even when we got stranded on the Bore's planet?" I asked sweetly.

She laughed.

"That was fun."

"We spent a month in shit."

"That's unsanitary." Horace looked over to her.

The idle chit chat kept us distracted from the heat. But it didn't last long before we noticed a whirl of dust coming for us.

"Sir, up ahead. Movement." Ravin signaled for us to stop.

"Fuck." I spat my curse. *Someone was paying attention.* "Fan out. Cage, Ravin, Cameron, you're with me. Let's try and catch a ride."

We would be easy to see, our black suits stood out against the brown background of the world. I got low, aiming my scope, waiting, pacing my breath. A head came into view, I fired. The vehicle swerved to the left crashing into the one next to it. More shots fired out.

Catching on, the rest of the cars swung wide to escape our view. I hightailed it to an old Chevy truck and pulled the dead body out. I shoved Cameron behind the wheel as Cage hoped in the back and Ravin in the passenger seat. I hopped in the cab and took position in the sun roof. Cameron pressed on the gas, kicking up dust, swinging us around.

Wilts jumped into an old Jeep with Angel and Mills. Three cars revved their engines and went full speed toward them. Kicking the Jeep in reverse, Wilts drifted, heading in the opposite direction, the sound of their gunfire fading.

"Be just a minute," Wilts' voice radioed in.

"Copy." I fired. "Cameron, nothing's changed, head to their base."

"Yes, sir." The car sped up.

I was cautious with my ammo, as was Cage. We fired after each aim, doing our best to not miss with the bullets being returned at us.

"I'm out, who has a magazine?" Ravin hollered out from the passenger seat. Cameron took another hard turn.

"Try the jockey box." I fired, hitting the tires of the closest vehicle behind us. The rim shot out, causing the driver to lose control.

"What?"

"The jockey box."

"What?" His voice was getting irate.

"The. Jockey. Box." I matched his tone; now was not the time for his absent mind.

He plowed his way up in the sunroof with me, causing me to miss my shot. "What?"

"The fucking jockey box!"

He gripped my vest and shook me. "Mother fucker! If you say that one more time, I will throw you out of this vehicle." His eyes got wide. "No one will know."

"Jockey box."

He held true to his word. His grip tightened and before he attempted to lift me, I dropped my gun into the car and took my own grip on him. Using my body weight, I slammed him back, cursing before he charged at me. Our fists flew, as mad as I was I avoided hitting his head.

"You're a fucking child!" I yelled between hits. "Reload your goddamn weapon, before I shove it up your ass."

"Try it bitch." His elbow collided with my temple making my ear ring. Disoriented from the blow, he grappled me into a side headlock. I tucked my chin and pulled on his grip. I reached my arm up and around for his head, but before I could push him back, an energy slammed my body back; a painful explosive tingling pain radiated from my side. Whatever had hit me hit Ravin, too; his grip loosened, and he clutched his side. I looked in the bed of the truck to Cage, who had her weapon pointed at us. *The fucking bitch shot me!*

"Knock it off."

"He started it," Ravin and I reputed.

"I'm finishing it." Her words came out behind her teeth.

Glaring at me, Ravin dropped back down into the cab handing me my gun.

"I still need a magazine."

"Jockey box," I said facetiously.

He was back, nose to nose with me, his hands slamming on the roof of the car.

"The glove box." Cage slugged one of her magazines at him.

"Why didn't anyone say so? Fuck."

He dropped back down and in the next few seconds was firing his weapon again in time for more trucks to roll in on the chase for us.

"My ammo is running low. Cover me." Cage shouted before ducking down behind the tailgate. She disassembled her spare shotgun. Another bullet slammed into my shoulder, I turned in the direction of the bullet and fired.

"How good is your aim?" Cage asked, holding a makeshift bomb in her hand.

"Toss it."

She wound up her arm and pitched the bomb out to the largest cluster of cars, I aimed. Fired. I ducked down in the cab for cover, the sound from her bomb was deafening. The force of it shattered the back window and even lifted the back end of the truck up.

"God damn!" I was back in position gazing out, the blast had taken out several vehicles. "What the hell did you put in there?"

"I'll give you the recipe."

"Merci, Mama."

I caught sight of Wilts with the rest of the team come barreling up, drifting to the side of us. Angel and Horace leaning out the windows firing their weapons.

"Running low on ammo." Horace called out across the distance. "We need to get out of here."

"Copy."

Cameron sped up as the forest was coming into view.

"Angel." I called out catching her attention. "Let's light them up. Cage, hand me that plastic tubing down by your feet."

I tossed it across to Angel.

Securing her weapon to her side she kicked open her door. "Cameron, clear the door." I ordered. Slowly he veered toward her open door, nicking it causing it to fly off. Her foot wrapped around the seatbelt before she crawled out to the gas cap to siphon the gas, leaving a trail. We were less than a mile from the shrubbery.

A large truck smashed into the side of their Jeep, and losing her grip, gravity pulled her down. Prepared her secured foot kept her from hitting the ground by mere inches. Horace leaned out to pick her up.

"Not yet." She pulled away, lifting herself up on the roof of the car.

I laid down heavier cover fire as she ran leaping across onto the truck that had hit their car. The driver of the car swerved from side to side trying to off balance her. Unphased by his attempts, she made her way to the back, siphoning his tank as well.

Rolling over into the bed of the truck, she disappeared from my view. I counted the seconds until she appeared, busting through the rear window, holding her weight in her hands. She slid in feet first legs wrapping around the driver's neck and with a quick twerk of her body, his neck was snapped.

Sliding in, she pushed him out the door. Flooring the truck, she collided it with Jeep, latching it on the back end.

"Ready!" she called, leaping back to the jeep.

I took aim at a car over the gas trail and fired two bullets into the gas tank until it lit. One by one the cars lit up, Wilts flipped his car around sending it back in the direction of the enemy before jumping out with the others, rolling as they hit the ground.

Ravin hollered out a cheer.

"That is what I am talking about! Get 'em, Baby!"

"Cameron, circle around –" I looked over in time to see a large Hummer inches from us. "Cage, get in!" She turned her attention to the vehicle coming at us. Dropping her weapon, she dived in, landing on me. I dropped between the seat and the wall.

The force of the collision vibrated through my body. I brought one hand to the roof and my other wrapped around Cage holding her close to me as the tires left the ground and we started to roll. I felt like a ping pong ball, the rest of the glass shattered cutting my face. We didn't get a chance to slow before another car slammed into us, sending my head slamming back.

I woke to shouting and gunfire.

"Sam. Sam, wake up!" It was Ravin. I looked around; I was still in the car. My leg felt hot and I couldn't move. "Horace, medical attention to my location." I forced my eyes open, *where was Cameron? Where was Robyn?* My vision blurred in and out as I focused on the front seat that was pinning my leg. With my free leg, I started to kick at the seat until my other was free.

I crawled out of the car, my vision slowly coming back. Robyn laid unconscious, but alive. *Cameron?* Ravin was up ahead firing his weapon into the trees. I looked around, *where was he?* I didn't see him. I stayed down, using my body to block any bullets that could hit Cage before pulling out my pistol.

"I'll cover you," I called out to Ravin.

He tossed over his weapon, bobbing and weaving he charged into the bushes. I waited until their fire halted, and Ravin jumped out of the bushes covered in sweat and blood.

"Where is Cameron?" I pushed myself to my feet lifting Cage up with me. A sharp pain shot through my leg almost sending me to the ground. He took Robyn in his arms. "We need Horace." He jogged a hundred yards from the car; I was hot on his heels, ignoring the pain.

I fell to my knees over a mangled body lying on the ground.

"Cameron! Cameron, look at me." His body was crushed and blood was sputtering out of his mouth, eyes wide. "Ravin, radio Horace. Now!"

"Horace, come in. Cameron is injured."

A moment passed before he responded.

"I'm headed your way." Horace radioed in.

I removed my vest and pulled off my shirt to pressed it against Cameron's abdominal wound. *Don't die.* In all my years, I'd been lucky and never lost a soldier.

I could see that Ravin had already attempted to use the med-kit that he had to help stop the bleeding before he had to leave Cameron alone.

I watched the color draining from his face with each passing moment. I'd never seen him this terrified.

"Horace is coming. Don't quit." I brushed the tears away that were flowing down his cheeks.

"I, I just…wanted to h-help." His voice broke on each letter.

"You did, and you're going to keep helping. Focus on me." I took his hand in mine; I could feel the crushed bone beneath his skin.

"W-will Ch-Charlotte be kept s-safe?"

"She's safe, now shut the fuck up, Cameron, and save your strength. Focus on breathing. Ravin, where is Horace?"

He shook his head and radioed him again.

"Horace, what's your position."

He didn't respond. *Fuck, fuck, fuck!* The blood from his wound was soaking through my shirt.

"I-I d-don't w-w-want t-to go a-al-alone." His voice was getting softer, and his eyes filled up with more tears. He was going to die. He knew it. He was going to die far from home, away from his family.

"You won't. I'm right here." I leaned down.

"W-where a-am I g-going t-to g-go?" I could see the fear building in his eyes with each passing moment. Ravin shouted over the comm. again.

"Not far." I brushed a hand smoothing his hair back. "I'll meet you there." I prayed my words brought a smidge of peace. He gave me a weak smile.

"D-d-don't le-l-leave me h-here. I-I w-w-want t-to go h-home."

"I'll take you home myself," I promised.

"T-tell An-Ang-Angel I'll m-mis-miss her."

I kept my jaw clenched shut and nodded.

"You won't miss her for long, but she will kick your ass for leaving before her."

He smiled before his body shook as he struggled to breathe in, the peace my words gave leaving by the second.

"I'm right here, Cameron." My voice drew his attention back. "You're not alone. I'm right here."

He gave me a half smile as the life faded piece by piece from his eyes. I choked back a sob. The sound of approaching gunfire grew louder. I couldn't focus on anything but Cameron's lifeless body. He didn't deserve this.

Chapter Twenty-Three

Year 5032, October 8

Dr. Horace Mills – Nefertiti

"Horace, where are you? Cameron is down." Ravin's voice came over the comm. once again. "Where are you?"

"Pinned down." The blaze from the explosion was burning my skin. I was on one knee firing at the remaining amount of Formers, Angel and Wilts set up behind me. "Keep him alive." I clicked off my comm. "Wilts?" I called out.

"Fallback. Angel, move!" He stepped in front of me, allowing Angel to secure her weapon and zigzag her way toward the forest. "Mills." I followed suit, as Wilts laid down cover fire.

Angel took cover behind a large tree, and began laying down fire for Wilts and myself. I took cover next to her, the bark on the tree chipped away as the bullets hit. She didn't flinch. Wilts turned, hightailing it to us, diving behind the bush next to us rolling on to his back, gun ready and firing.

"Keep moving! We need to regroup." Wilts spoke over his gunfire. I turned my head for a split second, I saw blood covering his side. He'd been hit.

"Angel, help Wilts."

"Yes, sir." She moved over and helped Wilts to his feet; together we moved deeper into the forest.

I clicked on navigation to locate Ravin's position. All four of their symbols were clustered together. "West." I called out ahead. I clicked on my comm. "Ravin, get him stabilized. We are coming your way." Static filled my ear. *Fuck.* "Sammy."

Silence. The shrubbery around us was getting thicker. Their base was a good three miles away…

"Cameron is deceased, and Cage is unconscious." Duke's voice came in heavy over the comm. "We-" Gunfire broke through the comm., and I could hear it in the distance. *Fuck!* "Ravin and I are being pushed out. Meet at –" His comm. cut out and the gunfire increased.

"Duke?" I almost yelled.

"He's fine. We need to stop Wilts' bleeding." Angel touched my arm as she spoke.

"The ledge over there. It'll hide us long enough." I jumped down the eight foot drop, helping Wilts and Angel.

"It's a flesh wound." Wilts grunted in pain as I examined the bullet wound. He clicked on his comm. "Duke. Ravin. One of you bastards check in."

I strained my hearing, hoping for any sound that they were okay. "Flesh wound or not. Angel cover us." I removed Wilts' vest and peeled back his ripped shirt.

This was hardly a flesh wound. I dumped a packet of gunpowder on his wound.

"Hold still." I took his hand and lit a lighter with another. A glam snapped up filling the air with a pop. The pressure from his hand made my bones creak. "Breathe." I let the fire burn before I placed my hand over the fire to smother it."

"Damn, you do that again, and I'm going to shoot you." His head slammed back against the earth. "Shit." He clicked on his comm. "Duke. Ravin. If you don't respond in the next ten seconds. I will hunt you down and kill you myself."

"God damn it, quit screaming! Head toward the lab, two clicks east is an armory. Gather what you can –" Duke's voice came in loud; his voice was still heavy before the transmission cut again.

I'd finished patching Wilts' wound before I helped him put his vest back on.

"Let's go." I gave him a hand. I focused my attention on Angel. "Are you injured?"

She shook her head.

"No, sir." Her breath was heavy but paced.

I gave her a kiss on the head.

"Let's go."

We followed Duke's coordinates to the armory. Once out of the ammo we had, we ran, keeping cover in the trees until we had to venture out into the small community they had built. Luckily, they were all out in the woods looking for us.

"There." Angel pointed out the small shed.

"How the fuck did they get all this?" I couldn't believe my eyes. It was a small shed, but it was filled to the top with weapons, ammo, and explosives. I shut the door behind us.

"I am in love." Wilts was holding an old Smith and Wesson handgun. "Up for a game of Russian Roulette?"

I snickered.

"Later."

"There are enough explosives here to blow this place to hell." Angel tossed a block of C-4 towards me. She was right, there were trunks full of the stuff. "We can link the blocks with a simple transmission from the ship, once we are in the air, we can blow this place."

Wilts and I shared a smile.

"What do we need to do?"

"Most of these weapons have chips; we can extract them, reprogram them, line the camp and boom."

"Start pulling and reprogramming the chips," Wilts delegated before clicking on his comm. "Sam…s come in."

A heavy static filled the comms until Duke's voice came through.

"Go ahead."

"Change of plan, there are some heavy explosives in the shed, we are going to rid this place and blow it once we are in the sky."

"Beautiful. Get it done. We have found an exit ship, but no Elba, Barren, or C.K."

"We will keep an eye out." Wilts clicked off.

Angel had already begun pulling chips from the weapons as fast as I was reprogramming them.

"What do you think they were going to do with all of this?" She looked at me.

I could see the horror in her eyes.

"It doesn't matter. They won't have the opportunity to do it."

She nodded.

"You won't leave this time, when we all get back? Right?" Her green eyes watched me, searching for answers.

I kissed her temple and pulled her in. I didn't want to leave her again; I was more than proud of the person she'd become. I didn't want to leave Sam either.

"No." I gave her a smile. "You're stuck with me now." She smiled at me and squeezed me tighter. "Back to work, honey, so we can go home."

"Yes, sir."

In ten minutes, we had filled up several bags of the rigged C-4. This place would be gone; no doubt about it. I handed bags over to Angel.

"There is extra ammo and guns. Be careful." I took her head in my hands and kissed her forehead.

"I'll be careful."

"Good girl."

She gave me a smile and hurried out the ammo shed. I looked over to Wilts who had several bags on his shoulder.

"She will be okay. Girl's tougher than me." He smiled at me. "This is almost over. Be safe, brother." He touched his forehead to mine.

"You too."

Chapter Twenty-Four

YEAR OCTOBER 8 5032

STAFF SERGEANT SAMUEL RAVIN – NEFERTITI

"We need to get Cage to the medical room." The ship we found was the largest one and our best bet to get off world, even then it looked like it would fall apart in take-off.

"Shouldn't be far from the cargo bay." Duke's words came out in breaths; in the last three days his body had been through the ringer. How he was still moving, I didn't know. I would never tell it to his face, but he was a tough son of a bitch. "Let's go." He repositioned Cameron's body, the blood and dead weight from it was causing his grip to slip. "Radio the others, we still need C.K."

"There is a ship about fifteen clicks from the lab. Follow Cage's transmitter."

"Copy." Wilts' voice drifted over the comm.

"Get Cage to the infirmary. Hook her up on an IV," Mills clicked in.

"Yes, sir. Angel?" I hadn't heard a peep from her since the cars. I knew she was safe, but I couldn't help but want to hear it from her.

"I'm fine. I'll see you soon." She clicked out as fast as she clicked in.

I looked over to Duke, who signaled for me to move forward. I shifted Cage's weight, raising my weapon. He took point. The ship was a mess, the metal was rusting, and every step on the cat walks creaked and shifted under our weight.

"This piece of shit is going to fall apart." I couldn't help but share my concern with him.

"One way to find out. At least it will beat the black hole."

"Speak for yourself. The black hole could open a door to another dimension. I like that risk better than exploding."

He chuckled at me.

"This is similar to most merchant ships; the infirmary is on the left under the engine for extra heat. We –" His words fell short as he peaked around the left side of the split hallway. Gunfire rang out, forcing him to duck back. "Fuck. Twenty, at least. Fall back."

I turned, trying to protect Cage from the bullets. I took nest in the small storage closet. Duke wasn't as lucky. He ducked down behind a crate, refusing to leave Cameron's body behind. I tucked Cage behind me and laid down cover fire. "Sam!" He didn't budge from behind the crate.

"Barren!" He shouted over the gun fire. I scanned the area looking for him, in his hand he held C.K. The bastard surrounded himself with a group of six and was pushing down the hallway while the others pinned us down. "Cover me." He pushed Cameron's body out of the way the best he could. "He's going to a shuttle!"

Fuck. I nodded and sprayed bullets pushing the large group of men back. Ducking low, firing as he went Duke disappeared around the corner. I cursed as my last bullet left my gun. I rotated back in the small closet and reloaded my clip. I could hear the bullets bouncing off the walls. If this ship was going to fly before, it may not now with all the bullet holes.

"Sam. Watch your back. I'll be right behind you in a minute."

I peeked around the corner; the bastards had moved closer. *This is ridiculous! After this I am demanding a vacation.* I exhaled, ready to return fire; I didn't even get my head around the corner when a rapid popping from a machine gun filled the air. I heard a bullet whiz past my head, my eyes fixed on the hole it left inches from me.

Was this friendly fire? Had Sam turned around? Where did he get the gun? Whoever it was ceased fire leaving the smell of sulfur in the air and my ears ringing. I waited a second before looking around the corner.

"Miss me?" Elba asked sweetly. He held two machine guns in his hands. *Badass.*

"What took you so long?" I pushed myself up, lifting Cage with me. "Duke is after Barren. Take her. I'm going after him."

He dropped the weapons and cradled Cage in his arms.

"I'll be on the bridge, getting the ship ready for take-off. Where are the others?"

"Headed this way, sir." I picked up one of the weapons and charged down the hallway after Duke.

"Duke, what's your position?" His radio call remained silent. "Duke, come in."

"I'm inside the med room." I kicked my feet into gear.

"Did you apprehend Barren?"

"Negative, Barren's diseased."

"Are you hurt?" He didn't respond. "I repeat. Are you hurt?"

I turned and rounded the corner nearly crashing into Mills. He was covered in sweat and enemy blood. He too was on his way to check on Duke. We pushed through the small door to the infirmary. Medical supplies and utensils spewed on the floor. The beds were tipped over and riddled with bullet holes on the underside. *Where was he?*

I caught movement towards the back of the room. He was inside the quarantine cell. His back was turned towards us; he was looking down. Mills ran over to him but the door was locked.

"Open the door." Mills ordered.

"I can't."

Horror was etched into every bit of Mills' face. I moved to stand next to him. Barren's lifeless body laid in a pile on the floor; the vile containing C.K. was broken in his hand.

"No! You open this door right now!" Mills' voice cracked on every word.

Duke walked over to the door. His shoulder was drenched in blood and a large cut followed the outline of his jaw. "I can't open the door."

"Yes, you can. Open the door."

"Mills," I whispered. I put my arm around his shoulders. "He's infected. Charlotte's Kiss is –" He ripped his body away from me and pounded his fist on the door.

"Sam, open this door." He was yanking on the door handle.

"I'm not going to open the door, Horace." His bloodied glove pressed up against the glass on the door. "If I open this door, you'll get sick. Angel *would* get sick. I'm sorry."

Slowly, Duke backed away.

www.ingramcontent.com/pod-product-compliance
Lightning Source LLC
LaVergne TN
LVHW021204120125
800983LV00001B/126
9781648045257